HUNTED BY MY GROVELING ALPHA

A FATED MATES SECRET BABY FORCED PROXIMITY PRANORMAL WEREWOLF ROMANCE

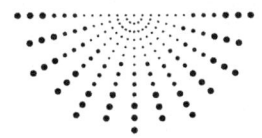

FLORA R. LEIGH

CONTENTS

Chapter 1	1
Chapter 2	9
Chapter 3	17
Chapter 4	27
Chapter 5	41
Chapter 6	51
Chapter 7	63
Chapter 8	72
Chapter 9	80
Chapter 10	93
Chapter 11	103
Chapter 12	117
Chapter 13	128
Chapter 14	137
Chapter 15	147
Chapter 16	156
Chapter 17	167
Chapter 18	174
Chapter 19	187
Chapter 20	199
Chapter 21	207
Chapter 22	220
Chapter 23	229
Chapter 24	241
Chapter 25	252
Chapter 26	261

Copyright © 2025 by Flora R. Leigh

All rights reserved.

No portion of this book may be reproduced in any form without written permission from the publisher or author, except as permitted by U.S. copyright law.

CHAPTER ONE

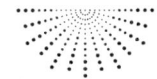

Phoebe

"We're out of options."

My fingers tightened, nails digging into the wooden armrest of my chair.

In that instant, I caught the scent of fear rolling off Elder Edmund—desperation mixed with shame, sharp as rotting wood. His voice was rough as sandpaper, and the tap of his cane against the floor echoed in my chest.

Rain hammered the windows in rhythm with my racing heart.

Over twenty pack members sat around the oak table, its damp wood scent mingling with the despair radiating from everyone—nearly overwhelming my sensitive nose. The crystal chandelier swayed overhead, casting dancing shadows.

"Darkfang Pack seized our last mining territory yesterday." Elder Mark's words carried bitter undertones. I could practically smell the hopelessness in his saliva. "The children's education, medical bills..."

"Enough." Elder Edmund's fury added sulfur to the air. He turned to me, his gaze piercing like needles.

My skin prickled instantly. I hunched my shoulders, trying to disappear into thin air.

"Phoebe." He deliberately lowered his voice, but I caught the tremor beneath. "You understand what Elena's disappearance a month ago means for us, don't you?"

My throat constricted as if invisible hands were choking me. I nodded stiffly, puppet-like. "Yes."

Elena Grayclaw—our pack's heir—vanished without a trace a month ago. Now, less than a week remained before her marriage alliance with Ironspine Pack. This union was our pack's only chance at survival.

"Her build, her appearance..." Elder Edmund's gaze crawled over my face like insects. "Very similar to yours."

Acid surged up my throat. No, they wouldn't dare...

"Phoebe, dear." Aunt Marian's hand was warm and damp as she gripped mine. Her familiar lavender scent now carried an undertone of bitterness. "Your scent abilities, your talent for mimicry... if you'd be willing to impersonate Elena, complete this marriage alliance..."

"It could save the entire pack." Elder Edmund's voice bordered on pleading. I could smell the desperation in his rapid breathing. "The Ironspine alliance is our only hope to reclaim territory and settle our debts. Phoebe, if you would just..."

Blood slowly turned to ice in my veins, cold flooding my system. Everyone's hope pressed down like stones on my chest—eight-year-old Tommy's innocent gaze, pregnant Lily stroking her belly, the last flickering hope in every pair of eyes.

The rain intensified. Tick-tock, tick-tock. Like a countdown.

"I..." The words squeezed from my dry throat, thin as a whisper. "How long would I need to pretend?"

"Until the marriage alliance is complete and our union is secure." Elder Edmund rushed toward me, his knees hitting the floor with a heavy thud. "Phoebe, you're our only hope. As the daughter of our late captain of the Beta Squad, you inherited your father's loyalty to this pack. You have the abilities, and having grown up together, you know her mannerisms better than anyone."

I closed my eyes. In the silence, everything became more vivid—

the pack members' terror, the children's innocence, the hope carried by an unborn child. This was my family. My duty.

When I opened my eyes again, everyone held their breath.

"All right."

The word slipped from my lips, light as a feather, heavy as lead. Relief erupted through the room in collective sighs. Aunt Marian's tears burned against my hand.

But I felt nothing except the hollow ache deep in my soul—I'd just traded away not my body, but myself.

Rain continued outside, but I knew the real storm was just beginning.

Three days later, the rain finally stopped.

Elias stood before the gates of Ironspine Pack's castle. At twenty-nine, he was tall yet graceful, with deep blue eyes that held steady wisdom. His ash-brown hair stirred in the breeze as he wore a dark gray suit with Grayclaw Pack's emblem pinned to his chest.

"Phoebe, I can't let you go in alone." His voice carried unusual weight now. I could sense his protective frustration—desperate to help yet powerless to act.

Massive iron gates towered before us, black metal carved with wolf totems, every line declaring Ironspine Pack's dominance. The castle's stone walls appeared even more forbidding under the overcast sky.

"My apologies, sir." The guard's voice was cold as steel. "By Alpha's direct orders, only Miss Elena Grayclaw may enter. No outsiders permitted."

Elias's fists clenched. I heard his knuckles crack. "I'm her escort..."

"Rules are rules." The second guard cut him off, hand moving to his weapon.

I drew a deep breath. The air carried Ironspine Pack's distinctive scent—power, authority, and an undercurrent of danger. Turning to face Elias, I saw worry and guilt warring in his eyes.

"Elias." I touched his arm lightly, feeling the tension in his muscles. "I'll be fine."

The breeze caught my shoulder-length chestnut curls, tossing them about. As I reached up to smooth my hair, Elias's expression grew more complex—I knew I wasn't breathtaking, but my delicate features and those bright green eyes that always seemed alert did bear some resemblance to Elena.

"You don't understand them, Phoebe." He kept his voice low. "Ironspine Pack is ruthless. Especially Drake..."

"Especially what?" I arched an eyebrow, the corner of my mouth lifting slightly. "An Alpha who's equally wary of this marriage alliance? Sounds like we're well-matched."

Elias blinked, then gave a rueful smile. "You always do this—worry inside but put on a brave face."

Worried? I asked myself. Yes, I worried about exposure, about failure, about disappointing my pack.

But there was also a flutter of... anticipation.

The rumors about him were countless—some claimed he was merciless, a killer without conscience; others insisted he was handsome as a sculpture yet never appeared in public; still others whispered he was enigmatic, rarely attending pack gatherings personally, always sending representatives instead.

In truth, apart from Ironspine Pack's inner circle, virtually no outsider had ever seen his face. This mystery made him both feared and legendary throughout the werewolf world.

Now I was about to meet this mythical figure myself.

"Remember the signals I taught you." Elias gripped my hand, warmth seeping through my gloves. "If there's any danger..."

"I'll handle it." I interrupted gently. "Trust me, all right?"

He studied me, complex emotions flickering in those deep blue eyes. Finally, he released my hand.

"Three days." His voice was barely audible. "If I don't hear from you in three days..."

"I know."

I turned toward the gates, adjusting the deep blue coat that had belonged to "Elena." The silk lining felt strange against my skin.

"Miss Elena Grayclaw, please follow me." The guard's demeanor instantly shifted to respectful.

As I crossed the threshold, I glanced back at Elias one final time. He stood beyond the gates, his worry and something I didn't care to examine making my chest tighten.

"Take care of yourself," I mouthed silently.

Then the heavy iron gates closed behind me.

The castle's interior opulence exceeded my imagination. Marble floors reflected crystal chandelier light, while oil paintings appeared mysterious and imposing in the amber glow.

"Miss Elena Grayclaw, welcome to Ironspine Pack. I am Victor, the head steward here." My guide was a man of about fifty with measured steps and professionally courteous detachment. "The elders require an audience with you."

"Now?" I asked, adding deliberate humility to my tone.

"Indeed. Please follow me."

I trailed him through lengthy corridors where heavy incense made the air nearly suffocating.

The council chamber doors opened slowly, revealing five elders seated upon a raised dais. They wore deep purple robes adorned with intricate golden emblems. The center elder had snow-white hair, a hawk-like nose, and eyes sharp as a jeweler appraising suspect merchandise.

"So this is Grayclaw Pack's heir?" The elder on the left spoke, his grizzled beard matching the contempt in his voice. "She looks rather... diminished."

I stood in the hall's center, feeling as though I'd been thrust onto a tribunal platform. Harsh light beat down from above while the elders remained shrouded in shadow, peering down at me.

"Indeed," agreed the right-side elder wearing a monocle, shaking his head. "Travel-worn and disheveled. Hardly the bearing expected of Ironspine Pack's future Luna."

My fists clenched at my sides.

"Not to mention her lineage," the white-haired center elder intoned darkly. "Everyone knows Grayclaw Pack's current... circumstances. Does the daughter of a failing pack truly merit our Alpha?"

Blood blazed through my veins, but I forced myself to maintain surface composure. Breathe, Phoebe. This is merely part of the trial.

"Honored elders," I began, striving to keep my voice steady, "I understand your reservations..."

"You understand?" The white-haired elder sneered. "A woman from a bankrupt pack—you believe we should simply accept you?"

"She requires... cleansing first," the left elder said in a tone that nauseated me. "After all, who can say what contamination she's brought from such a place."

The insults pierced like barbs. I felt heat rise in my cheeks—not from shame, but from rage. What did they take me for? Chattel?

"I shall arrange for someone to prepare a bath," Victor stated behind me, his voice equally distant. "To ensure she... meets our standards."

"Excellent." The white-haired elder waved dismissively, as if shooing away flies. "Once she's been cleaned, escort her to the designated chamber. Remember—she must be blindfolded. Our Alpha has no desire for her to observe more than necessary."

Blindfolded? I could scarcely believe what I was hearing. What manner of creature did they think I was?

Yet I could only nod. "I understand."

"Remove her."

Scalding water cascaded from above, washing away the grime of travel but not the humiliation burning in my heart.

Two servants lingered outside the bathing chamber, occasionally whispering among themselves. Though they spoke softly, my werewolf hearing caught fragments—"inferior pack," "unworthy," "Alpha's burden."

I closed my eyes, letting the water's rush drown out my fury. *Patience, Phoebe. All of this serves a purpose.*

After the bath, they dressed me in a gown of white silk—luxurious fabric yet modest in design, the neckline so high it nearly concealed my throat entirely. Matching soft-soled slippers made virtually no sound when I walked.

"Miss, please close your eyes." One of the servants—brown-haired, perhaps twenty, her voice timid—held up a length of black silk.

I drew a steadying breath and allowed her to bind the cloth across my eyes. The world plunged into darkness, sharpening my remaining senses. They guided me by the arms through what felt like an endless maze. Left turn, right turn, up a staircase, left again. I attempted to memorize our path, but the deliberate misdirection soon scrambled my sense of direction completely.

"We have arrived, miss."

The sound of a door opening, then I was gently guided forward.

"Please wait here," another voice instructed. "The Alpha will come when the time is appropriate."

Footsteps receded, the door closed. I reached behind me, my fingers finding the edge of a soft bed.

And so the waiting began. I perched carefully on the bed's edge, surrounded by darkness. I could hear only the gentle crackling of logs in the fireplace and occasional distant footfalls. Time seemed to stand still.

My eyelids grew heavy. The exhaustion of travel combined with mounting tension made sleep nearly irresistible. I gradually leaned back, curling onto my side on the bed. Just a moment's rest, I told myself...

I couldn't say how much time had passed when the soft click of a turning lock roused me from light slumber.

Through the haze of drowsiness, I sensed someone entering the chamber. The footsteps were careful, yet clear in the profound silence. My werewolf instincts snapped to attention, though my body remained frozen—whether from having just awakened or some inexplicable tension, I couldn't tell.

I maintained my position lying on the bed, straining to assess the situation through my other senses. The footsteps halted near the doorway. I could feel a presence—a tall figure radiating formidable energy.

That must be Drake.

I felt his gaze settle upon me, weighted like physical touch. The air grew thick with an unfamiliar yet potent scent—male werewolf pheromones mingled with hints of sandalwood and something primitively commanding.

My pulse quickened, but I forced my breathing to remain even, continuing my pretense of sleep.

He lingered by the door for an eternity—long enough that I began to wonder if he had already departed. Then the footsteps resumed, drawing closer to where I lay.

I concentrated more intently, sensing him come to a stop very near indeed. Close enough that I could hear his quiet breathing, could feel the warmth radiating from his body.

He was studying me.

This sensation of being observed so intimately was peculiar—both unsettling and strangely... thrilling? I could imagine his expression at this moment—perhaps puzzlement, perhaps disappointment, or some complex emotion beyond my comprehension.

Time seemed suspended. I could hear the soft dance of flames in the fireplace. I could hear my own heartbeat thundering in my ears, and wondered if he could detect it as well.

Then, quite unexpectedly, I felt a whisper of warm breath across my cheek. He had leaned down, drawing even closer.

My breathing nearly ceased entirely, every muscle in my body going rigid. What was his intention?

But nothing came to pass. After several heartbeats, that warmth receded and the footsteps resumed.

He was withdrawing.

I heard him release a soft sigh, the sound laden with emotions I could not decipher—weariness? Disappointment? Something else entirely?

The footsteps moved toward the door, growing fainter. Once more came the soft click of the lock, followed by the whisper of the door closing.

Silence reclaimed the chamber.

Tomorrow, the true test would begin.

CHAPTER TWO

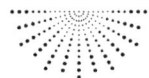

Drake

"Alpha, we've rooted out the Darkfang spy."

Kay pushed open the office door, holding a blood-stained document. Lean and wiry, he perpetually wore black tactical gear, his scarred face appearing even more menacing under the harsh lights. As my shadow beta, he handled matters that couldn't see daylight.

I didn't look up, continuing to review the financial reports spread across my desk.

I rubbed my temples, golden-brown hair slipping between my fingers. At twenty-seven, I was in my prime for werewolf leadership—six-foot-five, broad shoulders tapering to a narrow waist, and those eyes people called "glacier blue"—enough to command respect from most. But tonight, none of that could ease the exhaustion gnawing at me.

The Ironspine Pack's business empire demanded every ounce of my attention, especially at times like this.

"How many does that make?" My voice echoed in the spacious office.

"Third one this month." Kay placed the file on my desk. "Kitchen maid who's worked here two years. Tried to poison your dinner tonight."

I looked up, feeling the familiar throb at my temples. Moonlight streamed through the floor-to-ceiling windows, casting silver patterns across the mahogany surface. This was the second headache tonight—the first came from seeing that woman asleep in the guest room.

Elena.

No. I couldn't think about her. Not now.

"Handled?"

"She's in the basement." Kay's tone remained flat. "Begging for mercy, claims she was coerced."

I massaged my forehead. Two years was long enough to earn trust, to infiltrate our inner circle.

"Her family?"

"Three children. Youngest is five." Kay paused. "Says Darkfang threatened to kill them all."

"Rules are rules. Get rid of her." My voice came out colder than intended. "But the children... arrange protection. Get them somewhere far from Darkfang territory."

The Ironspine Pack had dominated the werewolf world for three centuries—not through mercy, but through unwavering strength. Every betrayal demanded consequences, regardless of justification.

Kay nodded. He never questioned my decisions, which made him invaluable.

"Also," he produced another file, "updated dangerous personnel list."

I accepted the thick document—three pages that deepened my mood. Each name carried detailed annotations: position, clearance level, threat assessment. I recognized most of them; some had served the pack for over a decade.

"Marcus the steward," I read aloud. "Eight years managing East Wing security."

"Attempted to breach your private quarters last night. Guards intercepted him." Anger crept into Kay's voice. "Claimed routine inspection, but the timing was suspicious."

I calculated quickly. East Wing—only two corridors from Elena's room. If Marcus truly worked for Darkfang, then she might be...

"Double the guard detail around Elena's quarters," I ordered. "Anyone approaching needs clearance and escort."

Kay raised an eyebrow. "Alpha, do you care about this woman?"

Care? An hour ago, I'd stood beside her bed, moonlight filtering through the curtains to cast gentle shadows across her face. She'd looked so peaceful, so... vulnerable.

That vulnerability sparked something entirely inappropriate for an Alpha—the urge to protect her, even to smooth away the worry lines creasing her brow, to see if I could ease whatever troubled her dreams.

The impulse confused and irritated me. I was Drake Ironspine, Alpha of the Ironspine Pack. My decisions should stem from logic and pack welfare, not inexplicable sympathy for a stranger.

This marriage alliance was crucial for consolidating our position in the werewolf hierarchy. Though the Grayclaw Pack had fallen on hard times, their bloodline and historical significance remained valuable.

"She will be Ironspine Pack's future Luna," I said finally. "Protecting her serves pack interests."

Kay remained silent, but I caught the skepticism in his eyes. He'd served me too long, knew me too well.

"How's the Pack Meeting going?"

"Proceeds as scheduled in three days. Representatives from all branch families will attend, including several... problematic ones." Kay flipped to the final page. "Alpha, for security reasons, I recommend postponement."

"No." I rose and moved to the window.

Moonlight illuminated my features—the sharp jawline and aquiline nose that typically wore an impassive mask. But tonight, thoughts of the woman upstairs softened my expression slightly.

"Darkfang wants us paralyzed by fear, wants us to alter established plans. If I retreat now, I signal that Ironspine Pack can be intimidated."

"But Alpha..."

"Enhance security protocols," I interrupted. "Place all suspicious personnel under active surveillance. Prepare comprehensive contingency plans. If they attempt disruption during the meeting, they'll discover what Ironspine strength truly means."

Kay considered this for several seconds before nodding. "Understood. And the mating ceremony?"

The mating ceremony—another migraine-inducing subject.

"Proceeds after the Pack Meeting."

"Have you met her?"

I didn't respond, but my fingers unconsciously touched my chest pocket, where I kept an Alpha seal ring—tradition dictated presenting this to my future Luna during our formal introduction.

Tonight, I'd simply watched her sleep, doing nothing.

"Go," I said. "Report any irregularities immediately."

Kay moved toward the door but paused without leaving. He placed additional files on my desk with practiced silence.

"Alpha, regarding Miss Elena Grayclaw..." Kay retrieved another document. "Emergency intelligence report just arrived."

I accepted the file marked "CLASSIFIED"—data my intelligence network had compiled over three days. The first page displayed Elena's photograph from Grayclaw Pack records: emerald eyes, expression cold and aristocratic.

I continued reading. Birth date, physical measurements, education history... everything matched official records perfectly. Then came recent activity tracking.

"Last confirmed sighting in Grayclaw territory one month ago," I read the crucial information. "Complete communication blackout until three days ago."

"Correct." Kay stepped closer. "But Alpha, certain details seem... inconsistent."

"Explain."

"Behavioral patterns. The real Elena never apologizes unprompted and would never display such... deference before elders." Kay hesitated. "Plus minor habits differ."

I looked up.

"Elena habitually touches her right earring when nervous. Tonight's woman bites her lower lip instead."

I reexamined the file. The photographed woman shared perhaps seventy percent similarity with tonight's visitor, but careful comparison revealed...

Subtle jawline differences. The authentic Elena possessed sharper features; tonight's woman appeared softer.

"You suspect an impostor?" I closed the file, voice calmer than anticipated.

"I suspect everything, Alpha. That's my job." Kay met my gaze directly. "Particularly during sensitive periods—any anomaly could indicate a trap."

I stood and approached the window. Night air carried mountain pine scents. If Kay's suspicions proved accurate, who was the woman sleeping upstairs? Why impersonate Elena? What was her true agenda?

"Darkfang's gambit?" This wasn't an inquiry but a confirmation.

"Possibly. Deploy a substitute to sabotage the alliance, create interpack conflict." Kay analyzed methodically. "Worse scenario—assassination mission."

Assassination. The word conjured memories of warm breath against my cheek earlier. If murder were her intent, that moment offered a perfect opportunity. I'd been completely exposed, defenseless.

Instead, she'd slept peacefully, breathing unchanged even when I drew near.

"Continue investigating," I decided. "But maintain discretion. If she's truly an impostor, I need her real identity and objectives."

"Additional surveillance personnel?"

"No." I faced Kay. "Maintain current protocols. If she harbors ulterior motives, she'll eventually reveal them. Besides..."

I paused, remembering her curled form on the bed. Instinct suggested this woman posed no immediate threat.

"Besides what, Alpha?"

"Nothing." I returned to my desk. "Continue your investigation carefully. No one else notices irregularities—including the elders."

Kay nodded and headed doorward, stopping at the threshold again.

"Alpha, if she proves fraudulent, what's your intention?"

"Truth first." I secured the intelligence report in my drawer. "But regardless of identity, if she threatens pack security, I'll handle it personally." Ice entered my voice.

"Your plan?"

My mind raced. If she was indeed fake, what purpose drove this deception? Internal Grayclaw power struggles? Darkfang conspiracy?

"Assassination seems unlikely," I reasoned. "If killing me was the goal, earlier presented ideal circumstances. Her reactions suggest fear rather than malice."

"Kay, implement Plan B."

Plan B—our years-old contingency for when my identity required concealment. Kay would temporarily assume my public role.

"You're certain, Alpha? Activating this protocol now..."

"Perfect timing." I interrupted. "If she's an impostor, I need to observe her true intentions covertly. If she's an enemy assassin, I should be the primary target."

Kay remained silent briefly, then nodded. "Duration?"

"Until the Pack Meeting concludes." I opened my desk drawer and withdrew a distinctive ring. "During this period, you are Drake Ironspine."

Kay accepted the ring—a symbol of pack authority. Combined with our similar builds and careful disguise, it would deceive most observers.

"The elders..."

"They know this protocol exists," I confirmed. "If necessary, Victor will coordinate with you. Regarding the mating ceremony..."

The most complex element. Tradition required the Alpha to personally perform the marking ritual. But with Kay substituting...

"We'll address that when the time comes," I concluded. "Priority now is determining her true identity."

Kay tested the ring's fit. "If she discovers the deception?"

"Then she's more dangerous than anticipated." My tone turned glacial.

Kay understood my implication. Ironspine Pack survival superseded all other considerations.

"One more thing," I added. "Monitor all her activities discreetly. I need to know every action, every word."

"Understood. Your cover identity?"

I'd already formulated the plan.

"Senior business consultant for Ironspine Group, specializing in inter-pack commercial agreements and asset consolidation. The name 'Alexander Gray' allows me to approach her regarding marriage alliance business terms without suspicion. I require detailed understanding of Grayclaw Pack's financial status—legitimate reason for contact."

Kay considered this. "Documentation needed?"

"Ready by morning," I confirmed. "Remember—from this moment, you are the Alpha. Every decision must reflect Drake Ironspine's character."

"Cold, decisive, ruthless?" Kay ventured a rare jest.

I didn't smile. "Rational, cautious, and perpetually prioritizing pack interests."

Kay stood and adjusted his collar. "Very well, 'Alpha.' I'll begin preparations."

"Wait." I stopped him. "Regarding that woman... if she truly means no harm, if she's merely caught in this political marriage..."

I left the thought unfinished, but Kay comprehended.

"You wish to protect her?"

Protect? Perhaps. Or merely curiosity. Something about her compelled my interest, made me want a deeper understanding.

"I want truth," I said finally. "Whatever that truth may be."

Most critically, I needed to understand her real purpose here.

After Kay departed, silence reclaimed the office. I reopened the intelligence report, analyzing every detail meticulously.

Two hours later, I reached my conclusion. The woman sleeping upstairs definitely wasn't the genuine Elena Grayclaw. The question remained—who was she?

I gazed toward the ceiling, as if I could penetrate the floors to see her peaceful expression. Tomorrow's formal meeting promised intrigue—would she maintain this masquerade or reveal her authentic self?

Either way, I anticipated the answers.

CHAPTER THREE

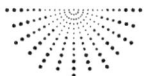

Phoebe

The woman in the mirror truly looked like a Luna.

The deep blue silk gown hugged my figure perfectly, the hemline swaying softly at my ankles. The sapphire necklace caught the light, echoing the color of my eyes.

The maids had spent two full hours preparing me—arranging my chestnut curls into an elegant updo and applying subtle makeup that enhanced my features.

But I knew this was just a beautiful mask.

Through the window, I could see the perfect full moon hanging in the night sky, its silver light washing over the earth.

The Full Moon Banquet—for werewolves, this was both a sacred night of peak power and a dangerous time when instincts ran wild.

The restless energy in the air made my skin tingle, reminding me of that ancient legend. Under the full moon, fated mates would feel the most primal call from deep within their bloodline.

I took a deep breath, trying to suppress the flutter in my chest. The fated mate legend sounded beautiful, but that was someone else's fairy tale. My marriage to Drake had been a business transaction from the start—it had nothing to do with some ethereal destiny.

"Miss Elena, the Alpha is waiting downstairs." Victor's voice came from outside the door.

Tonight would be my first public appearance as "Elena Grayclaw," accepting the "blessings" of the Ironspine Pack.

The metal doorknob felt cold under my palm, which had started sweating from nerves.

I opened the door to find Victor standing respectfully in the hallway.

"Please follow me."

We walked down the thickly carpeted corridor. Our footsteps were completely muffled, leaving only the soft whisper of my hem.

At the stair landing, I spotted him immediately.

A tall figure stood in the center of the great hall, his back to the staircase. The deep black tailcoat fit perfectly across his broad shoulders and lean waist. His dark hair was slicked back without a strand out of place, exposing the strong line of his neck.

This had to be Drake.

But...

I frowned, struck by an inexplicable sense of wrongness. His build was certainly tall and powerful, his presence commanding enough, but something felt off.

Different from the man who'd stood by my bed last night.

Last night's man had carried a more intense presence, as if the very air in the room trembled because of him. His aura had been more primal and dominating, dangerously attractive like a wild predator. This man, though equally tall and strong, seemed more restrained, more like he was...

Like he was deliberately imitating someone.

I shook my head. Maybe I was overthinking it. After all, I'd been blindfolded last night, half-asleep—my perception might not have been accurate.

"Miss Elena." Victor's gentle reminder brought me back.

I realized I'd reached the bottom of the stairs. The man turned around, and I finally saw his face clearly.

Handsome features, deep blue eyes, and a well-defined jawline.

Definitely an impressive Alpha. But when our eyes met, there was no spark.

No racing heart, no mysterious attraction, not even the nerve-wracking pressure I'd felt last night.

"Elena." He extended his hand, his voice deep and magnetic. "Welcome to the Ironspine Pack. I'm Drake."

I placed my hand in his palm. His hand was large and warm, but the touch brought no special feeling whatsoever.

"Drake," I replied softly, letting a proper smile curve my lips. "It's wonderful to meet you."

His gaze lingered on my face for a few seconds, as if studying something. Then he gently placed my hand on his arm.

"Ready?" he asked. "There are many people tonight who want to meet the future Luna. The Full Moon Banquet holds great significance for our pack."

I nodded, feeling the muscle definition of his arm. Very solid, very powerful, but lacking that intense presence that had left me breathless last night.

Maybe last night's mystery had just been the darkness and the unknown. Or perhaps, since we weren't fated mates, there simply wouldn't be that legendary powerful attraction.

We walked toward the banquet hall entrance. The heavy oak doors slowly opened, warm light and cheerful voices spilling out.

"The Alpha of the Ironspine Pack and his fiancée, Elena!" the announcer's booming voice echoed through the hall.

All conversation stopped instantly. Dozens of eyes turned toward us.

A wave of burning heat swept up my neck and cheeks. I fought to maintain my smile.

Applause erupted. I could sense genuine blessings, curious scrutiny, and some hostility I couldn't quite decipher.

Drake guided me into the crowd, his steps steady and confident. I tried to match his pace, my hem swaying softly at my ankles. The music in the hall was beautiful and soothing, but I still felt an underlying tension.

For the next hour, we were constantly surrounded. Everyone wanted to talk to me, learn about the Grayclaw Pack, and express their "blessings" for the marriage alliance. I mechanically repeated appropriate responses, my face locked in a permanent smile.

Drake was perfectly competent throughout. He'd respond to questions at the right moments, provide support when I needed it, and even skillfully redirect overly sharp inquiries. But I felt—he was too perfect, perfect like he was executing a mission.

"Drake, I'd like a drink," I said.

"Of course." He responded immediately. "What would you like?"

"Anything, as long as it's not alcoholic." I deliberately softened my voice. "Full moon nights make people lose control too easily. I want to stay clearheaded."

"Wait here." His gaze swept the crowd, then he headed straight for the refreshment table.

While Drake went to get drinks, I stood alone. Conversations rose and fell around me, crystal clear in the restless atmosphere of the full moon night.

"...Sera doesn't look too happy tonight." Two women whispered behind me.

"Of course not. She and the Alpha grew up together. Everyone thought..."

"Shh, keep it down. The new Luna's right there."

I pretended not to hear, but my ears perked up.

"Sera really is beautiful, and she's an elder's daughter. Perfect breeding, too."

"Too bad the Alpha chose a marriage alliance. But look at Sera's expression—she's obviously not giving up easily."

Childhood sweethearts... So there was already such a "Luna" in Drake's life, someone who met everyone's expectations.

Just then, Drake returned with my drink.

"Thank you." I touched his arm lightly. "Be careful not to drink too much yourself."

"Drake." A clear female voice called from behind us.

I turned to see a breathtakingly beautiful woman walking toward us.

She had waterfall-like golden hair and a tall, graceful figure. Most striking were her eyes—brilliant blue eyes gleaming with proud light. She wore a deep red evening gown, the color vivid as burning flame.

"Sera." Drake's voice sounded slightly tense. "Come meet Elena. Elena, this is Sera. We grew up together."

So the earlier conversation was right. I extended my hand proactively, my face wearing a proper smile. "Wonderful to meet you, Sera."

She hesitated a moment before reluctantly responding to my handshake—brief, cold, purely ceremonial contact.

"Elena." Her voice was clear and pleasant, edged with coolness. "Welcome to the Ironspine Pack."

Her tone was calm, almost polite, but the condescending feeling was unmistakable. Like a noblewoman receiving a guest of lower status—courteous but distant.

"Thank you." I maintained my smile. "Drake just mentioned you grew up together. You must have many interesting stories to share."

I kept up the surface politeness.

Sera nodded slightly, her gaze moving between Drake and me. But strangely, her look toward Drake didn't hold the possessiveness or jealousy I'd expected. Instead, there was a kind of... detachment?

"Indeed, many memories." She said coolly, then turned to Drake. "Drake, will you attend tomorrow's Pack Meeting?"

Her tone asking this question was natural, but I noticed Drake stiffen slightly.

"Of course. I'll participate in all important decisions." He answered somewhat cautiously.

Sera nodded, no unusual expression on her face. "Good. Elena, I hope you'll adapt to life here."

She nodded at me in acknowledgment, then turned and left gracefully. No extra words, no deliberate provocation, not even prolonged attention.

I watched her retreating figure, confusion rising in my chest. This was completely different from what I'd expected. Logically, if Sera really had those special feelings for Drake, facing his fiancée, shouldn't she be more... hostile?

But her behavior was more like a polite but not particularly interested observer.

Maybe I was overthinking it. Perhaps Sera was just more refined than the rumors suggested, better at hiding her emotions. Or maybe she simply didn't have those rumored special feelings for Drake at all.

I shook my head lightly, telling myself not to overthink. But that sense of wrongness still wouldn't leave me.

An hour later, I finally couldn't take it anymore.

The cheerful noise throughout the banquet hall suddenly felt suffocating.

"Drake, I'd like to get some fresh air." I touched his arm lightly, my voice carrying appropriate fatigue. "It's a bit stuffy in the banquet hall."

"Do you need me to come with you?" He asked politely, but I could sense he didn't really want to leave.

"No need. I just want some quiet time alone." I smiled and shook my head. "Keep entertaining the guests. I'll be back soon."

Drake nodded, seeming relieved. "Be careful. Don't go too far."

I left the banquet hall, walking slowly down the corridor leading to the garden. The castle was quiet at night, with only distant music and occasional laughter. The full moon's silver radiance fell on the marble floor, casting geometric patterns of light and shadow.

The night breeze carried the fragrance of the rose garden, letting my tense nerves relax slightly.

Just as I was about to turn back, low voices came from ahead.

I moved closer carefully and saw two figures conversing in the moonlight at the end of the corridor. One I recognized—an elder I'd seen at the banquet, white-haired, wearing deep purple robes. The other...

My breathing suddenly stopped.

A tall man, moonlight outlining his broad shoulders and lean silhouette. He wore a deep gray suit. Even with his back to me, I could clearly feel that intense presence.

That familiar, powerful aura instantly awakened my memory—the man who'd entered my room last night?

"...security measures have been strengthened," the elder's voice drifted over. "There won't be any more accidents."

"Good." The man spoke, his voice deep and magnetic, carrying natural authority. "About the Pack Meeting..."

Before he finished, he suddenly stopped and slowly turned around.

Our eyes met in the moonlight.

The moment our gazes locked, the wolf sleeping inside me suddenly awakened. A primal call from deep in my bloodline made me understand everything instantly.

My wolf was roaring, celebrating, submitting to its mate.

Fated mate.

The full moon had not only heightened my senses but awakened the most primal instincts of my wolf nature. I could feel it restless inside me, desperate to get closer to this man, to be completely conquered by his scent.

In that instant, the world seemed to stop. All sounds disappeared, leaving only the rush of blood through my veins and the low whimper of my wolf—the trembling of finding home.

His face was sharply defined in the moonlight—high cheekbones, thin lips pressed together, and those deep blue eyes—cold yet carrying some heart-stopping danger.

An electric current shot from my spine straight to my brain. I nearly lost my balance and had to slam my palm against the wall to steady my weakening body.

He stared at me for a moment, some emotion flashing quickly through his eyes. Then he said something low to the elder. The elder nodded respectfully and quickly disappeared down the other end of the corridor.

Now, only the two of us remained.

He didn't leave, his gaze still pressing down on me heavily. Even across the distance, it felt warm and burning, like a tangible touch making my heart race.

Finally, he turned and walked toward the castle's depths.

I knew I should return to the banquet hall, continue playing Elena's role. But my body seemed to have its own will. My wolf had already lost control. Werewolf instinct drove me, like pack members called by moonlight, involuntarily following the Alpha's steps.

I began following him.

My footsteps were nearly silent, maintaining sufficient distance. His pheromones in the air were like guiding markers, making it effortless to track his direction.

His pace was steady, clearly very familiar with the castle's layout. We passed through several ornately decorated corridors, moonlight streaming through stained glass windows, forming colorful patterns on the floor.

The fated mate attraction drove me to keep following, like a moth to flame—knowing the danger but unable to resist.

Finally, he stopped at a relatively secluded balcony. From here, you could see the castle's back garden, rose bushes giving off a faint fragrance in the moonlight. The distant banquet hall blazed with lights, but here was so quiet you could only hear the night wind rustling through leaves.

He turned around, his gaze looking straight toward the pillar where I was hiding.

"Come out." His voice was calm but carried undeniable authority.

My heart nearly stopped beating. I'd been discovered.

I slowly emerged from behind the pillar, moonlight falling on my hem, making the silk fabric shimmer. He stood before the balcony railing, his tall figure even more imposing in the moonlight.

"What are you doing?" He asked, his voice carrying a hint of confusion and wariness. "Miss Elena Grayclaw."

He knew who I was. But who was he?

I opened my mouth but found I couldn't speak. How could I explain? Say I was attracted to him? Say I thought he was the man from last night? Say I felt the fated mate pull?

"I..." My voice was barely a whisper. "I don't know."

That was the truth. I really didn't know what I was doing.

He frowned, stepping closer. Moonlight fell on his face, letting me see the complex emotions in his eyes—suspicion, curiosity, and something I couldn't read.

"You don't know?" He took another step forward. Now, less than six feet separated us. "Then tell me, why were you following me?"

His scent hit me, his powerful aura making me dizzy. My mind told me I should apologize, should find an excuse to leave. But my body seemed beyond my control.

"I..." I struggled to find the right words, but my brain was blank.

He took another step forward. Now we were close enough that I could see golden flecks in his eyes, feel the warmth radiating from his body.

"Answer me." His voice became lower, carrying some dangerous charm.

I looked up at him, those blue eyes deep as the ocean in moonlight. An unprecedented impulse surged in my chest.

Possessed by some impulse, I rose on my tiptoes and gently kissed his cheek.

His skin was warm, carrying a faint sandalwood scent. In that instant, flame-like heat spread through my entire body, making me unsteady.

He went completely rigid.

I froze too, realizing what I'd done. I had just... kissed a complete stranger?

"You..." His voice became hoarse, a dangerous light flashing in his eyes.

Suddenly, he grabbed my wrist. His hand was large and strong, but it didn't hurt me. Just that contact felt like being struck by lightning.

We stared at each other, the air thick with tense electricity. The full moon's radiance fell on us, coating this scene in silver light.

The fated mate attraction exploded completely in this moment, breaking through all reason and social convention. I could feel my heartbeat thundering, blood surging like lava.

He lowered his head, his breath falling by my ear, warm and rapid.

"Do you know what you're doing?" His voice whispered in my ear, carrying irresistible magnetism.

I shook my head, my voice thin as a feather. "No."

The next second, his lips covered mine.

The kiss started light and careful, as if giving me a chance to pull away. His lips were warm, carrying a faint mint taste. But when I didn't push him away, instead rising slightly on my toes to respond, the kiss instantly became deep and passionate.

One hand still gripped my wrist, the other caressed my cheek, his thumb brushing over my cheekbone. That touch made my skin burn, made me tremble involuntarily.

I could feel his restrained power, his body tense as if fighting something. But when my hand unconsciously gripped his suit jacket, his control seemed to completely collapse.

The kiss became deeper, more fierce. His scent completely surrounded me, making me feel like I existed in a world belonging only to the two of us. Moonlight fell on us, rose fragrance drifting in the night breeze, distant music blurring into the background.

Not until we both needed air did he slowly release me. But his forehead still pressed against mine, our breaths mingling, both slightly rapid.

At this distance, I could see the shock in his eyes and some complex emotion. In that moment, I realized this kiss had been equally unexpected for him, equally earth-shattering.

CHAPTER FOUR

Phoebe

I didn't push him away.

Instead, I found myself completely lost in sensations I'd never experienced before. My blood felt like it was filled with countless tiny sparks, burning away my sanity bit by bit. The full moon's radiance called to my primal instincts, making it impossible to resist this man's magnetic pull.

"Open your eyes," his voice was low and husky, carrying a command I couldn't defy. "Look at me. Really see who I am."

I trembled as I opened my eyes, falling into those ice-blue depths that blazed even more intensely with desire. Raw hunger and wild possessiveness swirled within them like a storm.

I stared into his eyes, letting myself drown in that dangerous sapphire ocean.

This seemed to please him. Another savage kiss descended, carrying the crisp bite of mint and his own scorching essence, stealing every breath and coherent thought from me.

The full moon's power, the fated mate bond, and this mysterious man's overwhelming magnetism—everything conspired to make me lose myself completely.

Electric pleasure coursed through my body like lightning, making my knees buckle. He swept me up effortlessly.

Through shadowed hallways, kicking open a heavy carved door, I was gently laid upon soft velvet sheets.

His movements shed their earlier restraint, now filled with an Alpha's inherent hunger for conquest. Every caress of his fingers seemed to ignite flames across my skin.

The dress slipped from my shoulders with practiced ease. Cool air kissed bare flesh, sending delicious shivers through me.

I bit my lip hard, but soft moans still escaped. My nails carved shallow crimson trails across his back. That hint of pain only inflamed him further, his movements growing wilder.

We melded together, every inch of space between us vanishing.

As consciousness began to fragment, I heard him growl broken words against my ear—part vow, part curse.

"Remember this feeling... remember me."

All thoughts of duty, responsibility, and political marriage dissolved. Only primal need and possession remained.

The full moon's magic blurred every boundary—reason and desire, strangers and fated mates, reality and fantasy—everything intertwined until I couldn't distinguish between them.

I only knew that in his arms, I felt whole for the first time in my life.

His hands roamed my body with a reverent hunger that bordered on worship, his calloused palms tracing the swell of my breasts, the dip of my waist, the flare of my hips as if he were charting the contours of some forbidden temple. Each touch was deliberate, possessive, his fingers splaying wide to claim every inch of exposed skin, memorizing the sacred territory of my form like a map etched into his very soul. The cool silk of the velvet sheets beneath me contrasted sharply with the heat radiating from his body, pressed so close that I could feel the hard ridge of his arousal grinding against my thigh, insistent and unyielding.

When his mouth followed the same divine path, trailing hot, open-mouthed kisses down the column of my throat, I arched beneath him with a gasp that tore from my chest, my back bow[...] pulled by invisible strings. His lips were fire—searing [...] latching onto the peak of one nipple with a suck that s[...] liquid pleasure straight to my core. He swirled his tongue ar[...] hardened bud, teeth grazing just enough to sting, drawing out br[...] less whimpers that echoed off the stone walls of the moon-drench[...] chamber. Silver light from the full moon streamed through the arched windows, casting ethereal shadows over our entwined forms: the taut lines of his shoulders flexing as he held me down, the curve of my leg hooked over his hip, inviting him closer. We moved together in a perfect, ancient rhythm, my hips rolling up to meet the teasing press of his cock against my slick folds, the friction building a pressure that made my clit throb with desperate need.

"Elena," he whispered my fake name like a prayer, the sound rough and reverent against the damp skin of my breast, his breath fanning hot over my sensitized flesh. He knew it—my name, my secrets—while I remained adrift in anonymity, this stranger who felt like destiny incarnate. His touch was achingly tender one moment, fingers ghosting feather-light over the quiver of my belly, then ruthlessly demanding the next, pinning my wrists above my head with one large hand while the other delved between my thighs. He parted my legs wider, exposing me completely to his gaze, and I felt the cool air kiss my dripping pussy, making me clench around nothing. "So wet for me already, Elena. Fuck, you're dripping down your thighs."

My body responded to him with an intensity that stunned me, every nerve ending ablaze as if he'd ignited gunpowder beneath my skin. His fingers—two thick digits at first—slid through my soaked folds, circling my swollen clit with maddening precision before plunging deep inside me. I cried out, the stretch burning sweetly as he curled them against that spot deep within, pumping in and out with a rhythm that had my walls fluttering greedily around him. Juices coated his hand, the obscene wet sounds filling the room, mingling with my ragged moans. Every sensation was magnified beyond anything I'd ever dreamed possible: the scrape of his stubble against my inner thigh as he lowered his head, the velvet heat of his tongue ng me like a man starved. He sucked [...] ing low in his throat, the vibration [...] y core until stars burst behind my [...]

bucking wildly, chasing the building [...] irm, his free hand splayed across my [...] ia," he growled against my pussy, the [...] ant to feel you shatter on my tongue [...] ess, tongue-fucking me deep, nose grinding against my clit as he feasted, his fingers joining to stretch me wider, scissoring inside my clenching heat. The pressure built unbearably, my thighs trembling around his head, until I shattered with a scream that echoed like a siren's call. My release gushed over his mouth, coating his chin, and he drank it down greedily, lapping every drop as if it were nectar from the goddess.

But he didn't stop. Even as the aftershocks rippled through me, leaving me boneless and panting, he rose up, shedding the last of his clothes with a predator's grace. His cock sprang free—thick, veined, the head flushed dark and glistening with pre-cum—and my mouth watered at the sight, even as a flicker of apprehension twisted in my gut. It was massive, curving slightly upward, promising to ruin me in the most exquisite way. He stroked himself once, twice, eyes locked on mine, that ice-blue storm raging with unchecked lust. "You're mine tonight, Elena. Every fucking inch."

When he finally made us one, positioning the blunt tip at my entrance and thrusting forward in one slow, inexorable slide, the universe exploded into starlight behind my eyes. The stretch was exquisite agony, my pussy yielding to his girth inch by torturous inch, walls clamping down like a vice as he bottomed out, his balls slapping against my ass. "Fuck, so tight," he groaned, forehead pressed to mine, our breaths mingling in harsh pants. "Made for me, weren't you? This perfect little cunt, sucking me in like it never wants to let go." We moved together as if we'd been crafted for this singular moment, for each other alone—his hips snapping forward in deep, punishing strokes that hit that spot inside me over and over, my nails raking down his back in red welts that made him hiss and fuck me harder.

His eyes never left mine, those sapphire depths holding me captive as we ascended together, sweat-slicked skin sliding, the bed creaking under the force of our joining. I wrapped my legs around his waist, heels digging into his ass to pull him deeper, and he rewarded me with a brutal grind of his hips, his pubic bone rubbing my clit until I was sobbing his nameless plea. "Please—oh goddess, don't stop—harder!" The words tumbled from my lips unbidden, raw and desperate. His name—I didn't have it, but it fell from my lips like a sacred invocation anyway, a guttural "You—fuck, you!" that dissolved into a keening wail as another orgasm ripped through me, my pussy convulsing around his cock, milking him with rhythmic squeezes.

Ecstasy crashed over us in devastating waves, his thrusts turning erratic as he chased his own release. "Elena—shit, I'm—" With a guttural roar that vibrated through his chest, he buried himself to the hilt and came, hot spurts of cum flooding my womb, marking me from the inside out. The sensation—his seed pulsing deep, overflowing to trickle down my thighs—pushed me over the edge again, a second climax tearing through me on the heels of the first, leaving me a trembling, incoherent mess.

We collapsed in a tangle of limbs, chests heaving, hearts pounding in unison. Even then, his hands continued their gentle exploration, tracing lazy patterns over the bruises blooming on my hips, the bite marks on my breasts—tender now, reverent, as if he couldn't bear to stop touching me, claiming me even in repose. He pressed soft kisses to my temple, my jaw, murmuring nonsense words that soothed the raw edges of my oversensitive body.

We made love again and again through the endless night, each joining more desperate than the last, our bodies slick with sweat and the mingled evidence of our releases.

We were both painted with passion's artistry—my skin bearing the evidence of his devoted worship: purple hickeys trailing from neck to navel, fingerprints etched on my thighs, the sticky remnants of his releases drying between my legs. His back was a canvas of my complete surrender, crisscrossed with the scratches of my nails, deep red lines that wept tiny beads of blood where I'd clawed in the throes of ecstasy. We lay spent, limbs entwined, the air thick with the musky scent of sex and sweat.

When exhaustion finally claimed us, I drifted into sleep wrapped in his protective embrace, his arm banded around my waist like an iron vow, his cock—still half-hard—nestled against my ass as if even in slumber he couldn't bear to be parted. I felt safer and more complete than I ever had in my existence, the fated bond humming like a live wire between us. If I'd known what daybreak would bring—the shattering of this illusion, the cold light of duty crashing back in—I might have clung tighter to those precious hours of perfect belonging, whispering pleas into the night for time to stretch just a little longer.

Dawn light crept through the curtains, slowly climbing across the rumpled bed.

I awakened to a symphony of aches throughout my body. Opening my eyes, I first encountered an unfamiliar, ornately decorated ceiling. Then the powerful male arm draped possessively across my waist.

I froze completely, carefully turning my head. A devastatingly handsome but unknown face lay mere inches away. In slumber, he'd lost last night's predatory intensity, appearing peaceful, almost innocent. Yet my heart hammered frantically against my ribs.

Fragments from the night before flashed through my mind—him commanding me to see who he truly was, his tender yet consuming kisses, him breathing my name like a prayer...

Had any of this been accidental?

More crucially, what had I done?

I was Phoebe, not Elena. I'd come here to save my pack, to fulfill a marriage alliance. And now I'd spent the night surrendering myself to a complete stranger.

If they discovered this, if the truth surfaced...

Horrifying visions flooded my mind. Ironspine Pack elders furiously denouncing me as a fraud, a traitor. Drake gazing at me with revulsion, publicly annulling our betrothal. News reaching Grayclaw

Pack—the devastated faces of my people, children weeping from hunger...

They'd declare I'd defiled the sacred alliance between our peoples, trampled upon the hallowed marriage contract. Ironspine Pack wouldn't merely exile me—they'd demand Grayclaw Pack surrender the real Elena as reparation. And when they discovered Elena had vanished long ago...

Grayclaw Pack would face utter annihilation. Not from poverty, not from warfare, but because of me—because of my betrayal, because I couldn't master my desires.

Everyone who'd placed their faith in me would perish in despair, and I'd become the most infamous traitor in pack history.

My hands began trembling violently.

I'd committed an unforgivable transgression.

Not merely because I'd betrayed this arranged marriage, but because I realized last night meant infinitely more to me than a simple "accident."

That profound sense of completion, of finding my place in the universe, of my very soul singing with euphoria...

I'd fallen irrevocably in love with a man I knew absolutely nothing about.

And this man possessed the power to obliterate everything I was fighting to preserve.

I had to escape before he awakened, had to pretend none of this had ever transpired. But as I carefully extracted myself from his embrace, overwhelming reluctance washed through me.

I dressed as silently as possible. The navy evening gown appeared hopelessly wrinkled in the morning light, perfectly mirroring my chaotic mental state.

The castle was beginning to stir. Occasional early-rising servants passed through the corridors. I attempted to appear nonchalant, but internally, I was in complete turmoil.

Once back in my chambers, I collapsed onto the bed's edge, arms wrapped protectively around myself, hands still trembling.

Last night replayed endlessly in my mind like a vivid film. Every exquisite detail had burned itself into my memory, leaving me feeling simultaneously ashamed and desperately longing.

I told myself it had been nothing more than full moon madness, mere hormonal impulse. But my body's honest response betrayed that lie—I could feel his marks upon me, could recall that unprecedented sense of absolute wholeness.

This feeling was far too dangerous—so perilous I nearly bolted back to that room, back to his waiting arms.

But reason commanded otherwise. I was Phoebe, masquerading as Elena, bearing the sacred mission to rescue my pack. Last night had already been a catastrophic mistake. I couldn't compound it with another.

Over the following days, I skulked about like a guilty child.

Whenever Drake appeared, I experienced indescribable guilt and mounting panic. He remained impeccably courteous—tenderly inquiring about my well-being, graciously accompanying me to meals, flawlessly portraying the devoted fiancé before others. But every shared glance, every concerned inquiry felt like daggers piercing my conscience, reminding me I'd betrayed this sacred arrangement, violated our agreement, abandoned my mission here.

"Elena, you appear rather fatigued today," Drake observed with genuine concern over breakfast. "Perhaps I should summon a physician?"

I could barely meet his kind eyes, hastily shaking my head. "That won't be necessary, I simply... haven't been sleeping well."

"Then you must rest more. You needn't attend this afternoon's garden activities." His gentle voice only intensified my torment.

This fundamentally decent man was fretting over a woman who'd betrayed their betrothal. If he knew the truth...

I battled back tears, managing only a few bites before fleeing the dining room.

I could sense his bewildered gaze following me, but explanation was impossible. How could I confess I'd spent a night of passion with another man?

On the third evening, as I attempted to organize my turbulent thoughts in the garden, he materialized.

"We need to talk."

That achingly familiar voice emerged from behind me, instantly paralyzing my entire body.

I turned slowly. He stood beneath the rose arbor, sunset's golden radiance creating an otherworldly halo around him, rendering him simultaneously tangible and phantasmagorical. That same overwhelming presence that commanded attention without effort.

In the sunset's illumination, I could observe his features more clearly. Even more magnificent than memory suggested, yet undeniably colder.

"You..." my voice wavered treacherously. "Who are you?"

"I'm Alexander Gray," he stated with perfect composure. "Senior business consultant for Ironspine Group, specializing in inter-pack commercial agreements and asset integration."

Business consultant? That explained the elders' deferential treatment, his presence within Ironspine Pack's stronghold.

"What brings you here?" I asked, genuinely surprised.

He approached with measured, purposeful steps. "You've been avoiding me."

Absolutely correct. I had been avoiding—evading him, that night's searing memories, my own internal chaos.

"Regarding that night..." He halted directly before me, close enough that his subtle sandalwood scent enveloped me. "I intend to assume responsibility."

Responsibility?

Momentary confusion gave way to understanding. In werewolf society, when an Alpha engaged intimately with an omega—particularly one already promised to another—the Alpha bore an obligation to accept accountability.

But that represented precisely what I feared most.

"No." The words erupted forth, unnaturally sharp in the garden's tranquility. "It's completely unnecessary. That was merely an accident, a regrettable mistake. The full moon's influence caused us both to lose our sanity. Simply... pretend it never occurred."

The instant I uttered those words, I felt my heart being savagely shredded. Each syllable scraped through my throat like broken glass, making breathing nearly impossible. My hands clenched into white-knuckled fists, nails carving crescents into my palms, desperately using physical pain to combat the emotional anguish.

I was lying. Lying directly to my fated mate.

The wolf within me howled in agony, snarled in fury, writhed in torment at my betrayal. It yearned to shatter reason's constraints, to reveal the truth to this man—that night hadn't been accidental but destiny's design. Yet I could only ruthlessly suppress it, forcing it to endure this self-inflicted torture alongside me.

The lie's bitterness coated my tongue, making me physically nauseous.

I witnessed something flicker across his features—wounded surprise? Barely contained rage? The sunset's shifting angles cast dancing shadows over his face, obscuring his true expression.

"Never occurred?" He repeated my words, voice dropping to a dangerously low register. "Is that truly your assessment?"

Evening breeze stirred around us, rose petals cascading between our forms like silent witnesses to my deception.

I felt my pulse thundering like war drums, blood surging through my veins as if struggling to burst free from my flesh. But I had to persevere, even if it meant eviscerating my own heart before my destined mate.

"Yes." I forced steadiness into my voice despite the internal maelstrom. "I'm about to marry Drake. This represents an alliance between our peoples. I cannot permit one reckless night to destroy everything."

Every word drew blood from my soul. But the words were necessary. I had to protect this arrangement, safeguard my pack.

He studied me with unnerving intensity, those azure eyes harboring emotions too complex to decipher.

"Drake." He repeated the name like a curse, voice acquiring that perilous edge, each syllable radiating menace. "Exactly how well do you know him?"

The question bewildered me completely. "What do you mean?"

"I mean," he advanced another step, now close enough that I could distinguish gold flecks within his irises, "do you truly understand the man you're marrying?"

"Of course, I..." I began responding, then halted mid-sentence. Did I genuinely know Drake? Beyond his polished exterior, what else had I learned about him?

"Mr. Gray," I struggled to inject formality and distance into my tone, "I appreciate your... concern. But my position remains crystal clear. My marriage to Drake represents our packs' salvation. I cannot and will not betray that sacred promise."

"Even if it means betraying your own heart?" His voice softened, yet the underlying power made me tremble.

"Heart?" I laughed bitterly. "Mr. Gray, emotions are utterly irrelevant in political marriages. We're adults. We comprehend duty and obligation."

"Are you certain this is your final decision?" he inquired, voice carrying terrifying calm.

"Absolutely." I attempted to project unwavering conviction. "Mr. Gray, we're mature individuals. We must accept responsibility for our actions. But certain mistakes are best addressed through forgetting them entirely."

Silence stretched endlessly between us. The sun vanished completely, plunging the garden into purple twilight. The distant castle blazed with warm light, yet here felt eerily quiet, containing only the night wind whispering through rose bushes.

Eventually, he retreated a single step.

"I understand perfectly." His voice resumed that distant frigidity. "Since this represents your choice, I'll respect your decision."

He pivoted to depart, but after several paces, glanced back.

"However, Miss Elena Grayclaw," his tone carried ice I'd never encountered before, "I strongly suggest careful consideration. Some people, once lost, could never be found again."

"I've considered everything thoroughly," I managed to respond.

He granted me one final look, penetrating enough to make me feel completely exposed, as if he could perceive directly through every deception.

"I'm granting you time," he declared, voice soft as night wind yet carrying unmistakable steel. "Consider carefully what you truly desire. Determine what matters more—the perfection others expect, or your heart's authentic voice. But remember, my patience has definite limits."

With that pronouncement, he turned and strode purposefully from the garden, rapidly vanishing into gathering darkness.

I remained motionless, watching his silhouette dissolve into sunset, unprecedented emptiness consuming my chest.

Had I made the correct choice?

For my pack, for this crucial alliance, for everyone depending upon me, I'd chosen duty over my heart's desperate plea.

But why did I feel as though I'd sacrificed something infinitely precious? As if I'd discarded my very soul?

Complete darkness descended. I stood in the garden, letting the evening breeze tangle my hair. Stars emerged overhead one by one, bearing witness to my internal struggle.

I reassured myself I'd made the mature decision. I was Elena now, not Phoebe. I carried a far more important mission to complete.

But my heart recognized the truth—I'd just rejected my fated mate, spurned the man who made my wolf tremble with recognition.

And this decision might become my life's most devastating regret.

Two weeks elapsed. I believed I'd reclaimed my equilibrium.

Daily existence fell into predictable patterns—sharing breakfast with Drake, accompanying him to various meetings, performing as the ideal future Luna before everyone. He remained perfectly courteous and gentle, while I strived to appear competent. Superficially, everything progressed according to plan.

But my body was undergoing subtle transformations.

Initially, I attributed it to stress-induced discomfort. Morning nausea, hypersensitivity to certain food aromas, inexplicable exhaustion... I convinced myself these were normal responses to environmental adjustment.

Until this morning.

I was arranging my hair at the vanity, preparing for today's Pack Meeting, when suddenly, overwhelming nausea struck. I rushed to the bathroom, stomach convulsing violently.

When I shakily regained my footing, gripping the marble sink, my reflection revealed a pallid face filled with terror.

No, this was impossible.

But my rational mind clearly understood the implications. Missed menstrual cycles, morning sickness, olfactory sensitivity... every symptom indicated a reality I dared not confront.

I was pregnant.

Carrying Alexander Gray's child.

I collapsed onto the cold bathroom tiles, trembling hands instinctively protecting my abdomen. A tiny life was developing within me—the biological fusion of that man and myself.

Terror crashed over me like a devastating tsunami.

If Ironspine Pack discovered I carried another man's child instead of Drake's, if they uncovered my fraudulent identity... not only would I face exile, but Grayclaw Pack would suffer complete annihilation. They'd perceive this as ultimate deception and betrayal of our sacred arrangement, an unforgivable desecration of Ironspine Pack's honor.

I recalled the elders' words during the Pack Meeting—"Grayclaw Pack's current situation is already precarious. Any mistake could prove our death sentence."

And I had committed an irreversible transgression.

I had to confess the truth to Drake.

This thought reverberated incessantly through my mind. Regardless of the pain, the terror, I couldn't permit the entire pack to suffer for my error. Perhaps... perhaps if I revealed everything, if I pleaded for his mercy, hope might still exist.

Maybe he'd demonstrate understanding, offer forgiveness, and even help me preserve this secret.

Or he'd be utterly revolted, cancel our betrothal, and condemn Grayclaw Pack to destruction.

But I possessed no alternative.

After dinner, I summoned my courage and knocked upon Drake's study door.

CHAPTER FIVE

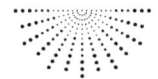

Phoebe

The oak door to the study felt ice-cold beneath my fingertips.

I stood there, taking a deep breath, trying to steady my racing heart. The hallway carried the faint scent of candle wax, and oil paintings cast dancing shadows in the dim light. Distant footsteps echoed occasionally through the castle, but here, everything was unnaturally quiet.

I had to tell Drake the truth. Whatever the consequences, I couldn't keep living this lie.

I knocked softly. "Drake?"

No answer.

I knocked again, louder this time. "Drake, it's me, Elena. I need to speak with you about something important."

Still silence.

I tried the handle—unlocked. The study was empty. Neat bookshelves lined the walls, heavy volumes perfectly arranged. Papers were scattered across the mahogany desk, but no Drake.

Perhaps he was elsewhere?

I closed the door and decided to search for him. My footsteps whispered against the thick Persian carpet as I moved down the corridor. The castle felt ghostly at this hour, nothing but the distant ticking of grandfather clocks and my own thundering heartbeat.

Rounding the corner, I spotted a tall figure ahead.

Instantly, recognition slammed into me. That commanding presence, that aura that made my wolf whimper and strain against my ribs...

It was him. Alexander Gray.

But what was he doing here? At this hour, in this place?

"Mr. Gray?" I called out hesitantly.

The figure turned.

The moment our eyes met, my heart hammered against my chest. Those piercing blue eyes, that face that had undone me beneath the moonlight... Yes, it was definitely him. My fated mate.

But the way he looked at me chilled me to the bone.

No warmth. No recognition. Not even a flicker of emotion. He regarded me like a complete stranger, his gaze terrifyingly calm, cold enough to stop a heart.

This was wrong. All wrong.

In the garden, even when I'd rejected him, even when I'd wounded him, there had been fire in his eyes—anger, disappointment, pain. But now... now there was nothing.

As if I were invisible. As if I meant absolutely nothing.

He glanced at me once, then turned and continued walking, his stride confident and dismissive. The entire encounter lasted perhaps three seconds, as though I didn't exist.

I remained frozen, feeling the world tilt beneath my feet.

"Wait..." I wanted to call out, but the word died in my throat.

He was already gone, vanished around the corner without a backward glance.

I pressed against the wall, legs trembling. What had just happened?

Why was Alexander Gray wandering Drake's castle? Why this arctic indifference? Had our conversation in the garden truly damaged him so deeply that he'd decided to treat me as a stranger?

Deep in my chest, that gnawing unease intensified.

I couldn't simply let him walk away.

My wolf was snarling, clawing, demanding I pursue him. The pull from somewhere primal and blood-deep was impossible to ignore.

"Wait!" I hurried after him, my voice bouncing off the stone walls. "Please, wait!"

He didn't pause, didn't even slow. I was nearly running to catch up.

"Mr. Gray, I need to speak with you." I was breathless as I stepped into his path.

He stopped, but those arctic blue eyes remained unchanged. "Miss Elena, it's quite late. You should return to your chambers."

His voice was devastatingly calm, as though addressing a complete stranger.

Why? Why was he speaking to me like this? As if our garden conversation had never occurred, as if that night beneath the full moon existed only in my imagination.

"No, please listen." I drew a shaky breath, struggling to organize my thoughts. "I... I want to tell you the truth. About that night, about who I really am, about everything."

He arched an eyebrow, but his expression remained granite-still. "The truth?"

"Yes." My hands were trembling, but I forced myself to continue.

"First, I must tell you—I have feelings for you. That night wasn't an accident or impulse. It was the call between fated mates. I know I rejected you before, hurt you, but I..."

I had to say it. Had to let him know how I truly felt.

Perhaps my rejection in the garden had wounded him. Perhaps that explained this coldness. If I was honest, if I bared my soul, surely he would understand?

"Stop." He cut me off, voice flat as winter stone. "Miss Elena, I believe you're mistaken about something."

No, I wasn't mistaken. I could feel the connection between us, that soul-deep pull couldn't possibly be false.

"I'm not mistaken!" I said desperately. "I know this sounds complicated, but please let me finish. I... I'm not really Elena Grayclaw."

That finally provoked a reaction, but not the shock I'd expected. Instead, a flicker of bored irritation crossed his features.

Why? Why would he react like that?

"I'm Phoebe," I pressed on. "I'm impersonating Elena to fulfill this arranged marriage, to save my pack. But when I met you, I realized..."

"Realized what?" His voice turned arctic. "That you could use your feminine wiles to extract greater advantages?"

His words struck like a physical blow.

No, that wasn't it at all. How could he reduce our sacred bond to something so calculating?

"That's not it! I realized we're fated mates. I realized I love..."

"Enough." His voice turned razor-sharp, severing my words. "Miss Phoebe, you may cease this performance."

I went rigid. He... he'd called me Phoebe? My heart began racing, but not from joy—from terror.

"You're not surprised?" I whispered. "I tell you I'm not Elena, and you show no surprise whatsoever?"

He released a laugh devoid of any warmth. "Why should I be surprised? Did you believe your masquerade was convincing?"

My world began spinning. No, this couldn't be happening.

"You... you knew from the beginning?"

"From the very first moment." His words fell like hammer blows. "The real Elena Grayclaw vanished a month ago. Grayclaw Pack dispatched you as her replacement, thinking you could deceive us all."

From the beginning? That meant... when he'd approached me during the full moon, he'd known I was an impostor? He'd known my true identity and still...

"Then... why didn't you expose me? Why..."

"Why did I sleep with you?" He stated what I couldn't bring myself to say. "Because it was an error in judgment. Full moon pheromones caused a momentary lapse in control. Nothing more."

Each word was a dagger to my heart.

An error? Nothing more? Impossible. That soul-deep resonance, that feeling of perfect completion...

"No... it wasn't like that. I could sense what you felt for me..."

"Sense what?" He regarded me with open mockery. "Miss Phoebe, perhaps you overestimate your charms?"

I couldn't draw breath, as though invisible hands were crushing my windpipe.

How could he look at me with such contempt? How could he speak in such dismissive tones? Was this man standing before me truly the same one who'd held me with such tenderness beneath the stars?

"But... we're fated mates. I can feel that calling..."

"Fated mates?" He repeated the words with disgust. "An impostor, a deceiver—you believe fate would choose someone like you?"

Deceiver. He'd called me a deceiver.

Every syllable lashed across my heart. Yes, I was living a lie, yes, I was impersonating another, but that wasn't my choice—it was to save my people. And what we'd shared... that hadn't been deception.

Tears began blurring my vision, but I refused to surrender.

"Please don't say that... That night, you made me see who you truly were. You said 'remember me'..."

Those words, those passionate declarations—surely they'd meant something?

"Merely pillow talk, Miss Phoebe." His voice could have frozen flame. "You didn't actually believe those words carried deeper meaning?"

Pillow talk? I felt my heart being systematically destroyed.

Those words that had haunted my dreams, those phrases I'd treasured as declarations of love, had become something so trivial in his mouth.

I stepped forward, reaching to touch him, desperate to prove our connection was real.

Perhaps if I touched him, he'd remember that perfect night. Perhaps this was merely a facade, protecting something vulnerable beneath.

I extended my hand toward his arm, but he jerked away with violent force.

The movement was so sharp I nearly lost my footing, stumbling backward. That gesture of revulsion, as though I were something contaminated he couldn't bear to touch.

"Don't touch me." His voice dripped with disgust. "Miss Phoebe, I strongly suggest you leave now."

Leave? He wanted me gone?

The words made my knees buckle, but I steadied myself.

"The promise you made in the garden—does it still stand?" My voice emerged weaker than intended, fingertips growing numb. "You said you'd give me time. Is it because I rejected you then that you've... changed your mind?"

I paused, choosing directness. "My choice hurt you, and that was my fault. But I'm here now—that's my answer. Can't we... can't we simply talk?"

He averted his gaze, his profile drawn tight. After an endless moment, he released a barely audible scoff.

"There's nothing to discuss." His tone held no emotion, only complete detachment. "The past should remain buried."

This was worse than anger. This was soul-crushing indifference.

"Why..." I heard my voice crack, all composure finally crumbling. "Won't you give me even one chance... to make this right?"

"Because your very existence here is a mistake." His words were ice. "An impostor, a liar—how long did you imagine you could maintain this charade?"

A mistake. My presence was a mistake. That night that had made me feel whole for the first time—in his eyes, it was merely an error.

"Final warning," he turned to leave. "If you value your life, leave this place. Don't show up again. Don't mention that night again. Otherwise..."

He left the threat unfinished, but his frigid tone was warning enough.

Just then, I heard approaching footsteps.

A familiar figure emerged from the corridor's far end.

Sera.

She wore an elegant midnight-blue gown, her golden hair catching the dim light. When she spotted us, her lips curved into a flawless smile.

"Honey," her voice was silk and intimacy, the tone reserved for beloved lovers. "What are you doing here?"

Honey? She called him honey?

I looked at the man beside me. His expression transformed instantly. That arctic coldness melted away the moment she appeared, replaced by a warmth I'd never witnessed.

"Sera." His voice became velvet, utterly different from the ice he'd used with me. "It's quite late. Why aren't you resting?"

"I was searching for you." Sera glided to his side, linking her arm through his with practiced ease. "There are matters regarding tomorrow's meeting I wanted to discuss."

Her gesture was so natural, so intimate, as though they'd always been thus. And he... he didn't resist, showed no discomfort whatsoever.

"Of course." He nodded, then glanced at me with undisguised revulsion. "Miss Phoebe, you should retire to your chambers."

Only then did Sera seem to notice me, her gaze lingering on my tear-ravaged face before adopting an expression of perfect concern.

"Elena? What's the matter? You look dreadful." Her voice held flawless sympathy, but I caught something else beneath it.

When she looked at me, triumph flickered in her eyes. What stunned me was what I read in her expression and bearing—a terrible revelation.

Her possessiveness over this man. That victor's smugness. That pity reserved for defeated rivals—all written clearly across her features.

So Sera's affections weren't directed at Drake at all. She loved Alexander Gray.

She had won. Utterly and completely.

"I'm fine." I barely managed the words, my voice a broken whisper.

"Are you sure?" Sera continued. "You appear to have been weeping. Are you feeling unwell?"

"She's perfectly fine," Alexander answered for me, tone dismissive. "Merely tired."

Then he turned to Sera, his voice warm once more. "Shall we go?"

I watched them depart together, Sera's arm still threaded through his. Their silhouettes looked perfectly matched, utterly harmonious, like destiny itself had crafted them for each other.

While I stood there—an unwanted interloper.

No wonder he'd been so cold. No wonder he'd dismissed our intimacy as meaningless. To him, I truly was inconsequential.

My wolf was keening, wounded by this betrayal. That connection I'd believed was fated had been nothing but wishful delusion.

Grief crashed over me like a tsunami, drowning reason. I couldn't breathe; my heart felt crushed in an invisible fist. Every hope, every cherished fantasy, shattered in that moment.

I hadn't merely lost love—I'd lost faith in destiny itself, lost all hope for the future.

Darkness crept into my vision, ears ringing. I tried to brace myself against the wall, but my legs had completely given out.

Before consciousness fled entirely, I heard rapid footsteps, someone calling my name. But the voice sounded impossibly distant, ethereal.

Then everything went black.

Consciousness drifted in darkness, like sinking through deep ocean waters. Occasionally, muffled voices reached me from some far shore.

"...collapsed completely...physician says merely exhaustion..."

"...needs proper rest...should wake by morning..."

Footsteps receded, leaving the room in silence. I wanted to open my eyes, but my eyelids felt weighted with lead.

Time became meaningless until I heard a door opening softly. Light footsteps approached, careful not to disturb.

"Phoebe..."

A familiar, gentle voice spoke near my ear, thick with pain and self-recrimination.

Elias?

"I'm here too late, Phoebe. Far too late." His voice trembled with suppressed emotion. "If I'd sensed trouble sooner, if I'd insisted on accompanying you inside, perhaps..."

He paused. The bedside chair creaked softly.

"I've been waiting outside the castle walls for word, for your signal. But you never sent any message, never appeared at our arranged meeting point. I knew something had gone wrong."

His voice grew increasingly hoarse.

"From the moment I first saw you at fifteen, I knew I'd spend my life protecting you..." His words became whisper-soft. "But I never imagined it would come to this. You're so remarkable, so brave—why must you endure such treatment?"

His hand touched mine with infinite gentleness, as though I were made of fragile crystal.

"Look at you now—so much thinner, so pale. Ironspine Pack's security is formidable. I barely managed to locate you, but I overheard your conversation by accident and learned what transpired. I wasn't eavesdropping intentionally, but seeing you weep in that corridor broke my heart." His voice turned fierce. "Did that Gray bastard hurt you?"

I heard him rise, pacing the room.

"Whatever happened, whatever he said or did, none of it is your fault. You've already sacrificed far too much for the pack's sake. I cannot allow you to suffer further."

His voice hardened with resolve.

"Grayclaw Pack may need this marriage alliance for survival, but if this man cannot appreciate your worth..." His tone became diamond-hard, carrying a finality I'd never heard before.

"Then I'm taking you away. Even if Alpha punishes me, even if the pack condemns me, I won't let you endure more of this torment."

Take me away? But what about the Grayclaw Pack?

I fought desperately to open my eyes, to stop him from making such a rash decision, but my body refused to obey.

"Phoebe..." he whispered against my ear. "I'm getting you out of here."

No... I wanted to protest, but couldn't form words.

"I'll arrange everything before dawn—horses, routes. We'll use the back roads, avoid main thoroughfares, escape Ironspine territory before they discover your absence."

In the darkness, I wanted to respond, to tell him I heard every word. But consciousness was too heavy, dragging me back toward the abyss.

His hand stroked my forehead tenderly.

"Rest now. When you wake, we'll be going home. No more enduring their contempt, no more bearing burdens that were never yours to carry."

In that darkness, his promise shone like a beacon, piercing the fog of despair.

Perhaps... perhaps leaving truly was the wisest choice.

CHAPTER SIX

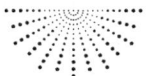

Drake

"Come in."

Kay pushed the door open, wearing that familiar grim expression.

"Alpha, everything you ordered has been handled. Castle security has been completely lifted—no interference whatsoever. Miss Phoebe and Elias have departed."

I nodded, struggling to keep my voice steady. "Good. Did you arrange protection?"

"Our most reliable people are shadowing them. They'll ensure she reaches her destination safely."

I stood at the window, watching the carriage disappear into the morning mist.

The wheels rattled rhythmically against the cobblestones, the sound growing fainter until it vanished completely down the path toward Grayclaw Pack territory. Through a gap in the carriage curtains, I glimpsed Phoebe's pale profile as she slumped against the cushions, looking so fragile, so utterly exhausted. Elias rode alongside on horseback, scanning their surroundings with the vigilance of someone guarding precious treasure.

I closed my eyes as memories crashed over me like waves. The moment I first saw her on that balcony, I knew everything was over. Not the arranged marriage—but my existence as a cold, rational alpha.

That instant of recognition—she was my fated mate—nearly shattered my control on the spot. For years, I'd dismissed fated mates as beautiful legends in our world. But when I saw her, the wolf inside me unleashed a roar unlike anything I'd ever experienced—pure, primal joy at finding home.

I should have turned and walked away. As Alpha of the Ironspine Pack, I had greater responsibilities, more pressing matters to handle. A woman masquerading as someone else shouldn't have become a variable in my carefully laid plans.

But when she kissed me first, every rational thought I possessed surrendered completely.

That soft touch, that intoxicating scent—it demolished every defense I'd constructed over the years in a single instant. I felt her nervousness, her inexperience, her inner turmoil. But I also felt her desire for me, that call resonating from the depths of our bloodlines.

"Open your eyes. Look at me clearly and see who I really am."

I remember exactly what I was feeling when I spoke those words. I wanted her to know that the man standing before her wasn't Kay playing a role, but the real Drake Ironspine. I wanted her to choose me, to accept me, while fully conscious and aware.

But the deeper truth was that I needed to see the honesty in her eyes. I needed to confirm that her response wasn't merely the full moon's influence, but something born of that inexplicable connection between us that transcended all reason.

When I saw the fascination and longing burning in her gaze, I knew I was utterly lost.

Every detail of that night was seared into my memory—her weight in my arms, the warmth of her skin, her heart racing with passion. But what haunted me most wasn't our physical union, but that overwhelming sense of completeness.

For years, I'd felt fractured, as if half of me was missing, always searching for something I couldn't name. But that night, with her in my arms, I finally understood what I'd been seeking—her, my other half.

"Remember this feeling... remember me."

My voice was nearly broken when I whispered those words against her ear. Because I knew it might be our final moment of intimacy. As Alpha, I had to protect my pack, had to face the storms gathering on the horizon. And she—an impostor—was never meant to remain at my side.

But in that moment, I still clung to a thread of hope that somehow I could find a way to protect both my pack and keep her with me.

Looking back now, how naive that hope seems.

She was gone.

This was what I wanted, wasn't it? I personally told her to leave, personally declared her presence a mistake. Now she had truly left, and I should feel satisfied.

So why did my chest feel like it was caving in? Why was my wolf howling inside me, desperate to chase after her retreating figure?

Last night in the corridor, when I saw her face streaked with tears, I nearly broke. I almost pulled her into my arms and confessed that it was all lies, that I'd never stopped missing her for a single moment.

But I couldn't. For her safety, to shield her from the bloodshed to come, I had to make her hate me, had to drive her away.

Even if it meant shredding my own heart in the process.

"Alpha, we have a serious problem." Kay's voice cut through my spiraling thoughts.

I turned around, noting the gravity in his expression, and dread settled in my chest like a stone. "What problem?"

"We found the mole. The Darkfang Pack spy—the one who witnessed you and Miss Phoebe together that night."

My hands clenched into fists involuntarily.

"Where is he?"

"In the basement. But Alpha..." Kay continued, his voice heavy, "the situation is worse than we anticipated. He managed to transmit intelligence before we captured him. Not only that, but we received an official challenge from Darkfang Pack this morning."

Icy fury shot straight to my skull, my knuckles white with the force of my grip.

"A challenge?"

Kay retrieved a letter bearing a black wax seal from inside his coat.

"They haven't specified exact grievances, merely claimed that Ironspine Pack has been 'treacherous' and demanded we surrender the relevant parties as a show of good faith, or face a declaration of war. Clearly, they're using vague accusations to gauge our response."

I accepted the letter and scanned its contents rapidly. Every word dripped with malicious threats and calculated scheming.

I placed the letter on the desk. "Standard tactics for them—manufacturing pretexts to seize territory."

"Precisely, Alpha. Our intelligence indicates Darkfang Pack has been amassing significant forces along our border recently. This is a coordinated effort."

I moved to the map, studying the boundary lines between our territories. Darkfang Pack had chosen their timing expertly—we'd just completed a security rotation, and our new defensive positioning wasn't fully established. If war erupted now, we'd be fighting from a disadvantage.

"There's worse news," Kay pressed on. "According to our sources, Darkfang Pack is already aware of Miss Phoebe's significance to you. They're dispatching tracking teams to capture her before she reaches Grayclaw Pack territory."

My blood turned to ice. This was precisely the nightmare I'd feared most. If Darkfang Pack seized Phoebe, they wouldn't merely use her as leverage against me—they would subject her to unspeakable horrors.

"Deploy additional guards," I commanded immediately. "Send our most elite warriors. Ensure she reaches Grayclaw Pack territory without incident."

"Already in motion. But Alpha, I fear it may not be sufficient. Darkfang Pack is deadly serious this time—they won't allow this opportunity to slip through their fingers."

I began pacing, my mind rapidly calculating the strategic implications. Darkfang Pack's ambitions extended far beyond Phoebe—they sought to crush Ironspine Pack entirely. Phoebe was merely a playing piece in their larger game.

"Take me to the spy."

The basement was shrouded in dim light, the air thick with dampness and the metallic tang of blood. The Darkfang Pack operative was bound to a chair, his face a patchwork of bruises, yet his eyes still gleamed with malevolent defiance.

When he spotted me, his lips curved into a taunting smile.

"Drake Ironspine," his voice emerged as a rasp, "finally deigning to visit?"

"You've already transmitted the intelligence." This wasn't a question—it was confirmation.

"Of course," he replied with smug satisfaction, "my masters were absolutely delighted to learn that the mighty Alpha of Ironspine Pack had been completely bewitched by some counterfeit. When word of this spreads, the entire werewolf world will mock you."

I maintained an outward facade of calm, but the wolf within me was growing increasingly agitated.

"More crucially," he continued, his eyes blazing with madness, "that little whore has become our primary target. We will locate her, and she will pay dearly for your transgressions. Picture this—when we finally capture her..."

"Silence." The words emerged through clenched teeth.

"Oh, struck a nerve?" He regarded me with mockery. "We'll make her beg for death, ensure she spends whatever remains of her pathetic life in absolute agony. And you—you'll be powerless to intervene, because once this war begins, you won't have the luxury of mounting any rescue."

The primal instinct to protect my mate erupted with volcanic force. My wolf shattered through every restraint of rational thought. One heartbeat later, my hand had closed around his throat.

"Touch even a single hair on her head, and I will erase Darkfang Pack from existence."

Terror flickered in his eyes, but he managed one final act of defiance. "Killing me changes nothing... She's already been marked for death. Darkfang Pack will never... never let her escape. And do you honestly believe you can wage war while protecting her simultaneously? Ha—"

I didn't permit him another word. My fingers contracted with sudden, crushing force. A soft crack of cartilage breaking, and all struggling and gasping ceased permanently.

"Dispose of the body." I released my grip and addressed Kay.

"Yes, Alpha."

Returning to my office, I positioned myself before the map, lost in strategic contemplation. The situation had grown far more complex than I'd initially assessed. Darkfang Pack's goals extended beyond capturing Phoebe—they intended to use this crisis as justification for total warfare. If I diverted forces to protect her, it would compromise our defensive capabilities. But if I abandoned her to fate...

No. I would never permit Darkfang Pack to harm her.

"Kay," I made my decision, "immediately deploy our most elite operatives. Not to shield Phoebe, but to systematically eliminate Darkfang Pack's tracking teams. I want absolute assurance that no threat can reach her."

"But Alpha, this will significantly reduce our available forces..."

"I'm fully aware of the risks." I turned to face him directly. "But this is non-negotiable. Phoebe's safety supersedes any strategic consideration."

Kay nodded, and I could see he understood the depth of my resolve.

"Additionally," I continued, "strengthen our diplomatic contacts with other packs. If Darkfang Pack truly intends total war, we'll require allies."

"Understood. One final matter, Alpha." Kay hesitated briefly. "Regarding Miss Phoebe... if war does erupt, what are your intentions?"

I remained silent for an extended moment. The answer to this question was both complex and agonizing.

"When the war concludes, assuming we both survive..." my voice dropped to barely above a whisper, "I will find her and reveal the truth. I'll explain why I inflicted such pain upon her, and tell her... that I never ceased loving her."

"And if she refuses to forgive you?"

I smiled with bitter irony. "Then I will dedicate the remainder of my existence to atonement, ensuring she never suffers harm again. Even if forgiveness remains forever beyond my reach, I will guard her until my final breath."

This was my fated mate, the woman for whom I would sacrifice everything. Even if hatred consumed her heart toward me, even if possession of her remained impossible, I would employ every resource at my disposal to guarantee her safety.

Darkfang Pack craved war? I would deliver war in abundance.

But first, Phoebe's security had to be absolute.

"One additional matter, Alpha." Kay's voice drew me back from my rage-fueled contemplation of Darkfang Pack. "The authentic Elena Grayclaw has been located and recovered. She awaits you in the reception room, requesting a personal discussion regarding the arranged marriage."

I nodded curtly. "Have her wait briefly. I need to address other urgent matters before meeting with her."

Kay acknowledged with a nod, then asked with noticeable hesitation, "Concerning Miss Phoebe..."

Phoebe.

Her name pierced my heart like a dagger. She was in that carriage at this very moment, weakly leaning against the cushions while Elias carefully escorted her toward home. And I had personally thrust her away, allowing her to believe my love had been fabricated.

"Knowledge of Phoebe's involvement will remain strictly confidential." I fought to maintain vocal stability. "According to official records, the arranged marriage never truly commenced."

"Yes, Alpha." Kay stepped backward, clearly preparing to execute his orders.

But just as he turned to leave, he offered quietly, "Perhaps keeping Miss Phoebe at your side would have been the wiser choice."

Keep her at my side? What decision had I actually made?

A surge of violent irritation exploded in my chest.

I had actually permitted her to leave me?

I had personally expelled my fated mate from my life.

I told her everything between us was elaborate deception, watched the light die completely in her eyes, and witnessed her emotional collapse before me. Then I stood helplessly as another man led her away, possibly never to return to my side again.

Logic insisted this served her best interests, protecting her from entanglement in the approaching carnage. But my wolf was roaring in fury at the loss of its mate. My heart was hemorrhaging from my own calculated cruelty.

Suddenly, uncontrollable rage detonated within me.

I lashed out violently at the nearby table. The massive oak structure toppled under my supernatural strength, scattering papers, inkwell, and quill pens across the floor. Ink spread across the carpet like spilled black blood.

Kay froze in shock, turning back to stare at me. In his perception, I should embody the calm, rational leader—the Alpha who never lost composure. But now I resembled nothing more than a beast consumed by madness.

"Alpha..."

"Get out." My voice emerged as a hoarse growl. "Leave immediately."

Kay offered no further words, departing swiftly and closing the door with deliberate gentleness.

I stood at the center of the chaotic room, fists clenched until my knuckles ached. The anguish in my chest surged like a relentless tide, making each breath a struggle.

I made the correct choice, I told myself repeatedly. For her protection, to spare her from the bloody conflict ahead, I had to force her departure. Even if it meant inflicting wounds upon her, compelling her to hate me.

But why did this "correct" decision cause such excruciating

torment? Why was my wolf howling as if it had lost the most essential part of existence itself?

After some time, Kay knocked softly before entering.

"Alpha, Miss Elena Grayclaw has arrived."

The woman who followed Kay possessed striking beauty—chestnut hair, emerald eyes, and indeed bore some resemblance to Phoebe. However, she radiated a sharpness that Phoebe lacked, a worldly composure born of experience.

I drew a steadying breath, attempting to regain emotional equilibrium.

"Please, enter."

Elena's gaze swept across the scattered debris, her mouth curving into a knowing smile.

"It appears I've arrived at an inopportune moment." She settled gracefully onto the sofa. "Mr. Kay mentioned you wished to see me, though perhaps I should return later?"

Rather than address her question, I returned to my position by the window. "Kay informed me of your reluctance to proceed with this arranged marriage."

"Correct." Her voice remained perfectly controlled. "Just as you clearly share that sentiment."

I turned to study her expression. "What exactly are you implying?"

"What I'm suggesting," she crossed her legs with practiced elegance, "is that he provided me with certain details regarding Phoebe's situation. I understand she assumed my identity to facilitate this marriage alliance on behalf of the Grayclaw Pack. While I remain ignorant of the specifics concerning your relationship, it appears... quite fascinating."

My expression hardened dangerously. "State your demands."

"Calm yourself, Drake." She laughed with genuine amusement. "I harbor no interest in your personal affairs. In fact, I'm grateful to Phoebe. Without her intervention, I would currently face forced marriage to a man I could never love."

She rose and approached the scattered papers, casually nudging a fallen quill with her foot.

"Initially, I expected Ironspine Pack's Alpha to be some cold-blooded politician willing to sacrifice anyone for advancement. But now it seems," she glanced back at me with sparkling eyes, "you're actually quite the romantic."

My fists clenched reflexively. "Miss Elena Grayclaw, I strongly advise you to..."

"Don't rush toward threats." She interrupted smoothly. "Blackmail holds no appeal for me. I simply want you to understand that I comprehend your choice. Deliberately harming someone you love in order to protect them—I understand that particular agony intimately."

I caught a brief flash of genuine sorrow in her eyes.

"I will cooperate fully with your arrangements," she continued. "Publicly, we'll announce that the marriage alliance was dissolved through mutual agreement. This preserves both your dignity and that girl's safety."

"What compensation do you require?"

"Freedom." Her answer came without hesitation. "Along with sufficient resources to establish an independent life in human society."

I nodded my agreement. "Those terms are acceptable."

"Excellent." She moved toward the exit but paused at the threshold. "One final consideration, Drake. If Phoebe truly is your fated mate, then fate will eventually reunite you. Fate never allows genuine mates to remain permanently separated."

"That reunion will never occur." My voice carried absolute finality. "I have wounded her beyond repair. Forgiveness lies beyond possibility."

"Perhaps." She shrugged with casual indifference. "But when that day inevitably arrives, ensure her safety above all else. And..." she paused meaningfully, "do not move against Grayclaw Pack. Regardless of their role in this deception, Phoebe came here to preserve them. If your love carries any authenticity, do not destroy what she sought to protect."

With those words, she departed, leaving me alone amid the ruins of my office.

Do not move against Grayclaw Pack.

Her counsel held merit. Regardless of my fury over this elaborate deception, regardless of how Grayclaw Pack's elders had exploited Phoebe's loyalty, I could not bring harm to the very people she had risked everything to save.

To do so would constitute the ultimate betrayal of her sacrifice.

I approached the window, gazing toward the direction of Phoebe's departure. The sun was setting, painting the sky in shades of deep crimson, as if the heavens themselves wept blood for our separation.

"Stay safe, Phoebe," I whispered into the gathering darkness. "Someday, I will prove that my love for you was never a lie."

Even if that day never dawned.

The room settled into profound silence, leaving me utterly alone.

I knelt and began collecting the scattered documents. Ink had penetrated deep into the carpet fibers, creating permanent dark stains.

My hands trembled—not from anger, but because this loss of control forced me to acknowledge that Phoebe's influence upon me ran far deeper than I had ever been willing to admit.

I collapsed onto the sofa, burying my face in my hands. Even now, even after personally driving her away, I could recall every detail about her with crystalline clarity. That touch, that sense of spiritual completion, that overwhelming feeling of finally discovering home.

This was the terrible power of fated mates—even when you desperately wished to forget, even when logic demanded forgetting, body and soul would invariably betray rational thought.

I had assumed time and distance would gradually dilute these feelings. I believed that focusing on responsibilities would restore my former peace. But during every quiet evening, during every moment of solitude, her image would resurface, reminding me of what I had once possessed and subsequently lost.

The office clock measured time with relentless precision, each tick emphasizing that she was moving farther beyond my reach.

I stood and walked to the liquor cabinet, pouring myself a generous measure of whiskey. The alcohol burned down my throat, but this physical discomfort paled beside the gaping emptiness in my chest.

Perhaps Elena spoke truthfully. Perhaps fate would never allow genuine mates to remain eternally separated. But even if we encountered each other again, could she possibly forgive last night's calculated cruelty? Could she ever understand why I found it necessary to inflict such pain?

I raised the glass toward the darkened window.

"To you, Phoebe," I said softly. "To the night we shared, and to the regret I can never make whole."

I emptied the glass in a single swallow.

Alcohol coursed through my bloodstream, but I understood that no quantity of liquor could numb my longing for her.

Because she had become an integral part of my very being, a heart I could never surgically remove.

Whether I chose to acknowledge it or not, Phoebe had completely conquered my heart, becoming simultaneously the meaning of my existence and my eternal torment.

This was the curse of fated mates—paradise when possessed, hell when lost.

And I now dwelt in hell.

CHAPTER SEVEN

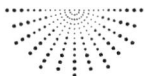

Phoebe

Five years.

I stood at the workbench of the Scent Workshop, sunlight streaming through the massive floor-to-ceiling windows and casting warm light on the perfume-making instruments, making every small bottle gleam like precious gems.

This studio in the heart of the human city had become my sanctuary, far from the turmoil of the werewolf world, far from those painful memories.

"Mommy, this smell is weird."

Four-year-old Ryan stood beside me, pointing with his tiny finger at a bottle of perfume I'd just finished blending. His blue eyes sparkled with curiosity—those eyes... Every time I looked at them, my heart ached.

"That's bergamot and cedar mixed together, sweetheart." I crouched down to meet his gaze. "It's a bit complex for you right now. When you're older, you'll understand these layers."

Ryan nodded and ran back to his corner to play with blocks.

He was always so quiet, so well-behaved. Never threw tantrums like other four-year-olds. Sometimes I wondered if it was because of the blood running through his veins—that man's blood, with its natural calm and control.

I shook my head, pushing away those unnecessary thoughts, and refocused on my work.

Perfume-making had become my salvation.

In this world filled with different scents, I could temporarily forget the past, forget those heartbreaking memories.

Humans might not have a werewolf's keen sense of smell, but their passion for beautiful fragrances was just as intense.

My studio had built up a loyal clientele over these five years. Business wasn't booming, but it was enough to give Ryan and me a peaceful life.

The door chimed as Elias walked in carrying grocery bags.

"Lunch time." He smiled at Ryan. "Little Ryan, what do you want to eat today?"

"Spaghetti!" Ryan immediately dropped his blocks and ran to Elias.

Elias had been with us these five years.

When we left the Ironspine Pack, he told me the Grayclaw Pack had found other ways to resolve their crisis—they no longer needed the political marriage. He said the pack members all understood my situation and wanted me to live peacefully. So we came to this human city, far from werewolf politics.

Elias gave up his chance to return to the Grayclaw Pack and chose to stay and help me run the studio. During the day, he was my assistant, handling clients and managing inventory. At night, he was Ryan's best friend, telling him fascinating stories.

"Any new orders today?" I asked while organizing my workbench.

"A lady wants a custom wedding perfume for next month's ceremony," Elias answered from the small kitchen. "And that elderly woman came back—says her husband loves that woody cologne from last time."

I nodded. These ordinary human clients with their simple needs gave me peace of mind. No political schemes, no pack feuds, no chains of destiny. Just simple business transactions, simple life.

"Mommy," Ryan suddenly appeared at my side. "Can we go to the park tonight? I want to see the swans."

I ruffled his hair. "Of course, sweetheart. After work."

Ryan beamed and ran back to his blocks. Watching his focused little face, complex emotions stirred in my chest.

This child was the most precious gift in my life—and my eternal reminder.

Every expression, every gesture reminded me of that man. Sometimes after Ryan fell asleep, I'd secretly study his profile. The resemblance to someone in my memory was uncanny.

But I never regretted having him. Even if that night was a mistake, even if that man never truly loved me, Ryan was innocent. He belonged to me—only to me.

Sometimes I thought about the people from Grayclaw Pack, about the elders who once trusted me. Elias told me they were all doing well, that the pack had found a new path. This comforted me and confirmed that my choice had been right.

"Phoebe." Elias's voice pulled me from my thoughts.

I looked up. He was focused on preparing lunch, his expression calm and gentle, just like every day these past five years.

"Mommy, someone's knocking," Ryan's voice came from the other end of the studio.

Elias and I exchanged glances, then I walked to the door. Through the glass, I saw a middle-aged man in an expensive suit. He looked ordinary, like a businessman.

I opened the door. "Hello, how can I help you?"

The man smiled and nodded. "I'd like to commission a custom perfume. I heard you're an expert in this field."

"Please come in." I stepped aside. "It's lunch time though. If you don't mind, we can briefly discuss your requirements."

The man surveyed the studio, his gaze lingering on the various fragrance bottles and blending equipment. But I noticed his eyes eventually settled on Ryan.

In that moment, I felt an unusual sense of alertness.

Something was off about this man, though I couldn't pinpoint exactly what.

But deep inside, the wolf that had slept for five years seemed to growl softly.

"Is this your child? Very cute," the man said, his voice gentle. "How old is he?"

"Four." My answer was curt. Instinctively, I moved toward Ryan and pulled him close.

Elias sensed something too. He casually repositioned himself between the man and us.

"Well then," the man continued, still wearing that benign smile, "about that perfume..."

But I was no longer listening attentively.

All my attention focused on protecting Ryan, because instinct told me this seemingly harmless customer might bring the very danger I'd spent five years trying to avoid.

After the strange man left, I couldn't shake my unease.

He'd eventually ordered a simple men's cologne, but throughout the entire process, I felt his attention was more focused on Ryan than anything else.

Maybe I was overthinking. Five years of peaceful living had made me hypersensitive to any disturbance.

"Phoebe," Elias set down a fragrance bottle. "There's something I want to discuss with you."

I looked up to see him holding an invitation with an elegant logo.

"What's this?"

"An invitation to Ironspine Group's supplier bidding conference." He handed me the letter. "They're looking for new perfume suppliers to create a luxury product line. I think this could be a great opportunity for us."

Ironspine Group.

That name made my hands tremble slightly.

Five years—I thought I could face anything related to that world calmly, but apparently I was still naive.

"I'm... not sure this is a good idea." I tried to keep my voice steady.

"Our business is stable enough. We don't need to take unnecessary risks."

"But this is a chance to expand our scale," Elias said gently. "Ironspine Group has significant influence in the human world. If we become their supplier, it would benefit Ryan's future too."

I glanced at Ryan playing with blocks in the corner. I did want to provide him with better living conditions, better educational opportunities. But I was also terrified of reconnecting with that world in any way.

"Are you sure this is just ordinary business cooperation?" I asked. "No other... complicated factors?"

"Absolutely," Elias said firmly. "In the human world, Ironspine Group is just a regular large corporation. Their cosmetics division has been seeking quality perfume suppliers. This is purely business."

I carefully read the invitation's contents. The bidding conference would be held next week. Participants needed to submit an original perfume creation with the theme "Perfect Fusion of Nature and Modernity."

This theme reminded me of my botanical aroma series I'd been developing.

It was my labor of love from these past years, inspired by my love of nature and longing for simple living. Every ingredient was carefully selected, maintaining the raw essence of plants while incorporating modern perfumery techniques.

"If it's just ordinary business cooperation..." I hesitated. "Maybe we could give it a try."

Elias's face lit up with a smile. "I knew you wouldn't miss this opportunity. Your botanical aroma series is absolutely unique. They'll definitely love it."

Over the next few days, I threw myself into preparations. I selected the three most refined pieces from my series: morning mint and lemongrass, afternoon jasmine and birch, and evening sandalwood and cedar. Each represented the natural beauty of different moments throughout the day.

Ryan was curious about my sudden busyness.

"Mommy, what are you doing?" He stood beside me, watching as I carefully poured perfumes into beautiful small bottles.

"Mommy's entering a competition," I explained while working. "If I win, we can make more money and buy you more blocks."

"Then I hope you win!" Ryan said happily and gave me a big hug.

His words warmed my heart. Yes, this was all for him—to give him a better future.

On the day of the bidding conference, I put on my most professional suit and brought my carefully prepared works to Ironspine Group's headquarters in the city center. It was a modern glass building soaring into the clouds, showcasing the company's power and ambition.

I'd originally planned to have Elias stay home with Ryan, but Ryan started getting upset when he heard about being separated from me all day.

"I want to go with Mommy!" He clung to my leg. "I'll be good and won't disturb Mommy's work."

Elias laughed and shook his head. "Phoebe, take him along. It's just a presentation anyway. Let little Ryan see the world."

"But it's a formal business venue..." I hesitated.

"It's fine," Elias said gently. "I'll watch him. Besides, maybe Ryan will bring you good luck."

Finally, I agreed. The three of us went to Ironspine Group headquarters together.

After entering the conference hall, staff guided us to the front-row participant seating. I sat in the chair marked with my name, with Elias and Ryan beside me.

"Remember, little Ryan," Elias whispered to Ryan, "when Mommy goes on stage to present, we need to sit quietly and cheer her on, okay?"

Ryan nodded vigorously, clutching his teddy bear. "I'll be really good."

The hall was already filled with a dozen or so perfumers—some representing famous brands, others founders of independent studios.

I seemed out of place among them—neither from a major brand

nor with an impressive background, just an ordinary perfumer from a small studio.

But when the judges began sampling each work one by one, I saw surprise in their eyes.

"This botanical aroma is quite interesting," a middle-aged female judge picked up my second piece. "The sweetness of jasmine and the freshness of birch create a wonderful balance—elegant yet vibrant."

"Indeed," another judge nodded in agreement. "This approach to combining nature and modernity is unique. No artificial traces, yet full of contemporary sophistication."

My heart raced. This was the first time in five years I'd received such high professional recognition.

"Miss Phoebe," the host looked at me, "could you briefly introduce your creative philosophy?"

I stood up, trying to calm my nerves.

"I believe perfume should be an extension of life, not decoration for life," I began. "Modern people often lose their connection with nature in complex urban living. Through this series, I hope that when people smell these fragrances, they'll remember morning dew, afternoon sunshine, and evening tranquility."

The hall fell silent as everyone listened intently.

"Every ingredient is nature's gift. My job is to help them find their rightful place in modern life. Not to change them, but to let them integrate naturally into our daily existence."

When I finished, soft murmurs rippled through the hall. I could sense that most judges were very interested in both my philosophy and my work.

After brief consultation among the judges, the host approached the microphone. "By unanimous decision, this bidding is won by Miss Phoebe from Scent Workshop! Congratulations on your original perfume receiving recognition."

I stepped forward to receive the contract notice and bowed to the judges' panel. "Thank you for your recognition and for Ironspine Group providing this opportunity. Scent Workshop has always been dedicated to exploring the most authentic expression of fragrances. This recognition means a great deal to us."

After my acceptance speech, the hall erupted in warm applause. The host smiled and continued, "Thank you, Miss Phoebe. This concludes our bidding conference. Thank you all for participating. The group has prepared exquisite refreshments and beverages in the adjacent banquet hall. Please move there for networking."

The joy of winning the bid continued to flow through the banquet hall. The crisp sound of champagne glasses clinking and guests' laughter and conversation intertwined, while the air carried the aroma of delicate desserts.

"Mommy, can we go eat those delicious things?" Ryan tugged gently at my sleeve, looking up with hopeful eyes at the elaborate dessert tower on the buffet table.

I bent down to meet his bright gaze. "Of course, sweetheart. Today's definitely worth celebrating."

Elias smiled and extended his hand to Ryan. "Come on, little gentleman. I'll take you to try that rainbow pudding."

"Really? Thank you, Uncle Elias!" Ryan jumped with excitement and took his hand, then turned back to confirm, "Mommy's coming too, right?"

"Yes, Mommy's coming with you." I couldn't help but smile.

A tall figure in a dark suit walked through the banquet hall's back entrance.

My breathing stopped instantly.

Even after five years, even if his appearance might have changed, that commanding presence, that Alpha aura that made the wolf inside me tremble—that would never change.

My fated mate. Ryan's father. The man who once shattered my heart.

In this moment, time seemed to freeze.

I clenched my fists, desperately trying to stay composed.

Five years—I thought I was far enough from that world, safe enough. But now I understood I could never truly escape.

Time had left few marks on him, only making him appear more mature, more unapproachable.

I fought to remain calm, telling myself this was just a coincidence.

Ryan lifted his little face, looking at Alexander Gray with those innocent blue eyes. Then he stretched out his small hand, pointed at Alexander Gray, and said in his clear, childish voice:

"Mommy, this man smells special."

No. This can't happen.

I hurriedly covered my son's mouth, hoping Alexander Gray hadn't noticed, but reality told me it was too late. Alexander Gray's gaze was completely focused on Ryan. I saw his pupils contract slightly, saw his clenched fists, saw some intense emotion he was struggling to suppress.

"Mommy," Ryan whispered in my ear, confusion in his voice, "why does that man's smell make me feel... safe?"

My blood turned ice cold.

Werewolf pups instinctively sensed the aura of Alphas related to their bloodline. It was instinct, a primitive reaction beyond rational control. And Ryan...

I looked up, inevitably meeting Alexander Gray's gaze.

In that instant, memories flooded back like a tide. The moonlit balcony, his warm embrace, his whispers in my ear, and that soul-trembling sense of completeness.

The attraction between fated mates never disappeared. Even after so much time, even after all the pain and misunderstanding between us, that call from the depths of our blood remained as powerful as ever.

The wolf inside me opened its eyes, revealing its intense longing and submission to this man before me. But my rational mind screamed warnings—danger, flee, protect the child.

The air in the banquet hall seemed to thicken as everyone held their breath, watching this scene unfold.

And I knew that no matter how desperately I wanted to protect Ryan, no matter how much I wanted to escape, the wheels of fate had already begun to turn.

CHAPTER EIGHT

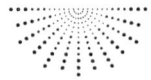

Drake

Five whole years.

I told myself she was doing fine. Told myself that someday I'd go find her.

The war with Darkfang Pack dragged on longer and bloodier than anyone expected. They didn't just want territory—they wanted to destroy Ironspine Pack completely. The fighting stretched on for four brutal years, and every time I thought I could break away to search for Phoebe, some new crisis would explode.

First year—constant border skirmishes. I had to lead every damn battle myself. Second year—assassins infiltrated the castle and nearly succeeded. Third year—neutral packs started wavering, so I spent months running between territories, keeping alliances alive. Fourth year—we finally crushed Darkfang Pack, but rebuilding ate up what little energy I had left.

I'd sent people to protect her for a while. Made sure she reached safety, made sure Darkfang's tracking teams got wiped out completely. My scouts reported that she and Elias never returned to Grayclaw Pack—they just vanished into some corner of the human world.

I thought about sending more people to find her immediately, but Darkfang was still breathing down our necks. Too much searching might expose her location and bring danger right to her door. I told myself that once the war ended, once everything was safe, I'd find her.

But when the war finally ended, when I finally had time to look—the human world was so vast, the trail so cold. I threw every resource I had at it, sent my best trackers, but she'd disappeared without a trace.

Each dead end hit harder than the last. Every empty lead just fed my frustration, my rage—at my own incompetence, at fate's cruel timing, at this whole fucked-up situation.

I even started wondering if maybe she didn't want to be found. Maybe she was completely done with the werewolf world. Done with me. Maybe she and Elias really were living happily somewhere, and I was just some fool who couldn't face reality.

But I never gave up. Even in my darkest moments, I never stopped looking.

Alexander Gray—that name I only used in special situations. The name I'd given her, and she'd never questioned it.

After she left, I used it whenever I appeared in public. Only Ironspine Pack's inner circle knew my real identity, and they understood that sometimes fake names meant better protection.

But this time was different. I wanted to face Phoebe as Alexander Gray, then tell her the truth—that I was Drake, Alpha of Ironspine Pack. Ask for her forgiveness. Just like she'd confessed her real identity to me all those years ago. I didn't know if I'd ever get that chance, or how long I'd have to wait. Even if it took my whole life, I'd do it willingly.

Until today. When I attended Ironspine Pack's bidding conference.

Fate put her in the most impossible place...

That familiar electric shock tore through every nerve in my body.

Even across the crowded room, even with her back turned, I could feel that pull from deep within my blood. The wolf inside me roared with joy at finding our mate. The attraction was so intense I could barely breathe.

It was her. Phoebe.

My fated mate, just dozens of steps away.

All rational thought surrendered.

I walked toward her without hesitation.

I pushed through the crowd, each step urgent and determined. The closer I got, the stronger her pull became. My heart hammered, blood boiling in my veins, just as out of control as that first time I'd seen her.

But when I looked over her shoulder, what I saw froze my blood solid.

Elias.

He stood right beside Phoebe, close enough to make my wolf snarl with threat. That intimate distance, that natural companionship—like they belonged together.

Jealousy slithered through my chest like a poisonous snake. Every muscle tensed. This man—this man who'd protected her since childhood—was still by her side. And me... I'd pushed her away with my own hands, sent her straight back into his arms.

Possessiveness burned through me like wildfire. I wanted to charge over there, tear him away from her, tell everyone she was mine—only mine. My fists clenched until my knuckles went white, instinct warring with whatever rational thought I had left.

Then I saw something that shocked me even more.

Elias was bending down, gently wiping cake crumbs from a little boy's mouth. His movements were so natural, so tender—like he was caring for his own child. The boy looked up at him with complete trust and affection.

But what really froze me in place was the child's face.

Deep blue eyes. Eyes exactly like mine. The strong nose, the determined jawline... every feature on that small face screamed an impossible truth.

Those were my eyes. My features. My bloodline.

The child turned toward me, and our gazes met across the room. Time stopped. I saw my own childhood reflection, saw the mark of Ironspine Pack blood, saw... my son.

My legs nearly gave out.

This child—this child Elias was treating so tenderly—was mine and Phoebe's?

The result of that full moon night?

Everything clicked into place. Phoebe's weakness when she left, the despair in her eyes, the hatred she felt for me... She'd been carrying my child when she walked away, and I'd hurt her like the bastard I was, left her to face it all alone.

The child blinked.

My heart felt like someone was crushing it in their fist, pain so sharp I could barely breathe.

What had I missed? My son's first smile? First steps? First time saying "daddy"? And all of it—all of it—had been witnessed by another man, shared with another man.

Anger, pain, regret—every emotion crashed over me like a tidal wave, threatening to drown me.

I had to go over there. Had to see her, had to see my child, had to...

My feet moved without hesitation.

The crowd parted naturally before me. My target was clear—Phoebe, and that child who carried my blood.

Elias sensed my approach first. His body went rigid, instinctively moving closer to Phoebe in a protective stance that made my wolf rumble dangerously. When our eyes met, the air crackled with tension between two dominant males.

He extended his hand, trying to defuse the situation with a polite handshake. "Alexander Gray. Didn't expect to see you here."

I completely ignored his outstretched hand.

My gaze locked onto Phoebe instead. She froze like she'd been turned to stone, spine rigid. I could smell the complex emotions in her scent—shock, fear, and a trace of something she was trying to hide... longing?

Elias's hand hung in the air for several seconds before slowly dropping. His jaw tightened, anger flashing in his eyes, but mostly wariness. He knew who I was, what I was capable of, and the history between Phoebe and me.

I didn't answer him. The little boy had captured my complete attention.

He looked up at me curiously. When his gaze fell on me, those deep blue eyes—identical to mine—sparkled with innocent curiosity.

As I continued toward them, his small hand suddenly grabbed onto my pant leg.

My heart nearly stopped beating.

My hand lifted without conscious thought, fingertips barely touching his soft brown hair. In that instant, two similar werewolf auras resonated—that natural connection only blood relations shared, the primal bond between father and son.

Electric sensation spread from my fingertips through my entire body. My wolf purred with deep satisfaction. This was my child, my blood, my legacy. The certainty was so strong, so undeniable, that wild joy flashed in my eyes.

But immediately after, guilt crashed over me like a tsunami.

"What's your name?" I forced my voice to stay calm, crouching down to his eye level, though excitement was about to explode from my chest.

"Ryan." He blinked those big eyes, then suddenly reached out to touch my face. "Sir, your eyes are just like mine! Mommy says my eyes are special."

My heart pounded violently. Ryan. That name echoed in my mind, each repetition bringing massive shock and satisfaction. My son. My Ryan.

"Yes," I said softly, voice trembling slightly. "Very special eyes."

I felt tense stares from two directions. Elias's pupils contracted to dangerous slits, his gaze like an icy blade fixed on me—he'd obviously figured something out. And Phoebe... her breathing became rapid and shallow, chest heaving, a trembling growl escaping her throat like a mother wolf protecting her cub, though her legs were visibly shaking.

But I didn't care.

My Alpha nature fully awakened. This was my mate, my child, my family. No one could take them from me—including Elias, who'd been by their side all this time.

My scent began releasing, carrying the dominance and possessiveness unique to Alphas. A silent declaration, a warning to all potential threats. These people mattered to me, and no one was allowed to hurt them.

Ryan seemed to sense this powerful aura, but he wasn't afraid. Instead, his eyes held a kind of recognition—like he instinctively knew I was his blood relative.

"Sir," he suddenly asked, his small face full of innocent curiosity, "do you know us?"

That simple question pierced my heart like a sword.

Yes, I wanted to say. I know your mother—she's my fated mate. I want to take you both home. I want to shoulder the responsibilities of a father, of a mate.

But I knew it wasn't time yet.

"Yes, Ryan." I stroked his hair gently, the tenderness in my eyes contrasting sharply with my earlier dominance. "I know your mother."

"Mommy!" Ryan turned excitedly, still gripping my finger tightly. "This man says he knows you!"

Phoebe slowly turned around. In that instant, time seemed to freeze.

Five years had left some traces on her face, but she was still breathtakingly beautiful. Those green eyes remained clear, just with added mature charm and... a maternal glow I'd never seen before. Her hair was longer than before, cascading over her shoulders, a few strands mussed from bending down to care for Ryan.

But when she saw me, those beautiful eyes flashed with complex emotions—shock, panic, anger, and a trace of pain she tried to hide.

"Alexander." Her voice was soft as a feather, but I could hear the tremor in it.

"Phoebe." I stood up, but Ryan still held my hand tight. We were only a step apart, but it felt like an entire world separated us.

She sucked in a sharp breath, the sound tiny and short like a startled animal. Her fingertips clutched her clothes until her knuckles went white, as if that fabric was her last connection to sanity. Her heels lifted slightly—ready to turn and flee at any moment.

Silence. Suffocating silence.

Elias stood behind Phoebe, his presence like a thorn in my heart. I heard his knuckles crack as he made fists. He was like a panther with every muscle coiled, claws temporarily sheathed, but every breath carried warning.

"Ryan's very cute." I looked at the little guy still gripping my finger, voice carrying a hint of testing. "How old is he?"

"Four." Phoebe's answer came too fast, like she wanted to end this topic immediately.

Four years old. I calculated the timing in my head. If he was four, then... then he really was born after that full moon night. My heart hammered so hard it felt like it might burst from my chest.

"He looks a lot like—" I started, but Phoebe cut me off immediately.

"Alexander." Her voice suddenly turned firm. "We need to go. Ryan needs his nap."

She bent down, speaking gently to Ryan. "Baby, time to go home."

"Mommy, can I stay a little longer?" He pouted. "This mister smells really good. I want to be close to him. He makes me feel safe."

Smell. The scent of blood relation. That bond made him instinctively drawn to me, just like I was drawn to him.

Phoebe's face went pale. She'd obviously realized this, too.

"Phoebe," I called her name softly, voice carrying five years of accumulated longing and pain. "Can we talk? Just a few minutes."

She shook her head—gentle but decisive. "There's nothing to talk about."

"There is." I took a step forward, Ryan moving with me, still holding my hand. "There's a lot to talk about."

I wanted to tell her I'd missed her every single day since she left.

I wanted to tell her my name wasn't Alexander Gray—I was Drake. When she'd told me her real name, I'd wanted to clarify my identity too, but the situation was so dangerous then, and I never got the chance. I'd let her leave with that cruel regret between us.

"Alexander Gray." Damn Elias interrupted our conversation, voice carrying warning. "Phoebe said she doesn't want to talk. You should respect her wishes."

My gaze instantly locked onto him, the air around us seeming to solidify into heavy lead. "This is between Phoebe and me. It's none of your business."

"Her business is my business." He was breathing hard. "I'm the one who's been there for her and Ryan."

Those words hit me like a sledgehammer. He'd been with them all along, while I... where was I? Fighting wars, handling pack business, searching for them—but I wasn't by their side.

This information flowed through my veins like poison. Jealousy and rage nearly consumed me.

Ryan seemed reluctant to give up, turning to Phoebe. "Can we invite this man to visit our house?"

Phoebe's face went even paler, panic filling her pupils. "Ryan, no."

"Why not?" Ryan asked innocently.

She stood up, something resolute flashing in her eyes. "Ryan, we're leaving now." Her tone became stern—this was a Phoebe I'd never seen before. A mother, who could become fierce to protect her child.

Ryan was startled by her tone, reluctantly releasing my finger. But his eyes were full of confusion and disappointment, like he couldn't understand why adults had to be so complicated.

Phoebe took Ryan's hand and turned to leave.

She pulled Ryan toward the exit, Elias close behind like a faithful guardian.

I stood there watching their figures grow distant. Ryan looked back at me once, waving his little hand, eyes full of reluctance.

My fists clenched, nails digging deep into my palms.

No. Not this time.

This time, I wouldn't let her leave again. I wouldn't let my son grow up without a father. I wouldn't let another man play the role that should have been mine.

Five years ago, I let her go because I thought it was best for her.

But now I knew—we had a child, a child who needed his father. And Phoebe... no matter how hard she tried to hide it, I could sense that trace of longing for me in her scent.

This time, I would fight. I would fight for my family.

CHAPTER NINE

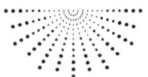

Phoebe

The afternoon I returned from the bidding conference, Elias told me he had to leave for a few days. I wanted to ask why, but seeing the evasive look in his eyes, I knew everyone had their secrets. I didn't press further and just told him to stay safe.

At the front desk of "Scent Workshop," I held Ryan tightly, feeling the warmth of his small body as I tried to draw strength from his innocence. But Gray's shadow and scent kept flooding my mind and nostrils like invisible chains, tightening around my sanity.

"Mommy, what's wrong?" Ryan looked up at me, his blue eyes full of concern.

Those eyes... identical to Alexander's.

I forced myself to smile. "Nothing, sweetheart. Mommy's just a little tired."

But I couldn't fool myself.

Five years. I thought my heart had grown strong enough, thought I'd forgotten that man.

The moment he appeared before me, the wolf inside me growled with excitement—craving his closeness. I fought desperately to suppress it.

No, I couldn't do this. I couldn't fall again.

He had rejected me, ignored my pleas, and coldly told me to leave. Back then, I felt like I'd fallen into an ice pit.

Why was he here? Had he discovered Ryan's existence? Or was he here to hold me accountable, or... because of me?

My heart pounded violently—half fear, half anticipation I didn't dare acknowledge.

My head spun, my thoughts a tangled mess.

I took a deep breath, trying to calm myself.

The phone suddenly rang, shattering my chaotic thoughts.

I glanced at the caller ID—an unknown number.

"Answer it, Mommy," Ryan urged innocently.

I took a deep breath and pressed accept.

"Hello?"

"Phoebe."

That voice made my world freeze. Deep and magnetic, carrying undeniable authority. Just hearing him say my name sent goosebumps across my skin.

It was him. Alexander.

My hand trembled uncontrollably, nearly dropping the phone.

Goddess, just his voice made me lose control like this?

The wolf inside me began pacing restlessly—it remembered his powerful presence, that intoxicating attraction.

"I want to visit your workshop and check on the project progress."

This wasn't a request—it was a statement. His tone brooked no refusal.

What? He—Alexander, senior business consultant for Ironspine Group—was personally following up on this small collaboration?

Check progress? Was this real or just an excuse?

He'd seen Ryan. Was he already suspicious?

"Check progress? Now?" I tried to deflect, my voice trembling slightly. "I'm not really available right now..."

"I'll be there in half an hour." He didn't give me a chance to refuse. "I already have the address."

The call ended, leaving me gripping the phone with shaking hands.

I bit my lip hard, trying to clear my head.

Just work, I told myself.

"Mommy, who's coming?" Ryan asked curiously.

"A work partner." I knelt down, stroking his soft hair, hoping he didn't notice my trembling hands.

"Ryan, sweetie," I ruffled my son's hair, "someone is coming to discuss work with Mommy. Go upstairs and play, okay?" I had to prevent more contact between them.

Ryan looked up at me and obediently said, "Okay," then climbed the stairs to the second floor.

To balance my career with caring for him, I'd chosen this street-facing commercial-residential building. The first floor housed "Scent Workshop"—my perfume studio. The second floor was our cozy home.

The workshop was spacious, and I'd deliberately created a little corner by the window for him, filled with toys and picture books.

When I worked at my desk, he would always play quietly in his own world—his thoughtfulness both comforted and broke my heart.

Half an hour later, the doorbell rang.

My entire body tensed. I took a deep breath, straightened my clothes, and walked to the door.

When I opened it, Alexander's imposing figure filled the doorway, those deep blue eyes looking straight at me. Instantly, his scent—sandalwood mixed with primal wildness—washed over me, intoxicating.

"Good afternoon, Phoebe." His gaze swept over the workshop interior, where various perfume ingredient bottles glinted in the sunlight. "Very nice work environment."

"Thank you." I stepped aside to let him in, trying to maintain distance. "This is the work area where I blend perfumes... Regarding project progress, I've completed the initial fragrance design..."

But when he passed by me, his warmth transferred instantly, making my heart skip a beat and the world go silent.

My skin erupted in fine tremors as an electric current shot from the point of contact through my entire body. The wolf inside me whimpered with longing.

I tried to focus on work, attempting to ignore the fatal attraction radiating from him. He stopped at the workbench, carefully examining several sample bottles.

"What are the proportions for these blends?" His voice was professional, as if he truly was here only to inspect work.

"The top notes use citrus and mint, the middle notes are..."

Just as I was explaining in detail, footsteps came pattering down the stairs.

My heart lurched—Ryan was coming down.

Ryan poked his little head around the stairway, blue eyes curiously looking toward the workshop.

The moment Ryan saw Alexander, he froze, then quickly ran down the stairs straight toward him.

No, don't... I tried to stop Ryan's enthusiasm mentally.

"Hi!" Ryan ran to him without hesitation, arms outstretched. "So you're the client Mommy mentioned! I'm so happy to see you again!"

I watched Alexander's expression instantly soften as he crouched down to catch Ryan's hug. His movements were gentle, naturally intimate—as if they belonged together.

My hands unconsciously clenched into fists, nails digging deep into my palms.

"Hello, little Ryan." His voice became much gentler. "I told you we'd meet again."

Alexander stood up with Ryan still clinging to his leg. He looked at me, eyes holding complex emotions—questioning, anger, and something deeper.

I could feel the Alpha pressure radiating from him intensify, carrying dangerous implications. The wolf inside me trembled, wanting both to submit and flee.

No, I couldn't show weakness. Right now, Ryan was mine alone, and I wouldn't let him take that away. If he was here about what happened five years ago, I'd face the consequences alone.

"Mr. Gray, will you play with me?" Ryan asked innocently. "I can show you my drawings! I drew lots of pictures!"

"Ryan." My voice came out sharp. "Mr. Gray is here for work, not to visit."

His eyebrow raised slightly. "Actually, I'd love to see Ryan's drawings." He crouched down to Ryan's eye level. "What did you draw?"

"I drew Mommy, Uncle Elias, and... a really amazing daddy!" Ryan said excitedly, completely oblivious to my changing expression. "Mommy says my daddy is someone really great. Even though he can't be with us, he definitely loves me!"

Alexander's eyes sharpened instantly. He slowly stood, his gaze locked directly on me.

"Is that so?" His voice was light, but the steel in his stare made me tremble. "Phoebe, who is Ryan's father?"

My breathing quickened.

"He's..." My voice shook as I tried to deflect the tense atmosphere. "Let's discuss work. Ryan, go to your room, okay?"

"Okay." Ryan reluctantly let go of Gray and returned to his room.

Alexander's gaze was deep and heavy as he approached me, his tone carrying undeniable pressure. "Phoebe, I think we really need to talk. About work... and about Ryan's father."

He'd finally asked the question directly. Those words struck like an ice-cold blade pressed against my deepest secret. About work? No, that was clearly just the opening. What he really wanted to probe was Ryan's parentage. How much did he know? Or was this another dangerous test? My mind raced but found only cold emptiness.

"He... his father died when Ryan was very young." I tried to keep my voice steady, but I knew my eyes betrayed my panic. "Car accident."

This was a carefully woven lie I'd told Ryan countless times—sometimes I almost believed it myself.

His stare grew sharper as he stepped closer.

I instinctively backed away until I hit the wall—nowhere to run.

"Car accident?" His voice was soft, but the doubt in it made me shake. "When?"

"When Ryan was six months old." My answer came too quickly—quick enough to sound rehearsed.

I saw suspicion flash in Alexander's eyes. My heart pounded so violently I worried he could hear it.

"Six months old." He repeated, then suddenly asked, "What was his father's name?"

My heart lurched. I'd never given this fictional person a name! Countless fake names spun and exploded in my mind.

Because Ryan had never asked such specific details.

"Jo... John." I stammered, picking a common name at random.

"John." Alexander slowly savored the name, his mouth curving in a meaningful smile.

This hastily fabricated name was like a cheap thread, and he'd already found it—now just one gentle pull would unravel my entire carefully woven story.

I knew he was beginning to suspect. My web of lies seemed so fragile, so pathetic before him.

"Mommy!" Ryan suddenly ran from his room, holding a drawing. "I found it! This is my best one!"

He excitedly ran to Alexander, holding up the paper.

My heart nearly stopped—it was a family portrait with me, Ryan, and a tall male figure. Though drawn with childish strokes, those deep blue eyes were unmistakable.

"Who's this?" Alexander crouched down, his fingers gently tracing the man's outline on the paper, the movement filled with indescribable emotion.

"This is my imaginary daddy!" Ryan said proudly. "Mommy says Daddy is very tall and strong, so I drew him tall! And... I think Daddy should have blue eyes like mine!"

He slowly raised his head, those deep blue eyes locked deadly on mine.

The surrounding sounds seemed instantly sucked away—I only heard my deafening heartbeat. Then his low voice rumbled like thunder rolling across the ground, making the floor beneath my feet tremble.

"Is that so? Blue eyes... just like mine?"

My breathing became ragged, fingers gripping my clothes until my knuckles went white.

"This... this is just coincidence. Ryan likes blue, so..."

I saw understanding flash in Alexander's eyes, followed by deeper emotions—possession, anger, and... longing?

He stood, looking at me deeply. "Phoebe, I need to thoroughly understand the workshop situation. This will require more time."

Over the following days, Alexander appeared frequently in my life.

Always with various reasons—checking project progress, discussing fragrance formulas, confirming product details. But I knew these were all excuses.

Whenever Alexander appeared, Ryan lit up like he'd discovered the most precious treasure. Ryan would drop his toys and fly to him, clinging to those long legs.

"Mr. Gray! You came again today!" Ryan's voice was always full of delight.

And Alexander—this cold, ruthless man with Alpha presence—became remarkably gentle with Ryan. He'd crouch down, patiently listening to Ryan's daily stories, bringing small toys, even playing hide-and-seek in the workshop.

All this both moved and terrified me.

"Mommy, I like Mr. Gray," Ryan said one evening, nestled in my arms. "I want him to stay with me always."

My heart clenched tight. The call of blood—even though Ryan was young and knew nothing, that instinctive closeness couldn't be faked.

"He has work cooperation with Mommy right now, so he comes often. But he has his own life and can't always be with us." I stroked his hair, my voice trembling.

That night, I sat alone at my workbench, watching moonlight through the window, my heart full of unease.

This should have been the world's most ordinary happiness—a father with his son, a powerful Alpha silently protecting his bloodline. This had been a luxury I didn't dare dream about during countless sleepless nights.

"That night was just an accident. Don't flatter yourself."

"If you want to live, get out of here now."

Those words still cut like knives in my heart. He had rejected me, pushed me away, letting me feel bone-deep cold at my most vulnerable moment.

Now he acted like nothing had happened, naturally integrating into Ryan's life as if he'd never been absent.

What did he want? Belated guilt, or... had he discovered that undeniable blood call in Ryan? My heart was a mess—craving this moment of false warmth while fearing the storm hidden behind it.

He was smart. With his observational skills, he'd discover the truth eventually. When that happened, what would he do? Take Ryan away? Separate us with various excuses?

I couldn't let that happen. Ryan was my everything, my reason for living. I couldn't lose him.

The next day, when Alexander came again, I gathered courage to confront him.

"Mr. Gray, I think you've been coming too frequently." I tried to sound calm. "The project is still ongoing—there's no need for daily checks."

He stopped, those blue eyes looking straight at me. "I'm just concerned about project progress."

"You can't come anymore." I forced my voice to sound firm, even as my heart nearly burst from my chest. "This isn't good for Ryan. He'll... become dependent on you."

"What's wrong with depending on me?" His voice carried dangerous implications. "Shouldn't he depend on..."

"No!" I cut him off, my voice sharp.

My body began trembling uncontrollably.

"Mr. Gray," I forced myself to look up, trying to sound cold and distant, "I think you've misunderstood something. Ryan is just a child—he'll become attached to anyone who's kind to him. But that doesn't mean..."

"Doesn't mean what?" He stepped closer, making my skin break out in fine tremors.

I took a deep breath, clenching my hands. "Doesn't mean you can keep appearing in his life. We all have our own lives and responsibilities. Right now we just have a business relationship."

I bit my lip hard, using the pain to stay clear.

The air suddenly grew heavy with invisible pressure, like the calm before a storm.

"Business relationship?" His voice was terrifyingly low, each word squeezed through gritted teeth. "Look me in the eyes and tell me we just have a business relationship."

I didn't dare look at him. I knew if I met those deep blue eyes, all my defenses would crumble.

"Yes." I answered mechanically, my voice cold. "Just business. So please maintain appropriate distance."

His fist clenched, knuckles white—like an enraged beast ready to explode.

I could feel him suppressing his fury. The wolf inside me whimpered uneasily, both fearing his anger and craving his possession.

But what right did that give him? He had no right to be angry. He had pushed me away first, told me to leave.

"Mr. Gray," I deliberately stepped back, even though each step felt like tearing something apart, "I'm sorry, but I need to work."

This was a dismissal—we both knew it.

He looked at me deeply, that gaze so complex I could barely bear it —anger, unwillingness, and something deeper.

Alexander stood, giving me one last look. "Phoebe, do you really think this will push me away?"

His voice was soft—like talking to himself—but the determination in it chilled my spine.

He turned and left, his back straight and proud.

The moment the door closed, my legs gave out, and I slowly slid to the floor.

Three days later—the cosmetics group's new product launch.

I stood at the display platform, palms slightly sweaty. This was my workshop's first time participating in such a large launch event, and the "botanical aroma" series would be featured as a key product. I took a deep breath, trying to calm my nerves.

Focus, Phoebe. This is your career, your life's work.

"Ladies and gentlemen, next we'll introduce the new fragrance series from Scent Workshop..." the host announced.

I straightened my deep blue suit and walked confidently onto the stage. Spotlights instantly focused on me, the harsh white light making me squint.

The audience was packed with industry professionals and media. I scanned the crowd, feeling strangely disappointed—Alexander wasn't there.

This was for the best, I told myself. No contact was the best outcome.

"Hello everyone, I'm Phoebe from Scent Workshop." My voice carried clearly through the speakers. "Today I'm presenting the 'botanical aroma' series, inspired by nature's most primal scents..."

I introduced the products while displaying samples. The audience response seemed positive—many were taking notes. I gradually relaxed, my voice becoming more confident.

"What makes this series special is our unique extraction technique, which preserves the plants' natural fragrance to the maximum extent..."

"Unique?"

A malicious voice suddenly interrupted my presentation.

My body instantly froze.

Sera stood up from the third row, wearing a wine-red dress with a pearl necklace glinting under the lights. Her mouth curved in a mocking smile—like an elegant but deadly viper.

Sera? Why was she here? My heart raced as countless thoughts flashed through my mind.

When I'd scanned the audience earlier, I'd noticed the Ironspine Group logo on the organizers' backdrop. As a core member of Ironspine Pack, her presence here made sense.

"Ms. Sera." I tried to stay composed, though my fingers unconsciously gripped the microphone tighter.

"Miss Phoebe," she said slowly, each word dripping with poison, "are you sure this formula is 'unique'? As far as I know, Ironspine Pack has a traditional fragrance formula extremely similar to your 'botanical aroma.'"

The entire venue went silent.

Blood rushed to my head. My breathing quickened, chest heaving violently.

She was lying! How could she slander me like this?

"Ms. Sera, what's your evidence?" I tried to keep my voice steady, but my throat felt parched. "This formula is my independent research with complete development records..."

"Oh? Really?" Sera gracefully walked to the front, her heels clicking on the floor—each step like stepping on my heart. "Then why are the main components and proportions so similar? Lavender, rosemary, cedar... even the extraction sequence is identical."

She pulled a document from her purse, waving it in the air. "This is Ironspine Pack's fragrance workshop formula from years past. Everyone can compare for themselves."

Whispers began spreading through the venue like ripples. Those once-friendly gazes turned suspicious and scrutinizing—like countless knives stabbing at me.

"This is slander!" My voice involuntarily rose with obvious trembling. "I've never had access to any Ironspine Pack formulas!"

My hands shook; the microphone nearly slipped. The wolf inside me roared with rage, wanting to tear apart this lying woman.

"Never had access?" Sera's smile grew more vicious as she slowly walked onto the stage, standing before me. "But as I understand it, you spent time at Ironspine Pack five years ago. And..."

She leaned close, her voice low but still picked up by the microphone. "Didn't you climb into one of our executives' beds? Stealing a formula would be easy for you."

My face instantly flushed red—whether from anger or humiliation, I couldn't tell. I felt the world spinning, ears ringing.

"You're lying!" My voice trembled, tears forming in my eyes. "This is defamation!"

"Defamation?" Sera stepped back, adopting an innocent expression for the audience. "I'm just stating facts. Everyone can judge for themselves—a woman who suddenly appeared then disappeared, returning with an 'original' formula... isn't that suspicious?"

The murmuring grew louder. People started taking photos, camera flashes blinding me. Standing under the spotlights, I felt like a criminal being judged.

"I... I didn't..." My voice grew weaker, my throat feeling blocked.

Alexander, where are you?

This thought suddenly surfaced, making me feel even more desperate.

"Since Miss Phoebe claims innocence," Sera turned to the audience, "why not have Ironspine Pack's professionals evaluate this? I've conveniently brought our head perfumer."

A middle-aged man stood from the audience—I recognized him as the unsettling client who'd visited my workshop a few days ago.

He took the sample Sera handed him, sniffed it carefully, then nodded. "Indeed, this scent... is eighty percent similar to our ancient formula."

"No!" I almost shouted. "This is impossible! My formula is..."

"Enough, Miss Phoebe." Sera cut me off, her eyes gleaming with victory. "Just admit it—you're a thief. You stole our formula and tried to profit from it."

My legs shook, barely able to support me. People in the audience were already starting to leave, potential partners looking disappointed and disgusted.

"I suggest," Sera raised her voice, "all companies considering cooperation with Scent Workshop think twice. Who knows what else she's stolen?"

I stood on stage feeling like a criminal nailed to a pillory. Tears finally spilled over, blurring my vision. I saw people shaking their heads, whispering, pulling out phones to send messages.

My hard work, destroyed just like that.

No, I couldn't let this happen.

"I can provide complete development records." My voice trembled, but I forced myself to continue. "Every formula evolution, every experiment's data—all documented. If similarities truly exist, I'll accept investigation by any professional institution."

I took a deep breath, looking out at the audience. "The reputation I've built over five years won't collapse because of baseless accusations. Please give me time to prove my innocence."

Even with my earnest explanations, it seemed no one chose to believe me.

I stumbled off stage, practically fleeing the venue.

Back in the dressing room, my phone went crazy with calls.

"Miss Phoebe, we're sorry, but considering the current circumstances, our company is postponing cooperation..."

"Let's wait until things are cleared up..."

"We need to reassess the risks..."

Call after call—all bad news. I collapsed in the dressing room chair as my phone slipped from my hands, hitting the floor with a sharp crack.

I hugged my knees, curling up in the chair.

Why was this happening? I hadn't done anything wrong...

The phone rang again—Elias.

"Phoebe, I saw the news." His voice was full of concern. "Where are you? I'm coming right over."

"I..." I choked up, unable to speak.

"Don't be afraid. I'll be right there." He hung up.

I closed my eyes, tears flowing endlessly.

Alexander, if only you were here...

But I immediately pushed that thought away. No, I couldn't depend on him. I had to rely on myself, didn't I?

But why, in my most desperate moment, did I still think of him? Think of his embrace, his warmth, that comforting sandalwood scent?

CHAPTER TEN

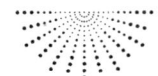

Drake

News of the press conference reached me within an hour.

Kay pushed open my office door, thrusting the tablet in front of me. "Alpha, you need to see this."

In the video, Phoebe stood under the spotlight, facing Sera's accusations. I watched her trembling hands, her forced defiance, the light slowly crumbling in her eyes.

My fist slammed into the desk. The solid wood groaned under the impact.

"That fucking idiot Sera!" I snarled, the wolf inside me howling with rage, desperate to tear apart everyone who'd hurt her.

Kay stood silently beside me. "Want me to handle it?"

"No." I forced myself to calm down. "She'll come to me."

Yes, Phoebe would come to me. When she was backed into a corner, when she needed help, she'd remember me. Even though she kept pushing me away, even though she said we were just business partners, in moments like this, she'd always remember the connection between us.

I sat in my office waiting. Phone face-up on the desk, volume maxed.

The first hour passed.

I told myself she needed time to cool off, time to think.

The second hour.

Maybe she was handling all those canceled contracts. I knew that feeling—partners abandoning you one by one, like knives twisting in your heart.

The third hour.

I started getting restless. The wolf inside paced anxiously. I picked up my phone, pulled up her number, finger hovering over the call button.

No, I couldn't make the first move. If she didn't want my help, my interference would only make her resist more.

The fourth hour.

Kay knocked. "Boss, Ms. Sera wants to see you."

"Tell her to fuck off." My voice was arctic cold.

"She says it's about Miss Phoebe..."

I shot to my feet. "Let her in."

Sera walked into the office, still wearing that arrogant attitude. But I could smell the tension radiating from her.

"Drake," she tried that sweet voice, "everything I did was for you. That woman doesn't deserve..."

"Shut up." I cut her off, walking toward her slowly, each step radiating Alpha authority.

Her face went white, instinctively backing away. "Drake, I..."

"You destroyed her." My voice was quiet, but dangerous enough to drop the room's temperature several degrees. "You used lies to destroy an innocent person."

"But she approached you with a fake identity. She's a fraud."

"I'm the fraud. Five years ago, to test her, I had Kay take my place as 'Drake' while I disguised myself as business consultant 'Alexander'. I thought it would protect Ironspine Pack, but I destroyed our future with my own hands."

My guilty rage was aimed at Sera, but also at myself.

"She didn't steal anything." I closed in until she had nowhere to retreat. "That so-called formula was fabricated by you. That 'master perfumer' was bought by you. You think I don't know?"

Sera's lips trembled. "I just... I couldn't accept it. Why should she get your attention? What is she?"

"She's my fated mate," I warned her again. "Don't you ever hurt her again."

"Get out." I turned away. "From today, you're cut from all Ironspine Pack business activities. If you go near Phoebe again, I'll make you regret being born."

Sera stumbled out.

The office fell quiet again. I stared at my phone screen. Still no calls.

The fifth hour.

I sent people for information. Word came back quickly. Phoebe had returned to her workshop, locked herself inside. Elias was with her.

Elias. Him again.

Why would she rather rely on him than come to me?

The sixth hour.

The sun started setting. I stood at the floor-to-ceiling window, watching the city slowly turn gold in the sunset.

She wasn't coming. I finally admitted the truth.

Even in her most desperate moment, she wouldn't ask for my help. This realization cut through me like a dull blade, slow and agonizing.

I deserved it. Five years ago, I pushed her away myself. What right did I have to expect her to come back to me now?

Night fell.

I still sat in my office, phone screen glowing harshly in the darkness.

She never called.

Eleven PM.

Kay pushed in. "Alpha, Miss Phoebe's still at the workshop. Lights are still on."

I shot up, grabbing my coat. "Get the car."

"Alpha, at this hour..."

"Get the car." I repeated, brooking no argument.

Twenty minutes later, my car stopped outside Scent Workshop.

The late-night street was empty except for streetlights casting yellow pools of light. Cold wind whistled through the gaps between buildings. The workshop was on the ground floor, light still visible through the glass storefront—the only light source on this street, like a lonely lighthouse in the darkness.

She was still inside, probably frantically mixing new perfumes, trying to numb herself with work.

I knew her too well. She always did this—buried herself in work when trouble hit, as if that could solve everything.

I pulled out my phone and dialed her number.

It rang forever. I thought she wouldn't answer.

Just as I was about to hang up, she picked up.

"Hello?" Her voice was tired and hoarse.

"Still working?" I tried to sound casual.

"Mr. Gray, it's late. What do you need?" Her tone was distant and guarded.

Alexander Gray? No, I wanted to tell her I was Drake.

My heart stabbed with pain. I'd help her through this crisis first, wait until her attitude toward me improved a bit. I didn't have the confidence to reveal the truth right now. Wait a little longer, just a little longer...

I took a deep breath. "I'm downstairs."

"What?" Her voice shot up. I could imagine her panicked expression.

"Come out. Let's talk."

"Nothing to talk about." Her voice went cold again. "Please leave, Mr. Gray."

"Phoebe," I softened my tone, "I know what happened today."

I could feel her struggling.

"So what?" she finally spoke, voice trembling slightly. "It's my business. Nothing to do with you."

"How is it nothing to do with me?" My voice rose involuntarily. "You're my..."

I swallowed that word again.

"Phoebe, you need help." I changed tactics. "Ironspine Group can issue statements, pressure those partners to reconsider. You don't have to carry this alone."

"I don't need it." Her voice suddenly turned hard. "I don't need anyone's charity, especially yours."

Charity? She thought this was charity?

"It's not charity," I fought to control my emotions. "It's... help between friends."

She laughed, bitter enough to break my heart. "Friends? Mr. Gray, when did we become friends?"

"Phoebe..."

"Enough." She cut me off. "Mr. Gray, thanks for your 'kindness', but I really don't need it. I can solve my own problems."

"How? By pulling all-nighters mixing new perfumes? By working yourself to death?" My voice turned stern. "You think that'll prove your innocence?"

"That's none of your business!" She was almost shouting.

Then the line went dead.

I stared at the dark phone screen, the wolf inside howling with fury.

She'd rather suffer alone than accept my help. This realization brought unprecedented defeat.

I looked at the ground-floor storefront. Lights still blazed, her silhouette moving busily inside.

She was fighting in there, and I could only stand here like an outsider.

No, I couldn't just stand by.

I called Kay. "Use Ironspine Group's influence to pressure all partners into reconsidering cooperation with Scent Workshop."

"Understood."

After hanging up, I stood outside the door. Something inside urged me—go in and see her, see Ryan.

I got out of the car and walked toward Scent Workshop's entrance. Just then, the door opened. Elias stepped out. Seeing me, he froze.

We stared at each other on the empty late-night street, cold wind threading between buildings, stirring up fallen leaves.

"What are you doing here?" Elias's voice was low, clearly hostile.

"I want to see Ryan," I said directly.

"It's past midnight." He stood in the doorway, blocking the entrance. "The kid's been asleep for hours."

"Then let me see Phoebe."

"She doesn't want to see you." Elias's tone hardened. "Mr. Gray, please leave. Stop disturbing her life."

I stepped forward, Alpha authority radiating naturally. "Disturbing? Seeing my son is disturbing?"

Elias's expression changed. "What do you mean, your son? Ryan is—"

"My son." I cut him off, voice cold and certain. "Five years ago, that full moon night, I was the one with Phoebe. Ryan has my blood, my scent. That can't be faked."

Elias's fists clenched, pain flashing in his eyes. "Even if that's true, so what? Who was with Phoebe through her difficult pregnancy? Who held her hand during labor? Who taught Ryan his first words, watched his first steps?"

Each question stabbed like a knife.

"Me." He continued, voice carrying a kind of pride. "These five years, every single day, every important moment, I was there for them. And where were you?"

"I was at war." My voice was low. "To protect them from Darkfang Pack discovering them, I had to..."

"Excuses." Elias sneered. "You had countless ways to find them, protect them, but you chose the easiest—let them leave."

I couldn't argue. Because he was right.

"But now it's different." I raised my head, meeting his eyes directly. "I'm back, and I'm not leaving again."

"Who do you think you are?" Elias was furious. "You think you can just walk in and out of her life? Five years ago, you broke her heart, now you want to waltz back like nothing happened?"

"I'm her Alpha." My voice carried undeniable authority. "Her fated mate. And you..."

I looked him over, the wolf inside growling. "You're just a guardian. A guardian who can never truly have her."

Cruel words, but true.

Elias went pale. Of course he knew this. He could never give Phoebe a complete mark, never truly become her mate.

"Even so," his voice shook but remained firm, "I won't let you hurt her."

"I won't hurt her."

"You already did once."

We locked in a standoff. Alpha pressure spread through the late-night street, even the streetlights seeming to dim.

Elias held firm, but I could see him struggling.

"Move aside." My voice brooked no refusal.

"No." He gritted his teeth, cold sweat beading his forehead.

"Elias," I softened my tone, "I'm not here to take them away. I just... just want to be part of their lives. Ryan needs a father. You should understand that."

His expression wavered.

"You can keep being their guardian," I continued, "but don't stop me from being a father."

Finally, Elias stepped aside, but I could feel his reluctance and anger.

I walked to the door and knocked.

"Phoebe, open up." My voice was calm but firm.

She didn't open the door. "Mr. Gray, please leave." Her voice came through the room, tired and resistant.

"I have a proposal," I said. "About your fragrance formulas."

"I've looked at your 'botanical aroma' series," I continued. "Excellent work, but there's room for optimization. Ironspine Group has the best perfume labs and supply chains. I can help you."

"I don't need your help." Her voice turned sharp. "I told you, I can solve my own problems."

"This isn't just your problem." I pulled out a document from my briefcase, explaining to her. "Ironspine Group's quarterly report shows that because of today's press conference, our cosmetics division stock dropped 3 percentage points."

"That's your problem, not..."

"You're our partner." I cut her off. "Your reputation damage directly affects the Group's business interests. As an investment representative, I need to intervene."

"Are you... threatening me?" Her voice trembled.

No, this wasn't a threat. I just wanted an excuse to see you.

"No..." My tone stayed calm. "Phoebe, let me help you. Not charity—business cooperation."

Elias suddenly interjected. "Enough, Alexander. You're using your power to pressure her."

I turned to him. "I'm discussing business with Phoebe. This has nothing to do with you."

"Her business is my business." Elias stepped closer, eyes burning with fury.

"Is it?" I sneered. "What can you help her with? Do you have labs? Supply channels? Media resources?"

Each question made Elias's face darker.

"Besides companionship, what can you give her?" I continued coldly. "And can companionship get her through this crisis?"

"At least I don't use power to oppress her!" Elias roared.

"Oppress her?" I raised an eyebrow. "I'm just stating facts. The gap between you and me can't be bridged by effort alone."

This completely enraged Elias.

Under the streetlight, his pupils contracted sharply. His right fist shot out with a whistling sound, aimed straight at my face. The cold wind was stirred by his punch, whipping fallen leaves into a frenzied dance in the air.

I tilted my head slightly. His fist grazed my cheek, the wind from his punch tousling my hair. Taking advantage of his forward momentum, I grabbed his wrist with my left hand, locked his shoulder with my right, and used his own force to slam him hard against the nearby wall.

"Bang!"

The dull impact echoed clearly in the late-night street.

Elias struggled to counterattack, his left elbow striking backward. I anticipated this, jamming my knee into his lower back while increasing pressure with my hands. His face was forced against the cold wall, blood seeping from his temple where he'd hit.

"Let me go!" he roared, his shoulders struggling violently, but my hands locked him like iron clamps.

He tried to kick backward. I twisted his arm behind his back at a sharp angle, leaving him unable to move. Lime from the wall crumbled from the impact, falling like snow in the lamplight.

"You think... you're so strong?" Elias panted, blood from his forehead streaming down his cheek, looking particularly striking under the streetlight.

I didn't answer, just increased the pressure. Alpha authority pressed down like a physical weight, making even the streetlights seem dimmer, the air thick and heavy.

Elias's legs began trembling. He was fighting the genetic instinct to submit with everything he had. Sweat mixed with blood slid down his face, hitting the ground with soft sounds.

"Calm down," I whispered in his ear, voice cold as ice.

He still tried to struggle, but I spun him around, his back slamming hard into the wall. This impact made him grunt, blood trickling from the corner of his mouth. My hand closed around his throat—not enough to choke him, but enough to make him feel the threat.

The late-night street held only our heavy breathing. Elias's shirt was soaked with sweat, clinging to outline his muscled form. His eyes still burned with defiance, but his body trembled involuntarily under Alpha pressure.

"You see," I released my grip, stepping back half a pace, watching him lean weakly against the wall, "this is the difference. You can't protect her, and you can't give her what she needs."

Elias tried to stand straight, but his legs gave out, nearly collapsing. His wrists showed purple fingerprints, the temple wound still bleeding, blood sliding down his cheek to drip on his white shirt, blooming into crimson flowers.

Just then, the door suddenly burst open.

"Stop it!"

CHAPTER ELEVEN

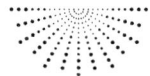

Phoebe

The dull thudding from outside made my heart clench.

"Bang!"

The sound cut through the night's silence like a hammer blow to my chest. Then came deep gasps and sounds of struggle echoing down the dark street.

I set down the essential oil bottle, which clinked softly against the lab table.

Elias and Alexander?

My breathing quickened.

Were they fighting?

I dropped everything and stumbled toward the door.

The moment I opened it, cold wind hit my face, carrying the night's chill and the mixed pheromones of two men. Elias leaned against the wall, blood seeping from his temple, shirt soaked with sweat, looking ready to collapse.

Alexander stood nearby, suit rumpled, tie loosened, sweat beading his forehead. But those deep blue eyes remained sharp, carrying that unmistakable Alpha intensity.

"Elias!" I ran to him, seeing the wound at his temple, my heart breaking. "How are you? Can you stand?"

"I'm fine..." he said weakly, trying to straighten up but clearly forcing it.

I whirled on Alexander. "Are you insane? What gives you the right to hit him?"

His expression was unreadable, but I had no time for his emotions.

"Elias, get inside." I supported his arm. "There's a first aid kit upstairs. You need that wound treated immediately."

"Phoebe, I..."

"Go!" My tone brooked no argument. "It's still bleeding. We need to disinfect and bandage it now."

Elias looked at me deeply, then glared at Alexander before slowly heading inside. I could see his unsteady steps, his shoulders trembling. Each step made my heart heavier.

He got hurt protecting me.

After Elias's footsteps faded on the stairs, I turned to Alexander. Night wind tousled his hair, but his gaze remained deep and penetrating.

Watching Elias's stumbling figure disappear upstairs, rage threatened to consume me.

I wanted to charge at Alexander, tell him to get out of my life, tell him I didn't need anyone's "protection."

But reason told me this wasn't the time for emotions.

"Come in." My voice sounded calm, though inside I was churning.

I wasn't letting him in because I forgave him, but because talking outside would only invite more trouble.

Alexander followed me into the studio. The moment the door closed, the cold wind and chaos outside were shut out, leaving just us and the warm interior light.

I directed Alexander to the living room, then hurried upstairs.

Elias was in the bathroom treating his wound, the blood cleaned away but the bruising still vivid.

"Let me." I took the antiseptic cotton from him, gently pressing it to the wound.

He winced but didn't pull away. "Phoebe, you shouldn't have let him in."

"I know." I said quietly. "But I might need his help. You're hurt—stay in the guest room tonight."

Elias was silent for a long time, finally saying, "Be careful. Don't let him hurt you again."

My hand paused, but I didn't answer.

After bandaging his wound, I went back downstairs.

Alexander stood in the studio with his back to me, studying the fragrance classification chart on the wall. Hearing footsteps, he turned.

"How's Elias?" he asked, his voice carrying barely detectable guilt.

"He'll be fine." My tone was cold. "Just shallow wounds."

The air instantly tensed.

The studio was filled with various scents—lavender, rosemary, cedarwood, and the new perfume I'd been mixing. These familiar fragrances usually comforted me, but now they felt complicated because of his presence.

His gaze swept around—the lab table with its bottles and vials, fragrance classification charts on the walls, the air still carrying traces of my recent work.

"You're mixing a new perfume?" he asked, his voice much gentler than outside.

"Yes." I didn't look at him, instead walking to the lab table to organize what I'd hastily abandoned. "Since all my partners pulled out, I need to develop new product lines."

My movements were mechanical, trying to hide my inner tension. The bottles trembled slightly in my hands, making soft clinking sounds.

"Phoebe." His voice suddenly turned serious. "Stop. Look at me."

My movements froze, but I didn't turn around.

"You think developing new products will solve this?" His voice carried an emotion I couldn't read. "What Sera did today wasn't just slandering your formula—she questioned your character, your professional competence. That kind of stain follows you forever."

My grip tightened on the bottle until my knuckles went white. "So what do you suggest?"

"The core issue isn't products," he said, slowly approaching. I could feel his warmth. "It's proving your innocence, rebuilding your reputation."

"I can..."

"What?" He cut me off, his voice sharp. "Fight the entire business community's suspicions alone? Phoebe, you're being naive."

I spun around, glaring at him. "So what should I do? Beg for your help? Like five years ago?"

The words escaped before I could stop them. I immediately regretted them, seeing pain flash in his eyes.

The air became heavy, as if time itself had stopped. We stared at each other, and that night five years ago seemed to replay—his cold rejection, my desperate tears, that feeling of complete abandonment.

"Phoebe." His voice became very soft, afraid to disturb something. "About before... once we handle this situation, can we talk properly?"

"Don't bring up five years ago." I turned away. "That's over."

"It's not over." His voice was closer now. I could feel him standing right behind me. "Phoebe, I know I hurt you. Now isn't the time to settle the past. You need pack support."

Pack support?

I slowly turned, looking into his deep blue eyes. There I saw determination, unquestionable resolve.

"What do you mean?"

"At the press conference, Sera accused you of plagiarizing Ironspine Pack's fragrance formulas." Each word was clear and forceful. "To clear this stain, you need public support from Ironspine Pack leadership. Only if they publicly vouch for you and clarify this slander can you completely clear your name. And I," he paused, "can help you get that opportunity."

My heart began racing. Pack support? What did that mean? It meant stepping back into that world of schemes and calculations, facing more people like Sera.

More importantly, it meant depending on him again.

I turned back to the lab table, picking up the bottle I'd set down. "I need time to think."

"Phoebe..."

"I said I need time." I cut him off, focusing on the perfume in my hands. "It's late, Mr. Gray."

He watched me for a while, finally saying, "I'll come tomorrow. We have many details to discuss."

After the door closed, I remained at the lab table, the test tube trembling in my hands.

Maybe he was right. Maybe I really did need outside help to get through this crisis.

But admitting that was harder than anything.

That night, I barely slept. Alexander's words kept flashing through my mind, along with Sera's vicious smile.

The next morning brought call after call—all from companies that had canceled yesterday, now reaching out.

"Miss Phoebe, about yesterday's incident, Ironspine Group has offered to guarantee, and our company has reconsidered..."

"After internal discussion, we believe Scent Workshop's product quality is trustworthy..."

"With Ironspine Group's guarantee, we have complete confidence in you and hope to restart cooperation soon..."

Ironspine Group was guaranteeing for me? I gripped the phone, confused and angry. What right did they have to guarantee for me? Who gave them that authority?

Was it Alexander? Was he helping me? Besides him, I didn't know anyone else with influence at Ironspine.

Could the renewed cooperation calls really be because he used his position as Ironspine Group's senior business consultant to help me?

Part of me was angry that he'd interfered without permission, but part of me was grateful for his silent efforts. He had genuinely helped resolve part of the crisis.

The doorbell rang, interrupting my thoughts.

I hurried downstairs. Alexander stood there with two cups of coffee and a breakfast bag. He wore yesterday's clothes and looked tired.

My resistance was softening. But this was all speculation—I needed confirmation.

"What's this about Ironspine Group's guarantee?" I asked directly.

He faced my question calmly. "Good morning, Phoebe. I think you need an explanation."

"I don't need charity from your corporation." I blocked the doorway.

"It's not charity, it's business mutual insurance." His voice was calm. "Ironspine Group needs quality suppliers, and your products are genuinely excellent. It's win-win."

"I didn't ask you to..."

"You didn't." He interrupted. "But Ryan needs a mother with an unblemished reputation, doesn't he?"

At Ryan's mention, half my anger evaporated.

I wanted to refuse. But thinking of Ryan, of those canceled contracts...

"I don't like being managed." I finally said. "Next time, at least ask me first."

"Besides," he continued, looking directly at me, "if you want to know why those companies changed their minds so quickly, you need to let me explain properly. Standing in the doorway discussing this isn't appropriate."

I bit my lip. He was right—I needed to know the truth. And... I hadn't washed up yet, and standing here in pajamas was embarrassing.

"Five minutes." My tone was commanding. "Talk, then leave."

Just then, Elias came downstairs. His temple wound was bandaged, but his color was still poor. Seeing Alexander, his body visibly tensed.

"Good morning, Elias." Alexander greeted him first. "About last night... sorry."

Elias looked at him coldly, said nothing, and went straight to the kitchen for water.

Awkward tension filled the air.

"Elias," I said softly, "Mr. Gray brought breakfast. Join us."

"No thanks." Elias finished his water. "I have things to do."

He left the studio, leaving Alexander and me facing each other.

"He's still angry." I sighed.

"As he should be," Alexander said quietly. "I was too impulsive."

I stepped aside, and Alexander walked naturally to the kitchen, unpacking breakfast. "Sandwiches, croissants, and little cakes Ryan loves."

Watching his natural movements, a strange feeling rose in my chest. This scene was too domestic, too much like... a real family.

"Alexander, you can talk now."

"Coffee first." He interrupted. "I'm guessing you didn't sleep well."

True. I'd spent all night thinking about his words, about getting pack support, about our recent interactions.

Morning sunlight filtered through the curtains, falling on him and casting soft shadows on his profile.

"I promised them there would be a pack press conference soon to prove your innocence. The key now is how you provide evidence to the pack and earn their recognition." Alexander analyzed calmly.

"Mommy, is Mr. Gray having breakfast with us today?" Ryan ran out from his room, interrupting our conversation.

I was about to refuse when Alexander knelt down to Ryan. "I came to help Mommy with work today. I can only play with you after work is done, okay?"

"Will you stay a long time?" Ryan asked hopefully.

Alexander glanced at me. "Depends on how long Mommy's work takes."

After a hurried breakfast, I settled Ryan in the living room with his blocks, then returned to the studio with Alexander.

"We need to organize all research records." He took off his suit jacket and rolled up his sleeves. "They need to see the complete creative process."

Watching him expertly flip through my notebooks, I couldn't help asking, "You understand perfume?"

"A little." He didn't look up. "Enough to help organize materials."

For the next two hours, we buried ourselves in work. He was efficient, quickly categorizing the scattered materials. Occasionally, our hands would accidentally touch, each time like electricity, making my heart race.

At ten AM, the doorbell rang.

"I'll get it." I set down the files.

Alexander's assistant stood outside with documents.

"Miss Phoebe, these are supplementary materials the boss said the pack needs." He handed me the files.

"Thank you." I took them.

"Miss Phoebe, I'm not troubled," I saw his hesitant expression, "but someone else is…"

"Please speak directly." My words seemed to give him confidence.

"I know as an assistant, I shouldn't meddle," he hesitated, glancing toward the living room to ensure Alexander couldn't hear. "It's about the boss."

"What about him?" My heart tensed inexplicably.

"He hasn't slept properly in a long time."

The assistant's voice was soft, but every word reached me clearly.

"The boss drives past this street every night but never dares come up. Last night he didn't go home at all—sat in his car all night."

My breathing hitched. Thinking of his tired appearance this morning, his unchanged clothes.

"Why tell me this?"

"Because only you can help him." The assistant looked at me seriously. "Only in front of you does his guard drop. Miss Phoebe, he needs rest, real rest."

After the assistant left, I stood alone at the door.

Because of me?

Deep inside, a corner I'd deliberately sealed began loosening.

That afternoon, I returned to the small office upstairs, organizing all the materials that could prove my innocence.

I arranged research notes chronologically, categorized and labeled each perfume sample version, even found original purchase receipts. These seemingly trivial things now became weapons to prove my innocence.

But I knew these "internal proofs" had limited persuasive power to outsiders. I needed more authoritative proof, like... the pack support Alexander mentioned.

At that thought, my hands stopped. Did I really have to depend on him? Could I trust him again?

Ryan's laughter came from downstairs. I couldn't help walking to the stairway to look.

"Mr. Gray, can you build with blocks?" Ryan brought out his favorite Lego set.

"Of course." Alexander put down his phone, focusing on building something with Ryan on the carpet.

"Put the blue one here!" Ryan directed.

"Why blue?" Alexander asked patiently.

"Because this is the sky! Mommy says the sky is blue!"

I secretly peered down and saw Alexander's movements pause, then he asked softly, "What else has your mommy said?"

"Mommy says Daddy is tall and handsome, just like Mr. Gray!" Ryan said innocently. "Mr. Gray, can you always play with me? Like a daddy?"

The air went silent. My breathing quickened, not knowing how Alexander would answer.

"If... if Mommy agrees." Alexander's voice was soft, carrying careful hesitation.

Standing at the stair landing, I froze completely.

Ryan's question was like a key, unlocking a door I'd kept tightly sealed in my heart. I covered my mouth to stifle any sound, but tears flowed despite my efforts.

This was the scene I'd dreamed of countless times—Ryan having a father who loved him, us becoming a real family. Those late nights crying while holding Ryan, the heartache watching other children with their fathers, bearing all the pressure alone...

If Alexander truly wanted to, if he wouldn't push us away again...

But how could I be sure? The wounds from five years ago hadn't healed. Could I risk it again?

As evening approached, I checked the clock—already six PM.

Just then, my lawyer called.

"Phoebe, Sera's side has announced they're suing you for commercial fraud." The lawyer's voice was serious. "Though her accusations won't hold up, this will further damage your reputation. I suggest considering settlement..."

"Settlement?" I gripped the phone. "That's admitting guilt."

"But litigation costs are high, and media attention would be greater, affecting your studio..."

I hung up, my hands trembling.

So things were worse than I'd imagined. Sera didn't just want to ruin my reputation—she wanted to completely destroy my business.

I leaned against the wall, closing my eyes. Five years of effort, five years of hard work—would it all be destroyed like this?

Maybe... maybe accepting his help wasn't just about business. Maybe it was time to give Ryan a complete family, give myself a chance to start over.

He was right. Even if I produced original evidence, with my background, they wouldn't believe me.

I needed pack support. Only their word would be trusted. And Alexander could help me achieve that.

That evening, Alexander packed up materials to leave.

"I'll come again tomorrow." He picked up his jacket.

"Alexander." I stopped him, pointing to the obvious dark circles under his eyes. "You need rest."

"I'm fine."

"Planning to spend another night in your car?" I asked directly.

He froze. "How did you..."

"Your assistant told me." I took a deep breath. "You'll collapse if this continues."

He smiled bitterly. "Better than..." He stopped. "I'll go to a hotel."

"Is Mr. Gray leaving?" Ryan ran over, hugging Alexander's leg. "Will you come back tomorrow?"

"Of course." Alexander ruffled his hair.

"You've been working hard." Ryan looked up. "Mommy says when you're tired, you should rest well."

Watching this scene, I struggled internally. Reason told me to let him go, but...

I heard myself say, "If you don't mind, stay for dinner."

Alexander looked up at me, surprise and hope flashing in his eyes. "Phoebe, I..."

"Rest a bit," I emphasized. "There's a lot to prepare tomorrow. You need energy. This is for work, too."

"For work." He repeated, his mouth curving slightly. "Thank you."

I looked at him silently.

As sunset approached, orange light streamed through windows, falling on him. His profile looked sculpted in the light and shadow, but I clearly saw the darkness under his eyes—so deep it looked like bruises.

He really looked exhausted.

At nine PM, Ryan was asleep. Only keyboard clicking and occasional page turning filled the living room.

I walked over with warm milk. "Drink this. It helps with sleep."

"Thank you." He took the cup, our fingertips accidentally touching. That familiar electric sensation shot through my body, making my heart skip.

He seemed to feel it too, his fingers lingering on mine for a second before pulling away.

"Phoebe," his voice was hoarse, "thank you for letting me stay."

"This is just cooperation," I answered quickly, trying to hide my inner turmoil.

He smiled without refuting.

At ten-thirty, when I prepared to go upstairs, Alexander still sat on the sofa. His laptop's blue light illuminated his tired face, making him look pale.

"Alexander," I hesitated, "tonight, you can sleep in the guest room."

He looked up, surprise flashing in his eyes.

"If you don't mind," I added, feeling my cheeks warm. "The guest room bed is comfortable, better than sleeping in a car."

His expression became complicated. "How do you know about that?"

"Your assistant told me," I admitted. "He's worried about your health."

Alexander was silent for a while. "Alright. Thank you."

"Guest room is upstairs, second door on the left. The sheets are clean," I said and hurried upstairs, my heart racing.

What was I doing? Letting him stay?

But thinking of his exhaustion, his assistant's words about insomnia, I felt I'd done the right thing.

At midnight, a soft sound woke me.

I tiptoed out of my room and saw weak light still glowing in the living room. Alexander still sat on the sofa, head resting on his arm, breathing softly.

He'd fallen asleep sitting there.

I walked over quietly. His brow remained furrowed, as if he couldn't fully relax even in sleep. Up close, I saw more clearly the dark circles under his eyes—so deep they looked like bruises.

How long had he not slept properly?

My throat tightened, an indescribable ache rising in my chest. This man who usually seemed invincible now looked utterly exhausted.

I was about to wake him, to have him sleep properly in the guest room, but my hand stopped halfway.

He slept deeply, breathing steady and even. This might be the first time in ages he'd slept so quietly. I couldn't bear to disturb him.

I tiptoed back upstairs and got a light blanket from the closet. Coming back down, I moved even more carefully, even lightening my breathing.

The living room was quiet except for his even breathing. I slowly approached, gently covering him with the blanket.

Suddenly, his hand grabbed my wrist.

My breathing stopped. I jerked back in surprise, but his grip was light, more instinctive than intentional.

"Don't go." He murmured in his sleep, his voice carrying vulnerable pleading. "Phoebe... don't leave me again..."

My eyes instantly welled up. This was the first time he'd shown such vulnerability before me. That proud, cold Alpha who'd pushed me away now seemed like a child afraid of abandonment.

I tried to gently free my hand, but he gripped tighter.

"I was wrong... Phoebe... I'm sorry..." His voice was broken, painful.

Tears slid down my cheeks. I stood there, not knowing how to react.

Finally, I sat gently on the carpet by the sofa, letting him hold my hand.

The night was deep, only weak streetlight filtering through curtains into the living room. I watched his sleeping face, his finally relaxed brow, complex emotions surging in my chest.

Maybe my feelings for him had never truly disappeared.

About an hour later, his hand gradually relaxed. I carefully withdrew it, gently flexing my numb wrist, then tiptoed back upstairs.

I lay in bed, closing my eyes, but my mind was full of the recent scene—him grabbing my hand in his dream, that "don't go," and "I'm sorry."

This was the first morning after Alexander stayed over.

Bird calls outside woke me. Sunlight streamed through curtains—another new day.

I left my room and looked around, finding the blanket neatly folded on the sofa. He was gone?

A note lay on the coffee table.

I picked up the paper with his neat handwriting.

"Phoebe, thank you for the blanket and company. This was the most peaceful sleep I've had in a long time. I'll handle the pack meeting—don't worry. Also, remember to add milk to Ryan's breakfast; he needs more calcium during his growth period. —Alexander"

Looking at this note, my nose stung. His thoughtfulness and care were slowly melting my heart.

When I went to make breakfast and opened the fridge, I found fresh milk inside, along with Ryan's favorite strawberry jam.

Obviously, he'd bought them before leaving.

This man...

My throat tightened, but I didn't know if it was from emotion or sadness.

"Mommy, where's Mr. Gray?" Ryan ran downstairs, looking around.

"He had work to handle." I tried to make my voice sound natural. "But he got you a new jam."

"Really?" Ryan clapped excitedly. "Mr. Gray is so nice!"

Yes, he really was nice. So nice I couldn't keep lying to myself that I didn't care about him.

CHAPTER TWELVE

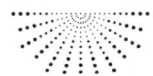

Drake

I stood by the floor-to-ceiling window in my office, watching the busy street below. Three days until the pack banquet. Everything had to be perfect.

Kay had just left with my instructions—ensure ironclad security for the banquet, and arrange Phoebe's entry route. She couldn't come through the main entrance. Too conspicuous.

A knock on the door.

"Come in."

Elena Grayclaw walked in. She wore a navy blue suit today, her blonde hair pinned up in a sleek chignon. All business.

"You wanted to see me?" She settled onto the couch with practiced ease.

"Need a favor." I turned to face her.

"About Phoebe again?" She arched an eyebrow. "Let me guess—you want me to speak for her at the banquet?"

I didn't deny it.

Elena laughed, the kind of knowing laugh that cut right through bullshit. "Drake, you know what? One word from you could solve everything."

"What do you mean?"

"With your position as Ironspine Pack Alpha," she leaned back casually, "if you publicly support Phoebe, who'd dare oppose you? You know damn well how much influence Ironspine Group has in the pack."

"But you'd rather make it complicated," Elena continued, amusement dancing in her eyes. "Have me step forward, let the pack make a 'fair' judgment, pretend you're just another voice in the crowd... All this trouble, just to buy more time with her, right?"

My expression didn't change.

"You have influence in the pack," I said evenly. "As Grayclaw Pack's representative, your support matters to Phoebe."

"Grayclaw Pack's representative?" Elena laughed softly. "I stopped representing Grayclaw Pack the day I left to live my own life. They've pretended I don't exist ever since. Now suddenly my bloodline matters?"

"But you're still Grayclaw's bloodline."

"Bloodline." She repeated the word with bitter irony. "Just like Phoebe's bloodline means she has to sacrifice herself for the pack?"

The air grew heavy.

"I'm not here to debate," my voice turned cold. "I'm telling you what needs to be done."

"Oh? Threatening me?" Elena wasn't fazed. "Don't forget, Drake—I help you because I choose to, not because I fear you."

She stood and walked over to me. "I'll support Phoebe at the pack banquet, but not for you. For her. She's sacrificed too much to save Grayclaw Pack. She deserves justice."

"That's enough."

Elena shook her head. "You're such a stubborn man. You love her deeply, but you put on this professional act. Think she can't see through it?"

"She doesn't need to see anything."

"When are you going to tell her you're Drake?" Elena asked.

"She's still resistant to me. Once everything's settled," I answered, guilt creeping into my voice.

"Drake," Elena's voice turned serious. "If you really care about her, stop playing this hide-and-seek game. She doesn't need a secret protector. She needs someone who'll stand beside her."

"Do what you're supposed to do." I turned my back to her, ending the conversation.

The door closed with a soft click, leaving the office silent again.

I walked back to my desk, where the pack banquet agenda lay open. As Ironspine Group's CEO, I'd attend as a corporate representative. But as Alpha...

If Phoebe knew I was both the cold Alexander Gray who'd rejected her and the real Drake, what would her reaction be?

Anger? Disappointment? Or... deeper hurt?

I closed the file.

Now wasn't the time for this. Three days from now, at the pack banquet, I had to ensure she got her vindication. After that...

I took a deep breath, preparing to play Alexander Gray again.

How much longer could this split existence continue?

Until she no longer needed my protection.

Or until I could no longer maintain this lie.

After Elena left, the office fell unnaturally quiet. The city's chaos was muffled by thick glass, leaving only the air conditioning's low hum.

I sat at my desk for five full minutes, finger hovering over my phone screen. Phoebe's number was right there, but I couldn't bring myself to call.

What are you afraid of? I mocked myself. The mighty Ironspine Pack Alpha, hesitating over a phone call.

Finally, I took a deep breath and dialed.

Each ring felt like an eternity. One, two, three... Just when I thought she wouldn't answer, the call connected.

"Hello?" Her voice came through tired, with Ryan's building blocks clicking in the background.

Just hearing her voice made my heart race.

"It's me." I kept my voice steady, leaning back in my leather chair. "The pack banquet's scheduled. Three days."

Silence on the other end, then her sharp intake of breath.

"So soon?" Tension crept into her voice. "My preparation..."

"You're ready enough." I cut her off, fingers drumming unconsciously on the desk. "The sooner we resolve this, the better. Delay only feeds more gossip. Bad for you and Ryan."

Mentioning Ryan softened my voice despite myself. Our son.

"You're right." She spoke quietly, then paused. "Thank you, Mr. Gray. I'll be ready."

"That's it?" I deliberately raised my voice, corners of my mouth lifting. "Phoebe, after everything I've done—arranging the pack banquet, convincing the elders to give you a chance, agreeing to escort you, all I get is a dry 'thank you'?"

I could picture her expression—probably biting her lower lip, brows slightly furrowed, those green eyes flickering with hesitation.

"What... what do you want?" Her voice turned wary, like a deer ready to bolt.

"Dinner." I leaned back, keeping my tone casual. "Tonight. As thanks. Fair enough?"

Her breathing quickened on the other end, followed by long silence. I could almost see her internal struggle.

"I'm... not sure about tonight..."

"Phoebe," my voice softened with a hint of pleading she couldn't detect. "Just dinner. You can't make me feel like my help was worthless. Besides," I paused, "we need to discuss some banquet details."

Perfect excuse. Professional. Gave her no room to refuse.

I heard her soft sigh.

"Fine." She finally gave in. "Seven tonight. There's a nice French place downtown..."

"I'll pick you up," I said immediately, not giving her a chance to refuse. "Six-thirty. Sharp."

"That's not necessary, I can..."

"I insist." My tone brooked no argument. "Six-thirty, Phoebe. Don't keep me waiting."

After hanging up, I stood in my office for a long time. The setting sun painted the city gold through the windows. I caught my reflection in the glass—I was smiling.

I arrived at the Scent Workshop thirty minutes early.

I'd chosen a charcoal gray tailored suit, no tie, top two shirt buttons undone. Casual but elegant.

Jazz played softly in the car. On the back seat lay a bouquet of white gardenias—not roses, too obvious. Gardenias were perfect. Elegant without being presumptuous.

At six twenty-five, the workshop lights went out.

At six twenty-eight, she appeared in the doorway.

My breathing stopped completely.

She wore an emerald green dress that fell to her knees, fabric flowing softly against her curves. The V-neckline revealed her delicate collarbones.

Her hair wasn't tied up as usual but fell naturally over her shoulders, catching the last rays of sunlight like spun gold.

Her makeup was subtle—just light lip color—but those emerald eyes outshone any jewel.

I got out to open her door. She stood there, fingers nervously fidgeting with her purse chain.

"Punctual," She said softly, her gaze lingering on me for just a second before darting away. But that second was enough for me to catch the flash of appreciation in her eyes.

"You're beautiful," I said honestly, my voice rougher than intended.

Her cheeks immediately flushed pink. "Thank you. We should... we should go."

I opened the car door for her. As she settled in, a familiar scent hit me—jasmine mixed with mysterious woody notes, and beneath it all, her unique essence. My hand tightened involuntarily on the door frame, fighting the urge to pull her into my arms.

The car's interior suddenly felt intimate and confined. She sat in the passenger seat, dress spread elegantly, hands folded in her lap. From my angle, I could see the gentle rise and fall of her chest, the graceful line of her neck.

"Where to?" I started the engine, my voice tight.

She gave me an address—a quiet French restaurant downtown. I knew the place. Elegant atmosphere, dim lighting. Very suitable for... dates.

Had she chosen it on purpose?

We drove in silence. Jazz flowed softly through the car, the saxophone's lazy melody mixing with her subtle fragrance to create an intoxicating atmosphere. At every red light, I stole glances—she gazed out the window, her profile ethereal in the streetlight, occasionally biting her lower lip unconsciously. That small gesture made my heart pound.

"Ryan..." I tried to break the silence.

"Elias is with him." Her response was quick, then, as if realizing something, she added, "They're watching cartoons."

Elias. The name made my hands tighten on the steering wheel.

The restaurant occupied a nineteenth-century building, flanked by sycamore trees along the cobblestone path. Vintage streetlamps cast warm light, creating an old-world charm.

The stairs to the second floor were narrow, carpeted in deep red. She walked ahead while I followed, watching her dress sway with each step, her heels clicking rhythmically on the wooden stairs.

"Careful with that step." The third step was loose. I instinctively reached out, hovering my hand near her waist—close enough to feel her warmth but restraining myself from actual contact.

Her body stiffened noticeably, breathing becoming rapid, but she didn't pull away. That almost-touch was more arousing than actual contact.

The restaurant was dimly lit, each table glowing with candlelight that danced on crystal glasses, casting flickering shadows. Lavender and fresh bread scented the air. Someone played piano in the corner, melody flowing like water.

We were seated by the window—private, overlooking the sycamores and distant city lights.

"What would you like to drink?" The waiter presented the wine list with professional courtesy.

Phoebe took the list, her graceful fingers trailing across the page. "White wine, please."

"A bottle of 2015 Chablis." I told the waiter, then turned to her. "From northern Burgundy. Mineral-forward, perfect with seafood."

She looked up, surprise flickering in her eyes. "You know wine?"

"A little." I leaned back as candlelight danced in my eyes. "Like you know fragrances."

She lowered her lashes, casting fan-shaped shadows on her cheeks.

The food arrived quickly. She ordered pan-seared sea bass; I chose steak. While cutting my meat, I noticed her stealing glances—her gaze traveling from my fingers to my wrist to my forearms. When I looked up, she quickly turned to the window, ears suspiciously red.

"Phoebe." I set down my knife and fork, studying her intently.

"Yeah?" She lifted her wine glass, sipping delicately. The wine made her lips glisten temptingly in the candlelight.

"These five years," my voice dropped low, "were you okay?"

She paused, fingers unconsciously tracing the glass rim. "Fine. Had my business, Ryan..." She hesitated. "Friends to keep me company."

"Elias," I said the name, tasting bitterness on my tongue.

She looked up, wariness flickering in those green depths. "He's my friend. Always has been."

"Just a friend?" I leaned forward, candlelight dancing between us, her pupils dilating slightly at the proximity.

"That's none of your business." She looked away, but I noticed her breathing quicken.

Under the table, my knee accidentally brushed hers. The contact sent electricity through my entire body. She jerked away like she'd been burned, but that brief touch made the air thick with tension.

"Sorry," I murmured, not retreating but maintaining that dangerous distance.

The restaurant's music had changed to a slow French chanson. The female singer's husky, languid voice, accompanied by accordion, told stories of love and loss. I couldn't understand the lyrics, but the melancholy melody struck straight to the heart.

"You..." She bit her lower lip—Goddess, how that made me want to kiss her. "Why are you really helping me? The real reason."

I watched her, watched candlelight dance in her eyes, her trembling lashes. Her scent grew stronger, mixing with the wine's fruit notes to create an intoxicating blend.

"Because I owe you." My voice turned husky. "Five years ago, I shouldn't have treated you that way."

Her grip tightened on the wine glass, knuckles white with strain. "That's in the past."

"It's not past." I suddenly reached out, covering her hand on the table.

Her hand was cold, trembling slightly in my palm. She tried to pull away, but I held gently, not letting her escape. Her pulse raced at her wrist like a frightened bird.

"Phoebe, look at me." My voice was low, almost hypnotic.

She slowly raised her head. Those emerald eyes held confusion, wariness, struggle, and... a flicker of desire she desperately tried to hide. That desire was so obvious it nearly stopped my heart.

"These five years," my thumb gently stroked her hand, feeling her skin's softness, "I haven't gone a single day without regret. Every night, when I'm alone, I think of you. Your smile, your voice, your..." I paused, voice growing darker, "everything about you."

Her breathing quickened, chest rising and falling visibly. Candlelight cast shadows on her collarbones, the skin gleaming invitingly.

"Gray..." Her voice trembled.

"Call me—" Drake. The name almost slipped out.

She blinked, confusion flashing through her eyes. "Call you what?"

"I mean," I quickly recovered, "Gray's too formal."

She gently pulled her hand away, the loss of contact leaving me hollow. "We're not friends. We barely know each other."

"No, we're not strangers." My voice turned urgent, body leaning forward. "That night..."

"Don't mention that night!" Her voice rose, drawing glances from nearby tables.

She immediately realized her outburst, face burning red like a ripe apple.

"Sorry." She ducked her head, voice small. "I just... don't want to talk about it."

"Why?" I stood and walked around the table to her side.

She instinctively leaned back, but the chair limited her movement. I bent down, hands braced on her chair's armrests, trapping her in my embrace. From this angle, I could see the panic in her eyes clearly, smell her tension-laced scent.

"Because you can't forget either, can you?" My voice was right by her ear, breath hitting her sensitive neck.

Her skin immediately broke out in goosebumps, like she'd been struck by lightning. I could see the fine hairs on her neck standing up, her earlobe flushing pink from increased blood flow.

"You're... too close." Her voice shook, hands pressed against my chest, but the weak resistance felt more like invitation than rejection.

"Close?" My nose nearly touched her hair as I breathed deeply, filling my lungs with her essence. "Compared to that night, when we were skin to skin, breath mingling, you trembling beneath me..."

"Stop." Her voice was nearly pleading, but her body betrayed her—she was trembling, not from fear, but from...

"Phoebe," I pulled back slightly but maintained the surrounding position, watching her flushed cheeks and moist eyes. "Tell me, in these five years, have you thought of me? Even once?"

Her eyes suddenly reddened, tears gathering. "What right do you have to ask? What right—"

"Because I think of you every day." My voice nearly broke. "Every damn night, I regret it. Regret not keeping you, regret those hurtful words, regret letting you face everything alone..."

"Enough." She pushed me away, standing. "I'm leaving."

I grabbed her wrist, grip unyielding. "Don't go."

"Let go." She struggled, but I could feel she wasn't using full strength.

"No." I pulled her close, close enough to share body heat, to see my reflection in her pupils. "Not unless you look me in the eye and tell me you feel absolutely nothing for me."

She looked at me, tears finally falling, sparkling like diamonds in the candlelight. "What do you want to hear? That I've thought of you every night these five years? That even after you hurt me, I still... still..."

She bit her lip, stopping herself from continuing. But those unfinished words said everything.

"Still what?" My heart pounded, blood boiling in my veins.

"Nothing." She broke free forcefully, turning to leave. "I'm going home. Ryan's waiting."

I followed her out of the restaurant. On the stairs, her heel suddenly twisted, throwing her off balance. I immediately stepped forward, catching her from behind around the waist.

For that instant, she was completely in my arms. Her back pressed against my chest—I could feel both our heartbeats. Her hair brushed my chin, tickling yet making me crave more.

"Thank... thank you." She frantically tried to leave my embrace.

But I didn't immediately let go. Instead, I rested my chin lightly on her shoulder, whispering in her ear. "Phoebe, give me a chance."

Her body went rigid.

"Let me make amends." My voice was soft, pleading. "Not from guilt, but because... because I want to be with you. Start over."

She trembled in my arms. "We can't go back. Some things, once broken, stay broken."

"Then we'll build something new." I gently turned her to face me. "Phoebe, I know I don't deserve it. I know I hurt you. But please, give me one more chance..."

"Why?" She looked up, eyes blurred with tears. "Why now? Why appear just when I'm finally trying to forget you?"

I reached up to wipe her tears, fingertips touching her soft skin. "Because I've realized that these five years without you, I wasn't living —I was just surviving."

She closed her eyes, more tears spilling.

I lowered my head, forehead touching hers, our breaths mingling.

"Phoebe, I know fated mate might sound like a curse to you, but for me, meeting you was the luckiest thing in my life."

My hands gently cupped her face. "From the moment I saw you, I knew you were my fated mate. That feeling... like finally finding my lost other half."

"Then why..." Her voice broke. "Why pushed me away?"

I looked into her tear-blurred eyes, heart breaking. The truth was on my tongue but couldn't be spoken—because Darkfang Pack threatened your life, because war was coming, because making you leave was the only way to protect you.

"Because..." I closed my eyes, struggling to weave a less hurtful lie. "Because I was too stupid then. I thought pushing you away was right. I thought... it was better for both of us."

Half truth, half lie. It was for her good, but not the kind she understood.

"I was scared." I chose something closer to truth. "Scared of that loss of control, scared that this connection would make me... lose you."

Because enemies would use you against me, because my identity would bring you danger. Words I could never speak.

She studied me, as if trying to see into my soul. "You're hiding something."

My heart lurched, but my expression remained calm. "These five years taught me that without you, nothing I have matters. That's the only thing I'm certain of now."

She looked at me, too many complex emotions in her gaze.

The air was thick with tension. I could feel her struggle, her desire. That fated mate attraction—even after five years, still irresistibly strong.

CHAPTER THIRTEEN

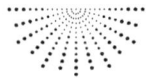

Phoebe

The pull of a fated mate crashed over me again, drowning me like a tide.

I stood on the stairs, his forehead pressed against mine, our breaths mingling. That scent of sandalwood mixed with raw wildness wrapped around me, making my sanity crumble piece by piece.

I should push him away.

The thought flickered through my mind, but it felt so pale and powerless.

"Phoebe..." His voice was low and rough, like the deepest notes of a cello, vibrating against my ear.

I could feel his body heat, could feel the rhythm of his heartbeat. That familiar feeling—five years ago, that night, we were like this too, so close, so... out of control.

"I..." I tried to say something, but the words stuck in my throat.

His hands still cupped my face, thumbs gently stroking my cheeks. That tender touch burned like flames against my skin, making my body tremble involuntarily.

This wasn't right. He rejected me five years ago, so why was he doing this now?

But my body was betraying my reason. When he drew closer, every cell in me screamed for more. The feeling was too intense, so intense it scared me.

"I'm drunk." I heard myself say, my voice laughably weak, "It must be the alcohol..."

"You only had half a glass." His voice carried a trace of bitter amusement, "Phoebe, stop lying to yourself."

He was right. I wasn't drunk, at least not on alcohol. I was drunk on his scent, drunk on the irresistible pull of a fated mate, drunk on... drunk on the feelings I'd been trying to forget for five years but never could.

The stairway was quiet, only our ragged breathing. In the distance, muffled music and conversation drifted from the dining room, but all of it seemed covered by a layer of mist, distant and unreal.

"What do you want?" My voice was shaking, "What exactly do you want?"

"You." His answer was so simple, so direct, "I only want you."

Those two words shattered my last defense.

I don't know who moved first—maybe me, maybe him, maybe both of us at once. I rose on my tiptoes, he lowered his head, and then our lips were pressed together.

In that instant, the whole world disappeared.

His lips were warm and soft, tasting of red wine and something deeper, something that belonged only to him. That taste made me dizzy, made me crave more.

The kiss started gentle, like testing, like asking. But quickly became urgent and deep. His hands moved to my lower back, pressing my whole body against his. My hands climbed to his shoulders without thought, fingers threading through his soft hair.

I could feel him trembling, just like me. This feeling of losing control was both terrifying and addictive.

When we finally broke apart, we were both gasping. His forehead pressed against mine again, eyes burning with deep fire.

"We..." His voice was so hoarse it was barely recognizable, "Hotel?"

Hotel. That temporary, escapist choice.

"No." I heard myself say, my voice carrying a certain finality, "My place."

He froze, surprise flashing in his eyes. "But Ryan..."

"He's staying at Elias's tonight." I interrupted, my cheeks burning, "Elias said he'd watch cartoons with Ryan first, then take him stargazing later."

It was true. Elias had texted this afternoon saying he wanted to take Ryan to see a meteor shower in the suburbs and would stay overnight at his place. I'd hesitated about agreeing at the time, but now it seemed...

Maybe fate had arranged it.

"Are you sure?" He looked at me seriously, "Phoebe, this is your home, your private space. If..."

"I'm sure." I interrupted him again, reaching for his hand, "Take me home."

The atmosphere in the car was suffocating.

I sat in the passenger seat, hands clasped tightly together. He drove faster than on the way here, but still steady. His other hand held mine, fingers interlaced, that simple touch making my heart race.

"You're nervous." He said suddenly.

"I'm not." My voice betrayed me.

He chuckled softly, bringing my hand up to kiss my fingertips gently. "When you lie, your voice gets higher."

My face burned redder.

The car quickly reached the building below Scent Workshop. Night had fallen deep, this street quiet except for the halos of streetlights. I fumbled for my keys in my bag, but my hands were shaking.

He embraced me from behind, chin resting on my shoulder. "Want me to do it?"

His breath against my neck made me nearly drop the keys.

"No... no need." I took a deep breath and finally opened the door.

The workshop was dark, only weak light from the streetlamps filtering through the storefront windows. Various spice scents mingled together, creating a unique atmosphere—this was my space, my territory.

Now, I was letting him into this most private space.

He followed me in, hands never leaving my waist. I could feel his restraint, and his desire.

We climbed the wooden stairs, each step making my heart race faster. On the second floor, I pushed open the bedroom door.

The room was tidy, moonlight filtering through the curtains, illuminating the bed and simple furniture. The air held a faint lavender scent—the essential oil I used for sleep.

The sound of the door closing behind us made my body shiver.

Then he turned me around and kissed me again.

This kiss was more fierce than before, more unguarded. His hands tangled in my hair, tugging gently, making my head fall back. I could feel his long-suppressed desire, and my own matching hunger.

"Phoebe," he murmured against my lips, "if you regret this, tell me now."

Regret?

I looked into his eyes, gleaming deep blue in the moonlight. There was desire there, restraint, and... love.

"I don't regret it." I hooked my arms around his neck, kissing him first, "Gray, I..."

I wanted to say "I like you," wanted to say "I never stopped liking you," wanted to say "I've thought about you every day for five years."

But my words were swallowed by his kiss.

His hands began unzipping my dress, movements gentle and slow, like handling precious art. I started unbuttoning his shirt too, fingers clumsy with nervousness.

"Don't be afraid." He took my hand, placing it over his heart, "Do you feel it? My heartbeat."

His heartbeat was violent and strong, as fast as mine.

"I'm nervous too." He whispered in my ear, "Because this is... for us... too important."

His words relaxed me somewhat. So it wasn't just me who was nervous—he was too.

"Mr. Gray," I looked up at him, moonlight illuminating my face, "I need to know something."

"What?"

"This isn't just... isn't just because of the fated mate attraction, right?" My voice trembled, "You... you really..."

"Love you." He completed my sentence, "Yes, Phoebe. I love you. Not just because of the fated mate, but because you're you. Your strength, your gentleness, your love for Ryan, everything about you."

Tears suddenly blurred my vision.

"I do too..." I choked out, "I love you too. Since five years ago, never stopped."

He kissed away my tears, tender and cherishing.

"Then let me prove it to you," he said softly, "let me show you with my actions how much I love you."

His kisses fell densely, from lips to neck, leaving burning trails. His fingers, clumsy yet urgent, began removing the barriers of clothing between us.

The rustle of fabric mixed with heavy breathing, amplified endlessly in the silent room.

When the last constraint fell away, when his burning skin pressed against mine without barrier, a tremor mixed with desire and subtle fear swept through me.

He stopped, forehead against mine, dark eyes like storm-filled night sky, locked tight on me.

"Phoebe..." He called my name, like a confirmation, like a final question.

In the haze of passion, I grasped a thread of clarity.

I looked into his eyes, feeling my heart's enormous, real thunder for this man before me.

He kissed me deeply, with an almost reverent yet possessive gesture, claiming me completely.

His touch explored every inch of my skin with deliberate slowness, as if he were memorizing the landscape of my body—not just with his fingers, but with the reverence of a man who had waited a lifetime to worship it. Each caress was a whisper of silk against flame, his calloused fingertips tracing the gentle curve of my collarbone, dipping into the hollow of my throat, then gliding down the soft swell of my breasts. Sparks danced across my nerves, igniting a slow-burning fire that made my skin flush with warmth, every nerve ending alive and humming under his tender attention.

I arched beneath him, my hands embarking on their own journey of rediscovery, mapping the hard planes of his chest where his heart thundered like a storm against my palm. My fingers splayed across the taut muscles of his shoulders, feeling the subtle tremor of restraint in his frame, the way he held himself back, savoring me as much as I savored him. The contrast of his roughened palms—scarred from years of quiet battles—against my yielding softness was intoxicating; it made me gasp, a soft, involuntary sound that mingled with the hush of our shared breaths, my body yielding to him like petals unfurling in the first light of dawn.

When he trailed kisses down my throat, each one a feather-light promise, I felt my pulse racing beneath his lips, a frantic rhythm that echoed the wild beat of my heart. He lingered there, his breath warm and steady against the fragile skin, before his mouth found the sensitive spot where my neck met my shoulder—a secret hollow he knew from stolen moments in dreams. His lips brushed it with exquisite care, a gentle nip followed by a soothing swirl of his tongue, drawing from me a soft moan that trembled on the edge of a sigh. The sound seemed to unravel him; his grip on my hips tightened just enough to ground us both, pulling me closer against the insistent heat of his hard length, yet never demanding—only inviting, like a tide drawing the shore into its embrace.

"You're so beautiful," he whispered against my skin, his voice a gravel-rough murmur laced with the ache of unspoken years, his words vibrating through me like a caress of their own. "I've dreamed of this... of you... for so long. Every night, every quiet moment, it was your face, your touch, that kept me whole."

His confession sent a rush of heat flooding through me, not just desire, but something deeper—a profound tenderness that wrapped around my heart like vines in bloom. I threaded my fingers through his hair, the thick strands silky and warm under my touch, guiding his mouth back to mine with a gentle tug that spoke of trust, of homecoming. This kiss was different—deeper, more desperate, yet achingly soft at its core. It was five years of longing compressed into a single, lingering moment of connection: our lips parting and meeting in a slow dance, tongues tracing lazy patterns of rediscovery, breaths mingling like secrets shared in the dark. His free hand cupped my cheek, thumb brushing away an errant tear of overwhelming emotion, his eyes—dark and fathomless—holding mine with a gaze that said everything words could not.

Emboldened by the intimacy of that look, I let my hands wander lower, tracing the ridges of his abdomen, feeling the quiver of his muscles under my fingertips as I explored the strength that had always protected me. He mirrored my gentleness, his hand sliding down my side in a languid path, palm flat against the dip of my waist, then lower still, to the curve of my hip where he squeezed softly, as if to say, I'm here, and this is ours. When his fingers finally ventured between my thighs, parting me with the lightest of touches, I gasped at the intimate reverence of it—his movements unhurried, exploratory, like he was coaxing a fragile flower to open under the sun. He watched my face with unwavering focus, his thumb circling in slow, deliberate spirals that built waves of pleasure from a simmer to a crest, each stroke attuned to my every hitch of breath, every subtle arch of my back.

My body responded with a forgotten eloquence, hips lifting to meet his hand in a rhythm as old as time, the slick heat of my arousal a testament to the love that had simmered between us for so long. Soft whimpers escaped me, mingling with his murmured praises—"That's it, love... let me feel you"—his voice a soothing balm that made the intensity feel safe, cherished. He leaned down to press feather-soft kisses along my jaw, my temple, the corner of my mouth, turning what could have been overwhelming into a symphony of shared vulnerability.

"Please," I whispered, the word a fragile plea laced with wonder, not entirely sure what I was asking for—more of his touch, more of his gaze, more of the man who had become my everything—only knowing I needed the depth of him to fill the spaces longing had carved in my soul.

He paused then, his hand stilling as he positioned himself at my entrance, the tip of him warm and insistent against my core. His eyes searched mine one last time, stormy with desire yet clear with unwavering certainty, a silent question that needed no words. "I love you, Phoebe. Only you," he breathed, the vow wrapping around us like a vow renewed.

When he slowly pushed inside me, inch by exquisite inch, filling me completely with a gentleness that belied his strength, I felt like I was coming home—not just to his body, but to the love that had always been waiting. The initial stretch, a sweet ache of accommodation, gave way to a fullness that felt perfect, inevitable, our bodies slotting together like pieces of a long-lost puzzle. We stayed still for a moment, foreheads pressed together, breaths syncing in the sacred hush, his hand cradling the nape of my neck as if I were the most precious thing in his world. In that pause, with the world narrowed to the beat of our hearts and the tender press of skin on skin, time itself seemed to bend, allowing us to simply be—loved, whole, and utterly entwined.

The pain was brief and sharp, quickly replaced by an unprecedented sense of fullness. As if some corner of my soul that had always been empty was finally filled perfectly. What followed was a rhythm wild and uncontrolled, like a voyage he commanded, tossing on wave crests.

I could only cling helplessly to his broad back, nails probably digging into his skin.

Strange pleasure accumulated like waves, crashing against my nerve endings. The world shrank to just this room, this bed, and his intoxicating scent.

When that devastating climax finally came, white light seemed to explode before my eyes, my whole being thrown to the clouds, then falling softly. In my ears was my own uncontrollable, tearful whimper.

The tide receded, leaving only exhausted, satisfied afterglow. I collapsed beneath him, breathing heavily, my whole body feeling dismantled and reassembled.

He didn't leave immediately, instead continuing to cover me with his heavy body, delicate and tender kisses falling like feathers on my forehead, eyelids, nose tip, finally lingering again on my slightly swollen lips.

"It's okay... my Phoebe."

His deep voice carried post-coital laziness and indescribable satisfaction, resonating in my ear.

That "my" made my just-calmed heartbeat race again, hot flush rushing to my cheeks.

I shyly buried my burning face in his neck, not daring to meet his eyes, but my body unconsciously pressed closer to him, feeling the reassuring vibration of that strong heartbeat.

CHAPTER FOURTEEN

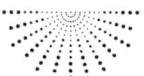

Drake

At eleven PM, I was alone in the office on the top floor of Ironspine Tower.

Outside the floor-to-ceiling windows, the city lights twinkled like scattered stars. I stood by the window, staring at my blurred reflection in the glass. The pack banquet was two days away. Everything was ready—had been ready for weeks—but here I sat anyway, pretending to be busy.

The documents on my desk had been reviewed countless times. Every detail was seared into my memory. But I couldn't leave. Couldn't face that empty apartment.

In two days, it would all be over.

I walked back to my desk and sank into the leather chair with a soft creak. The desk lamp cast a warm circle of light over the scattered papers, illuminating both the documents and my gnawing anxiety.

I had to tell her the truth. Tell her I was Drake Ironspine, not Alexander Gray.

The thought sat on my chest like a stone. I could already picture her face when she learned the truth—shock, anger, disappointment, and... betrayal.

I picked up my phone, its screen harsh in the darkness. Opening my conversation with Phoebe, I stared at last night's "good night" message. My fingers hovered over the keyboard.

What could I say? Where would I even start? Finally, I typed slowly.

"Still at the office. Freezing in here."

Send.

I leaned back and closed my eyes. The air conditioning hummed in the quiet office like monotonous background music.

My phone buzzed.

Phoebe. "Working this late?"

Seeing her reply, I straightened, an involuntary smile tugging at my lips. She was still awake. She cared.

"Too many pack banquet files to review. Getting a headache." I typed quickly, fingers flying. "And..."

I paused deliberately, waiting.

Phoebe. "And what?"

"I'm starving. Barely ate lunch."

It was true. I'd spent the entire afternoon thinking about her, about tomorrow's banquet, about the confession looming ahead. My stomach had been in knots all day.

Phoebe. "How can you not take care of yourself?"

Even through the screen, I could picture her frowning—that mix of scolding and concern that made my heart melt.

"I'm used to it." I replied, then added, "When you're alone, you forget to eat."

Suddenly, my phone rang. I took a deep breath and answered.

"Which office are you in?" Her voice was brisk, no-nonsense.

"Ironspine Tower. Top floor."

"I'm bringing you food."

My heart skipped. "You don't have to—"

"Already on my way." She cut me off. "Twenty minutes."

The line went dead. I stared at my phone, then couldn't help laughing—that helpless, bubbling-up laughter that comes from nowhere.

She was coming.

I jumped up and started tidying frantically. Stacked the scattered documents, cleared coffee cups from my desk, splashed water on my face in the bathroom, and straightened my tie. The man in the mirror had dark circles under his eyes from sleepless nights.

Twenty minutes felt like a century.

Finally, a knock.

I practically sprinted to the door, took a breath to compose myself, then opened it.

Phoebe stood in the hallway holding a thermal bag. She wore simple jeans and a white sweater, her hair in a casual ponytail with strands framing her face. No fancy styling, but beautiful enough to steal my breath.

"It's late..." My voice came out hoarse.

"Let's talk inside." She brushed past me. "The hallway's freezing."

Her shoulder grazed my chest as she passed. That brief contact made my breath catch. She carried the cool night air with her and the faint scent of jasmine.

She set the thermal bag on the coffee table and opened it efficiently. Steam rose immediately, filling the office with aroma—pasta, eggs, fresh vegetables.

"You..." I stood frozen, watching her arrange utensils. "You made this?"

Her face flushed, avoiding my eyes. "I had ingredients at home. Eat before it gets cold."

I sat on the couch and took the fork she offered. The pasta was still steaming, rich tomato sauce topped with fresh basil. The first bite burst with flavor—not the refined but sterile taste of restaurant food, but the taste of home. Of being cared for, remembered.

"Is it good?" She sat across from me, hands folded, watching nervously.

"It's perfect." I looked up seriously. "The best I've ever had."

She smiled, eyes crinkling into crescents. That pure, pleased smile hit my heart like a gentle collision.

I ate while she watched quietly. The office was peaceful, only the soft clink of utensils. This companionship was too precious. So precious I wanted time to freeze.

After I finished, she began packing up, moving naturally like she was in her own home. I stood and walked to my desk, pretending to review documents.

"These are all for the pack banquet?" She approached, standing beside me, leaning slightly to see the papers.

She was so close I could feel her warmth, smell the fragrance in her hair. My fingers clenched, fighting the urge to hold her.

"Yeah." I sighed deliberately. "Every document needs careful review. Still have so many left..."

She picked up a file and studied it. The lamplight fell across her profile, outlining soft features. The way she bit her lip in concentration made it impossible to look away.

I turned and gently wrapped my arms around her waist from behind.

"Alexander?" Her body tensed, the document nearly slipping.

Alexander? How desperately I wanted her to say... Drake. I regretted hiding my identity. What if she couldn't forgive me? What if she never spoke to me again? I couldn't bear the thought.

My body went weak with helpless dread.

"Let me hold you." I rested my chin on her shoulder, voice against her ear. "Just for a moment."

She didn't struggle. Instead, she slowly relaxed, leaning into my embrace. Her back pressed against my chest. I could feel her heartbeat—fast and strong.

"You're acting strange today." She said softly, puzzled.

"How so?" I tightened my arms, pulling her closer.

"I can't put my finger on it." She turned in my arms, looking up with searching green eyes. "Are you hiding something from me?"

My heart pounded. She was too perceptive, always catching my subtle mood shifts.

"No." I kissed her forehead, lips touching warm skin. "I just missed you."

It was true. Since last night, thoughts of her had consumed me completely.

Her face turned red like sunset clouds.

Moonlight streamed through the windows, casting silver light over the office. In that glow, she looked like a moon goddess. I couldn't hold back anymore. I leaned down and kissed her.

It started gentle, careful, like tasting morning dew. Her lips were soft and warm with a hint of tea. But soon, suppressed desire crashed over me. I deepened the kiss, exploring her mouth, tasting her sweetness.

Her hands climbed to my shoulders, gripping my shirt. I could feel her response—shy but eager—and it nearly shattered my control.

The office temperature was rising. My hands moved up from her waist, feeling her heat even through the sweater.

"Alexander..." She gasped between breaths, voice soft and breathless. "This is an office..."

"I know." I kissed down her neck, leaving a trail on her pale skin. Her skin was silk-smooth, carrying her unique scent.

"Someone... someone might come..." Her voice trembled, but her arms only tightened around my waist.

"They won't." I lifted her—she was so light it broke my heart—and set her on the desk, standing between her legs. "No one comes at this hour."

She sat on the edge, having to look up at me. The angle made her irresistible—swollen lips, dazed eyes, chest rising and falling.

I continued kissing her, fingers threading through her hair, gently massaging her scalp. She trembled in my arms, making small sounds like a kitten.

"Wait!" She suddenly pushed me away hard enough that I stepped back. Her face was apple-red, hair slightly mussed. "We really can't! This is an office!"

She jumped down, frantically smoothing her clothes and hair like a caught child.

"What if there are cameras..." Her voice was panicked.

"No cameras." I reached for her again, but she dodged. "My office doesn't have cameras."

"Still no!" She backed away, arms crossed defensively. "Alexander, know your place!"

Looking at her flushed cheeks and moist lips, my self-control teetered on collapse. But the determination in her eyes made me stop.

"Fine." I raised my hands in surrender. "You win."

She visibly relaxed, though desire hadn't completely faded from her eyes, making her even more tempting.

"I... I should go." She grabbed the thermal bag hurriedly. "It's late."

"I'll walk you out."

"No need. I drove."

"I insist." I picked up my jacket. "At least to the parking garage."

She didn't refuse. We walked side by side down the empty hallway, footsteps echoing on marble. In the elevator, we stood close, her arm occasionally brushing mine. Each contact was electric.

The parking garage was vast and mostly empty, scattered cars looking lonely. Night wind blew from the entrance, carrying autumn's chill. She instinctively moved closer, and I took her hand, intertwining our fingers.

Her hand was small, completely enveloped by mine. The warmth of joined palms made this cold night feel warm.

"After the pack banquet..." I suddenly spoke, voice echoing in the empty space.

"Hmm?" She looked at me sideways, puzzled.

"After the pack banquet, I have something to tell you." I stared ahead, not daring to meet her eyes. "Something important."

She stopped and turned to face me. "What is it? Can't you tell me now?"

"You'll know when the time comes." I squeezed her hand reassuringly. "Just... whatever I tell you, remember one thing."

"What?" Her eyes showed concern.

"I love you." I finally found the courage to look into her eyes. "That's a fact that will never change."

She froze, emotions flashing through her eyes—confusion, worry, a trace of fear. "Alexander, what are you..."

"You'll know soon enough." I opened her car door, cutting off her question. "Drive safely. Text me when you get home."

She got in, looking at me through the window with deepening confusion. I bent down and kissed her forehead through the glass.

I watched her car disappear into the night, red taillights growing distant. I stood there for a long time.

The autumn wind was cold, cutting through my thin shirt, but I didn't feel it. Something colder gripped my heart—fear of the future.

Would she forgive my deception? Would she understand why I'd done it?

Or would she hate me? Completely, utterly hate me, never wanting to see me again?

I didn't know. But I knew I couldn't continue this lie.

She deserved the truth. Deserved to make her own choice.

The next afternoon, I stood at Phoebe's door holding a large dress box.

Less than twenty-four hours until the pack banquet.

"You're here early." Phoebe looked surprised, hair loose around her shoulders.

"I brought you something." I held up the box. "For tomorrow's banquet. You need the right dress."

Her brow furrowed. "I have formal wear."

"I know." I entered and set the box on the sofa. "But this is the pack banquet. It needs to be more formal. And..."

I paused, looking at her. "I want to see you in this."

Her face flushed. "Alexander, you don't need to..."

"Try it on." I opened the box, revealing the dress inside. "If you don't like it, we'll find something else."

It was a deep blue evening gown, satin fabric gleaming softly in the light. The neckline was elegant off-shoulder, fitted at the waist, with layers flowing like water.

Phoebe gasped. "This is too expensive."

"Nothing's too expensive for you." I lifted the dress. "Try it?"

She hesitated, then took it. "Give me a minute."

She carried it upstairs while I waited. Ten minutes later, soft footsteps on the stairs.

When she appeared at the top, my breathing stopped completely.

The dress fit perfectly, deep blue highlighting her pale skin. The off-shoulder design showed elegant collarbones and shoulders, the fitted waist accentuated her slender figure, and the flowing skirt swayed like midnight waves.

She tugged at the skirt self-consciously. "Is it too..."

"Perfect." I walked over and took her hand, making her turn. "Absolutely perfect."

"Really?" Her voice held uncertainty.

"See for yourself." I led her to the full-length mirror.

The woman reflected was breathtaking—elegant, regal, like a goddess from a painting.

"Tomorrow there'll be a styling team too." I stood behind her, hands lightly on her shoulders. "Makeup, hair, making sure you're the most stunning woman there."

"I don't need to be the most stunning." She turned to face me. "I just need..."

"Need what?" I looked down at her.

"Need you beside me." Her voice was soft. "Tomorrow... I'm nervous."

I pulled her into my arms. "Don't be afraid. I'll be right there."

She leaned against my chest, the satin rustling softly under my hands. I could smell her fragrance—jasmine mixed with her unique scent, making my reason crumble.

"Phoebe..." My voice turned husky.

She looked up, those green eyes especially bright in the afternoon light. I couldn't help leaning down to kiss her gently.

The kiss started soft, like savoring precious wine. But quickly, suppressed desire took over. My hands found her waist, pulling her closer, while hers climbed to my shoulders.

"Wait..." She gasped, pushing me away. "The dress will wrinkle."

"Then take it off." My reason had been burned away.

"No!" Her face turned apple-red. "It's daytime!"

I took a deep breath, forcing calm. She was right. I couldn't be this impulsive. Tomorrow was the pack banquet. I had to stay rational.

After tomorrow, I'd tell her the truth.

The thought made my mood suddenly heavy.

"What's wrong?" She sensed my shift with usual perceptiveness.

"Nothing." I stroked her cheek gently. "Just thinking about after tomorrow..."

"What about after tomorrow?"

"After tomorrow, many things will be different." My voice carried weight she couldn't understand.

She frowned. "Alexander, you keep saying things I don't understand. What exactly..."

The doorbell suddenly rang, interrupting us.

"That should be the styling team." I released her. "I had them come look at the dress, plan tomorrow's look."

For the next two hours, stylists circled Phoebe, discussing hairstyles, makeup, accessories. I sat watching, my mind elsewhere.

Phoebe, after tomorrow, will you still trust me the way you do now?

After the stylists left, Phoebe changed back into regular clothes. The dress was carefully hung up, waiting for tomorrow.

"Thank you." She came to me. "For everything you're doing."

"It's what I should do." I took her hand and kissed her fingertips lightly.

"Alexander," she looked at me seriously, "you said you have something important to tell me after tomorrow. Can't you give me a hint?"

I was silent for a long time.

"Phoebe, if... if I'm not who you think I am, what would you do?"

She froze. "What do you mean?"

"If I've been hiding things from you, if I..." I stopped, not knowing how to continue.

Her expression grew serious. "Alexander, what are you saying? What have you hidden from me?"

"You'll know after tomorrow." I stood. "I should go. Get some rest. Tomorrow will be a long day."

"Alexander!" She grabbed my hand. "You can't just leave a bunch of riddles and walk away!"

I turned and pulled her into my arms, holding her so tightly I wanted to merge her into my body.

"Phoebe," I whispered in her ear, "whatever happens, remember I love you. That's real. It always will be."

Then, before she could react, I released her and left quickly.

Outside, the night wind was cool. I looked back at the house with warm light glowing through the windows.

Tomorrow, everything would change.

I just hoped it wouldn't be for the worse.

CHAPTER FIFTEEN

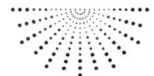

Phoebe

Chandeliers cast warm golden light throughout the Pack Banquet hall, illuminating every corner.

Outside the massive floor-to-ceiling windows, the full moon hung suspended in the night sky, its silver light streaming through the glass and weaving with the indoor lighting into a mesmerizing dance of shadows.

I stood at the entrance, taking a deep breath. The air was thick with complex werewolf scents—the commanding presence of those in power, the restless energy of young pack members, and subtle emotions I couldn't fully decipher. All mingling with the cloying sweetness of champagne, the sharp bite of cigars, and something else lurking beneath—something dangerous.

"Phoebe, are you okay?" Elias whispered beside me, his hand gently rubbing my back in comfort.

I nodded, though my heart was still racing.

Everything here brought back memories of that suffocating night five years ago—the chaos of the Full Moon Banquet, that night with Alexander, and the crushing despair I'd felt the next morning when my world collapsed.

At least that was behind me now. Alexander and I had found each other again. We were together again.

Stay calm, Phoebe. You're not that helpless girl anymore.

Though Alexander wasn't standing beside me now, I knew he was somewhere in this banquet hall, handling his own affairs.

I smoothed the deep blue gown Alexander had chosen for me. The silk fabric hugged my curves, making me appear both elegant and powerful. That's what I needed—to project confidence before these aristocrats.

I scanned the crowd, searching for Alexander among the guests. He'd promised he'd be here tonight, watching over me from the shadows... but there were too many people. I couldn't spot him yet.

Never mind. Focus on business first. After meeting with the elders, I'll find him.

"Elena's over there." Elias's voice drew me from my thoughts.

Following his gaze, I saw her—the real Elena.

She stood at the far end of the banquet hall, positioned directly beneath a crystal chandelier, her silver-gray gown shimmering softly in the light.

Standing beside her was...

My breath caught.

Drake. My husband in name only. The man I'd abandoned five years ago without a word of explanation.

He wore a dark suit that perfectly accentuated his tall frame. Though oddly, I'd never sensed any Alpha presence from him. What made my heart race was the realization that he'd already noticed me.

Guilt crashed over me in waves. I remembered how I'd fled the castle with Elias's help, how I'd vanished from his life without leaving so much as an explanation.

I hadn't even told him my real identity. I'd let him believe he'd married Elena, then simply abandoned him.

When Drake's eyes met mine, I saw him offer a slight nod—polite but distant, the kind of acknowledgment you'd give an ordinary guest.

Why was he so composed? Didn't he resent me? Or perhaps... perhaps he simply hadn't cared when I left?

"Phoebe?" Elias noticed my distress, taking my hand. His palm was warm and dry, offering comfort. "You've gone pale."

"I'm fine." I forced a smile, trying to look away from Drake. "Just... a little nervous."

At that moment, Elena seemed to notice our presence. Her gaze swept across the crowd and landed on me. I saw her eyes widen slightly before she gently touched Drake's arm and began walking toward us.

My breathing quickened. She was coming over. What would she say? What would she do?

From the corner of my eye, I watched Drake remain where he stood. His gaze followed Elena briefly, but when she headed my way, he simply raised his wine glass and turned to converse with other guests.

"Should we go somewhere else first?" Elias suggested, clearly sensing the tension.

"No." I took a deep breath, forcing myself to stand straight. "We're here now. Better to face whatever comes."

Elena glided gracefully through the crowd, her gown flowing with each step like a silver cloud. Guests unconsciously parted for her, their conversations pausing as she passed.

As she approached, I could see her features more clearly—delicate bone structure, green eyes, and that unshakable composure I could never replicate.

"Phoebe." Her voice was gentler than I'd expected, tinged with curiosity rather than hostility. "It's been a long time."

I hesitated for a moment, then realized I should respond.

"It's good to see you, Elena." My voice trembled slightly as I tried to sound composed.

Elena smiled faintly, that expression carrying emotions I couldn't quite read.

"Drake has mentioned you to me." She paused, her gaze lingering on me. "He said you were very... special."

Drake had spoken to her about me? What had he said? My heart began pounding, but I fought to maintain my composure.

"I think we should find somewhere quiet to talk," Elena continued, her tone remaining gentle but with an underlying firmness I could sense.

"About... some things that need to be clarified."

Elias shifted nervously beside me, his fingers brushing my arm as if to say: If you don't want to go, we can leave right now.

But I knew I couldn't run away. Not now. I couldn't flee like I had five years ago.

"All right." I nodded, even though every instinct screamed at me to escape.

Elena led me toward a relatively quiet corner of the banquet hall, where several velvet sofas were arranged in an intimate circle, away from the main social area. An elegant floor lamp cast soft, warm light, creating a cozy circle on the carpet. Through a translucent screen, you could glimpse figures moving beyond, but their voices were muffled.

Elias followed at a respectful distance.

"Please, sit." Elena gracefully gestured to a seat, settling herself on the sofa across from me.

I nervously smoothed my dress, my palms already damp with perspiration. How would she begin? Would she directly confront me about my deception from years past?

"Phoebe," Elena began, her voice still gentle, "I imagine you must be terribly worried... about what happened back then."

My heart lurched violently, nearly bursting from my chest. She knew. She knew everything.

"I..." I opened my mouth but couldn't find words. Should I apologize? Explain? Simply confess everything?

Elena seemed to notice my panic and waved her hand dismissively. "You don't need to be nervous. Those matters..." Elena paused, her eyes flickering, "have all been resolved. Drake... he understands the position you were in."

When she mentioned "Drake," her tone carried complex emotions I couldn't decipher. Was it sympathy? Something else entirely?

"Resolved?" I repeated, confused.

"Yes." Elena nodded quickly, then seemed eager to change the subject. "I heard you're having some professional difficulties?"

I blinked, struggling to follow her abrupt shift. "Yes, someone's questioning whether my formula plagiarized traditional Ironspine Pack fragrances."

"That's complete nonsense." Elena's tone became firm. "You've documented your evidence properly, haven't you?"

"Yes, original records with detailed timestamps of every experiment and modification."

Elena stood, glancing around before gesturing toward the far end of the banquet hall. "Do you see those elders over there? I can introduce you. Once they review your evidence, they'll support you."

"You... you're willing to help me?" I asked in disbelief.

Elena turned back to me, complex emotions flickering in her eyes. "Of course. And the pack will issue an official statement tomorrow, clearing up all rumors about the formula controversy."

I felt my eyes growing moist. This woman I'd once impersonated, this woman I'd expected to despise me, was extending help when I needed it most.

"Thank you, Elena. I... I don't know how to repay you."

She smiled softly, that expression carrying warmth I couldn't fully understand. "No repayment necessary. We're all just trying to do what's right, aren't we?"

Just as Elena prepared to introduce me to the pack elders, a sharp voice suddenly pierced the air behind us.

"How touching, this display of sisterly affection."

The voice sliced through our quiet corner like a blade through silk.

I turned to see Sera approaching, draped in a fiery red evening gown that made her look like a walking flame.

Her heels clicked sharply against the marble floor with each step, radiating menace.

But her expression burned even hotter than her dress—a volatile mixture of fury and jealousy.

"Sera." Elena's voice immediately turned wary. "Is there something you need?"

"Oh, there's definitely something." Sera sneered, her gaze boring into me.

"I think everyone here deserves to know exactly what kind of person our 'honored' guest really is."

Her voice grew louder, drawing attention from nearby guests.

Conversations gradually died down as all eyes turned toward our corner. The air seemed to thicken, even the crystal chandelier light becoming harsh and unforgiving.

My heart began hammering, but I fought to remain calm. "I don't understand what you're implying."

"Don't understand?" Sera pulled several photographs from her small purse, holding them aloft. "Perhaps these pictures will refresh your memory?"

Even from a distance, I could make out their content—images of me, but the angles and lighting had been manipulated to suggest intimate contact with some man. I recognized shots from late nights at my perfume studio, but they'd been maliciously edited and spliced.

"These photos..." I began to explain.

"These photos clearly reveal your true nature!" Sera cut me off, her voice rising. "A whore who betrayed her fiancé and cavorted with other men! I want everyone here to see what you really are!"

Whispers erupted around us like a tide, mixing surprise, curiosity, and schadenfreude. I felt like I was standing center stage, being scrutinized by countless eyes, each gaze piercing my skin like needles.

My cheeks burned with shame and rage.

"Enough." Elias's voice cut through the chaos like ice as he stepped protectively in front of me, blocking Sera's advance. "Ms. Sera, please retract these malicious accusations."

"Accusations?" Sera's voice turned shrill. "The photos are right here—the evidence speaks for itself!"

"Those photos are obviously doctored," Elias replied calmly. "Anyone can see the editing marks. And regardless of their authenticity, Miss Phoebe's private life is none of your concern."

Sera's face flushed crimson with humiliation and rage as she pointed at Elias. "Who the hell are you? Just some pathetic assistant, and you dare lecture me?"

"I'm Miss Phoebe's friend and colleague, and I have every right to protect her from malicious slander." Elias's tone remained steady, but I could feel his protective instincts radiating outward.

"Friend? Colleague?" Sera laughed bitterly, her voice loud enough for everyone nearby to hear. "You think I don't know the truth?"

Her voice echoed through the banquet hall like a stone thrown into still water, creating ripples. All conversation ceased, every eye focused on our confrontation.

Even the string quartet in the distance had fallen silent, plunging the entire hall into an eerie quiet.

Sera continued, her voice dripping with jealousy and resentment.

"You outsiders will never deserve to stand beside a true Alpha! Only I, who grew up with him, truly understand him!"

As she spoke, her gaze wasn't directed at Drake, but toward another section of the banquet hall.

The area near the floor-to-ceiling windows, where moonlight streamed in from outside, casting silver shadows across the floor.

I followed her gaze, and my heart stopped—

Standing there was Alexander. My Alexander.

He stood with his back to the window, silhouetted at the boundary between moonlight and lamplight, half his face shrouded in shadow, half outlined in silver. Those deep eyes watched our scene quietly, appearing especially profound and mysterious in the interplay of light and shadow.

He was watching us with complex emotions I'd never seen before.

"Wait..." My voice began to tremble. "Sera, when you say 'true Alpha,' you mean..."

"Stop playing innocent!" Sera shrieked. "Alexander is our true Alpha—Drake!"

In that instant, the world seemed to freeze. Every sound in the banquet hall vanished, leaving only my heartbeat thundering in my ears. The chandelier light became blinding, the moonlight turned frigid, even breathing became laborious.

Those words struck me like lightning from a clear sky.

So... Alexander was that husband in name?

Wait. If he was the Alpha, then that night five years ago...

Memory fragments began reassembling in my mind.

At the Full Moon Banquet, I'd been drawn by that powerful scent

The figure I'd followed, his Alpha presence had been so intense

That night, his possessiveness and desire were beyond what any ordinary werewolf could possess

So from the very beginning, from that full moon night, it had been Drake himself with me?

And the other man was just a decoy, a shadow used to mislead everyone?

But why... why would Drake do that?

Why had someone impersonate the Alpha? Why concealed his own identity?

My mind went blank, then began racing. Memory fragments from five years ago started reassembling—Alexander's powerful pheromones, his authority within the pack, his coldness and testing toward me...

If Alexander was the true Alpha, then that Drake... he wasn't.

I looked around and suddenly realized everyone's expressions carried strange shadows. In the dim lighting, every face appeared blurred, as if they wore masks in a performance I couldn't comprehend.

Elena had gone pale, her lips trembling slightly, seemingly anxious about Sera's revelation; the fake Drake in the distance continued chatting with other guests, but I noticed his posture seemed more like... protection? Or surveillance?

They all knew. Every single one of them knew, and only I had been kept in the dark.

A chill crept up from my feet, spreading through my entire body. I felt like I was standing in ice-cold water, everything around me becoming distant and surreal.

Fury at the betrayal began burning in my chest.

He'd watched me believe I'd betrayed my "fiancé," letting me struggle day and night in an abyss of guilt! And he'd even been cruel to me.

All of this was a performance he'd orchestrated. It was the source of my five years of suffering.

When we met again, he'd still used the name "Alexander" to approach me... deceiving me, hiding from me.

And now, here I was being slandered and mocked by others, turned into a laughingstock.

Those tender words, those passionate kisses, those nights that made me believe hope was rekindling... had they all been part of his carefully crafted game?

I was like a fool, performing earnestly in his scripted play while he sat in the audience, savoring my stupidity and naivety.

Damn you, Drake!

"Phoebe?" Elias noticed my distress, looking at me with concern.

I didn't answer. Instead, I gathered my skirt and turned toward the banquet hall exit. I had to get out of here.

"Phoebe, wait!" Elena called from behind.

But I didn't stop. Only one thought kept echoing in my mind: They were all lying to me. Everyone was lying to me.

I walked through the crowd, each step feeling dreamlike. The banquet hall lights became blurred, like watercolors dissolved in tears; the guests' laughter turned distant, like sounds from deep underwater; only the sharp click of my heels on marble rang clearly in my ears, one step, then another, like some desperate countdown.

Moonlight streamed through the glass doors from outside, cold and piercing. I pushed open the heavy doors as night's chill wind struck my face, carrying early spring's bite that stung my eyes.

Alexander Gray was the real Drake.

My heart plummeted into an abyss, like a heavy stone sinking into dark, icy depths.

CHAPTER SIXTEEN

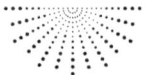

Drake

Sera's voice still echoed through the banquet hall, cutting through the air like a piercing alarm. I stood in the shadows by the floor-to-ceiling windows, my fingertips digging so hard into my palms that my nails nearly broke skin.

"Alexander is our true Alpha—Drake!"

I watched Phoebe's body go rigid.

Like a statue suddenly frozen in time, she stood in the center of the crowd, moonlight streaming through the crystal chandelier to bathe her in ethereal light, making her look so fragile, so utterly defenseless.

No. This wasn't how it was supposed to happen.

I should have told her the truth myself, somewhere private, just the two of us. Gently, carefully explaining everything. Not like this—not in a hall full of strangers.

She turned her head, her gaze cutting through the crowd to land squarely on me.

In that instant, I felt an invisible fist crush my heart.

Her eyes went wide, pupils blown with shock, reflecting the crystal lights like scattered stars. I saw her lips part, trying to speak, but no sound emerged.

Then I watched understanding slowly dawn in her eyes—that agonizing moment of realization, that soul-crushing despair of complete betrayal.

She understood.

She finally knew who had tangled with her that full moon night five years ago; who had pushed her away with cutting words; who had approached her again masquerading as a business consultant.

It was all me—the real Drake.

From beginning to end, it had all been me.

Whispers rose around us like a tide, carrying curiosity, shock, and barely concealed glee.

But I could only see her—watching the light in her eyes extinguish bit by bit, like a candle snuffed out by wind.

Just like that night five years ago, when I'd coldly delivered those brutal words, the light in her eyes had died exactly the same way.

No, I couldn't let her walk away like this again.

I couldn't lose her again.

I set down my glass and strode toward her. My footsteps rang against the marble floor. The crowd automatically parted, everyone stepping back with bowed heads in submission.

"Phoebe—" I began, my voice rough with tension.

But she didn't look at me. Instead, she gathered her skirt and turned toward the exit.

In that moment, something seized my heart—not anger, not fear, but something deeper, more suffocating. She was leaving again.

I turned to Sera, who still stood there wearing a satisfied smile, as if she'd just delivered some masterful performance.

"Enough, Sera." My voice carried the unmistakable authority of an Alpha.

All whispers died instantly. Even breathing became cautious.

"Sera." The words came out ice-cold, each one forced through gritted teeth. "Do you have any idea what you've just done?"

"Drake... I..." Her voice trembled. "I just wanted everyone to see her true color!"

"True color?" I stared coldly at the photos clutched in her hands. "With these pathetic tactics? Repeatedly framing her? I warned you never to hurt Phoebe again."

Sera's face drained of all color, her body shaking violently. She looked up at me, tears spilling uncontrollably.

"But... but Drake, I was doing this for you... she doesn't deserve..."

"Doesn't deserve?" I stepped closer, each word sharp as a blade. "Doesn't deserve to stand beside me? Sera, what gives you the right to make my decisions?"

Sera went white as parchment. Her mouth opened but no sound came. Tears streaked her makeup, mascara leaving black trails down her cheeks.

"Drake, I love you..." she choked out, her voice raw with desperation. "Since we were children, I've always... I've always loved you..."

I looked at her, complex emotions churning in my chest. Sera was my childhood friend. I knew about her feelings, but I'd never given her any encouragement beyond friendship.

"Sera, I've always considered you a friend." My voice remained steely. "But that doesn't give you the right to hurt Phoebe. She's my fated mate. I won't allow anyone to harm her—including you."

Sera swayed as if the words had shattered her last foundation. She covered her face, completely breaking down, barely able to remain standing.

Elena quickly moved forward to support her.

"Kay, take care of the banquet." I gave rapid orders to Kay, who was pushing through the crowd toward us, then turned to search for Phoebe.

But she was already gone.

My heart plummeted.

The deep blue gown was disappearing behind the archway. She held her dress high, spine ramrod straight, steps hurried but controlled—the bearing of someone making a final, irreversible exit.

No.

Panic crashed over me like a wave.

I ignored Sera's sobs and the guests' whispered gossip, striding after Phoebe with determined steps.

To hell with what they thought.

Right now, only she mattered.

I burst from the banquet hall into the crisp night air, autumn's bite sharp against my face. Moonlight spilled across the courtyard's stone pathways, stretching tree shadows into long, dark fingers. In the distance, a figure in deep blue hurried toward the parking area.

"Phoebe!" I called out, my voice ringing clear in the empty night.

Her steps faltered momentarily but didn't stop. If anything, she moved faster.

I caught up just as she reached her car, pressing my hand against the door before she could open it. "Phoebe, wait—let me explain—"

She whirled around and slapped me hard across the face.

The sharp crack echoed through the night. My right cheek burned, ears ringing from the impact. But worse than the physical sting was the arctic coldness in her eyes.

"Explain?" Her voice shook, but every word was crystal clear. "What could you possibly explain? How you had someone impersonate you? How you used a false identity to get close to me? Or how you stood by watching me make a complete fool of myself again?"

Moonlight illuminated her face. I saw tears gathering in her eyes, but she bit her lip fiercely, refusing to let them fall.

My heart felt like it was being torn in two. "Phoebe, I know I was wrong. I'm sorry!"

"'Sorry' and 'I was wrong' don't fix anything!" I could feel her barely contained fury.

Wind lifted her hair, dark strands clinging to her damp cheeks. Her whole body trembled.

I wanted to reach for her, to pull her into my arms and warm her with my body heat. But she stepped back, creating deliberate distance between us.

"Five years ago, when I found the courage to tell you the truth," her voice dropped to almost a whisper, so soft the wind nearly carried it away, "what did you do? You told me to get lost, to never show my face again."

The memory sliced through my heart like a razor. I remembered that morning—her pale face, the tears in her eyes, the cruel words I'd spoken, believing I was protecting her.

"That was because I had to make you leave." My voice began to shake. "Darkfang Pack was already targeting you. If you'd stayed with Ironspine Pack, they would have killed you—"

"So you drove me away like that?" Her tears finally spilled over. "Do you have any idea how terrified I was? I thought I'd ruined everything. I thought... I thought that night meant absolutely nothing to you."

Every word was like a dull knife sawing through my heart.

"That night was the most important moment of my life," I said quietly. "Because that night, I knew with absolute certainty that you were my fated mate."

"Fated mate." She repeated the words, her voice dripping with bitter irony. "Is this how you treat a fated mate? With deception, lies, manipulation?"

The wind grew sharper, making leaves rustle overhead. Distant music drifted from the banquet hall, its cheerful melody painfully incongruous with this moment.

"I know I was wrong." My voice carried a humility I'd never heard from myself before. "I was terrified. Afraid Darkfang Pack would hurt you, afraid... afraid that if you learned the truth, you'd hate me."

"Hate you?" She laughed, the sound hollow and bitter. "Well, congratulations—I'm hating you right now."

Those words cut deeper than her slap.

"Phoebe..." I reached toward her, but she stepped back again.

"Don't touch me." Her voice was cold as winter. "Don't look at me like that anymore. Don't say those things to me. I'll never believe you again, Drake. Never."

In the moonlight, her face was breathtakingly beautiful, but the ice in her eyes made me feel like I was drowning.

"Do you know how hard I tried?" Her voice suddenly became very soft.

"For five years after I left, I tried to forget you, tried to forget how badly you hurt me. When we met again five years later, I was foolish enough to give you another chance. You had countless opportunities to tell me the truth, but did you? You kept lying. Even when we were together again, you never told me."

My throat constricted, words barely forming. I'd thought about it so many times. But each time, my hesitation and self-doubt had silenced me.

"I thought this time was different." She continued. "I thought 'Alexander' genuinely loved me. But it was all just another elaborate lie."

"It wasn't a lie," I said desperately. "My feelings for you are real—they've always been real—"

"Enough." She cut me off, exhaustion making her voice crack. "I don't want to hear any more. I'm tired, Drake. I'm so damn tired."

She opened the car door, preparing to get in.

"Where are you going?" I asked reflexively.

"Anywhere, as long as it's far from you." She didn't look back.

Panic struck again. Almost instinctively, I grabbed her wrist. "No, you can't leave—"

She yanked her hand away, the motion so final it made my heart stutter. "Can't leave? Why not? Because you haven't finished playing your games?"

"Because I love you." The words erupted from somewhere deep inside, crystal clear in the hushed night.

Everything around us seemed to freeze. The wind stilled, leaves stopped rustling, even the moonlight felt suspended.

She stared at me, a kaleidoscope of emotions flashing in her eyes—surprise, doubt, pain, rage.

"What did you say?" Her voice was barely audible.

"I said I love you," I repeated the words with fierce conviction. "From five years ago until this moment, I've never stopped loving you."

Fresh tears spilled down her cheeks, catching the moonlight like liquid silver.

But she shook her head, her smile more devastating than any tears. "You know what, Drake? I used to dream of hearing you say those words. I desperately wanted to know that night wasn't just some meaningless accident to you."

She paused, her voice turning to ice. "But now? Those words are worthless."

My body went rigid, time crystallizing around this moment. I tried to speak but my voice had abandoned me.

"Phoebe—" The word came out as barely a rasp.

"Starting today," she looked at me with unwavering resolve, "everything between us ends. Our business relationship—I'll have Elias handle the transition with your company. As for our personal relationship... I don't think we ever really had one, did we?"

The words struck like a physical blow to my chest.

"No, please don't—"

"And one more thing." She cut me off. "Please don't appear in front of me and Ryan ever again."

"Ryan..." His name caught in my throat, bringing back images of that sweet boy with our combined features, clinging to my legs, calling my name with such trust.

"Phoebe, please, give me one more chance—"

"Chance?" She laughed coldly. "You've already had two. Five years ago, and now. Both times you chose deception."

She slid into the car, looking at me through the glass with such frigid detachment I barely recognized her.

"Goodbye, Drake." Her words were soft but final. "This time, it really is goodbye."

The engine roared to life, its sound jarring in the silent night. Headlights blazed, harsh white light washing over me and stretching my shadow long across the pavement.

I stood helplessly as the car pulled away, watching the red taillights grow smaller and smaller until they vanished around the bend.

Five years. It had taken me five years to find her again, five years to work my way back into her life. And I'd destroyed it all in a single night.

My right hand slowly clenched into a fist, nails digging crescents into my palm, but that small pain couldn't touch the gaping void in my chest.

This time, she would never forgive me. I had lost her completely. Lost her again.

In the distance, music still played in the banquet hall, but that celebration might as well have been on another planet.

The night was deep and mercilessly cold.

I don't know how long I stood in that parking lot—long enough for my body to grow numb with cold, long enough for the moon to shift overhead. But I couldn't move. As if staying rooted to this spot could somehow freeze time before she left.

"Drake!"

Kay's voice cut through the silence, urgent footsteps approaching on stone.

I didn't turn around, my gaze still fixed on that empty corner where her car had disappeared. She was long gone, but I kept staring as if sheer will could bring her back.

"Drake, are you all right?" Elena's worried voice followed close behind.

I closed my eyes and drew a deep breath. Cold air filled my lungs like shards of glass.

"Why are you out here?" My voice sounded eerily calm, foreign even to my own ears.

"The banquet's over." Kay stopped beside me, hesitating. "Drake, about Phoebe..."

"She's gone." I cut him off, opening my eyes to the star-scattered sky. The full moon hung high and bright, cold and distant as her gaze had been.

Elena moved to my other side. "I could go after her, try to help—"

"No." I shook my head. "She won't listen."

Besides, I had no right to ask her back.

"But..." Elena seemed ready to argue.

"She's right," I said quietly, my hand unconsciously clenching and releasing, palm still aching where my nails had cut deep. "I had two chances. Both times I chose deception. Why should she forgive me?"

Kay was quiet for a long moment. "The Darkfang situation—you were trying to protect her—"

"Protect?" I laughed bitterly. "I told myself I was protecting her, but really I was just using 'protection' to mask my own cowardice and selfishness."

Five years ago, I could have told her everything—that I was Drake, what that night meant to me. Instead, I chose the cruelest possible rejection, then convinced myself it was for her own good.

Five years later, I could have confessed the moment we met again —told her the other Drake was just a stand-in, that I'd never stopped missing her. But once again, I chose deception, approaching her with a false face, testing her feelings as if that could somehow atone for past sins.

What was the result?

I had simply ground salt into her wounds all over again.

"Drake..." Elena's voice carried deep concern.

"I need to be alone." I turned away, avoiding their worried expressions. "Go back inside. Kay, deal with the Sera situation."

Kay frowned. "But you—"

"I'm fine." My tone brooked no argument. "Just go."

Elena and Kay exchanged uncertain glances before finally nodding. Their footsteps gradually faded, the banquet hall lights dimming behind me.

I stood alone in the empty parking lot, surrounded by nothing but wind and the whisper of leaves.

She had said never to appear before her and Ryan again.

Ryan...

That precious boy with his soft curls and bright eyes—eyes that held traces of both of us. I remembered how he'd grabbed my pant leg that first day, the sound of his voice calling my name, the way he'd looked at me with such innocent trust...

I was going to lose my own son, too.

The emptiness in my chest expanded, threatening to consume me entirely.

I needed... I needed to go somewhere.

* * *

THE CAR CUT through the darkness, moonlight streaming through the windows to pool on the steering wheel. I didn't need GPS—my hands knew exactly where to go.

Grayclaw Pack territory.

The place where she used to live.

The car finally stopped outside a somewhat shabby neighborhood. Nothing like Ironspine's grand castle, with its manicured streets and bright lighting. Here, under the pale moonlight, weathered buildings stood in quiet resignation, cracks in their walls etched deep by shadow.

I stepped out into the biting wind, breathing air thick with the scent of damp earth.

Five years ago, she had left from this very place to come to Ironspine Pack. What had she been feeling then? Nervous? Afraid? Or perhaps nurturing some fragile hope for the future?

And what had I given her in return?

My feet seemed to carry their own memory, deeper than conscious thought, bringing me here again—to this place that held all my regret and desperate longing.

During the five years since Phoebe's departure, this territory had become an obsession I couldn't shake. I'd returned here countless times, walking the paths she might have taken, standing beneath trees where she'd played as a child. I'd frantically collected every trace of her existence, as if breathing the same air could somehow bring me closer to her.

The Grayclaw pack house sat silent in the cool wash of moonlight.

The three-story building showed its age—paint peeling from exterior walls that had once been lovingly maintained. A small courtyard stretched before it, ancient trees casting shifting shadows in the lunar glow.

I stood outside the gate without entering.

The silence was profound, broken only by my own breathing.

Wind stirred past, carrying the faintest trace of a familiar scent—her scent.

Jasmine, cedar, and something indefinably hers alone.

Even after five years, even though she'd long since left this place, the very earth seemed to hold whispers of her presence.

I closed my eyes and breathed deeply.

That delicate fragrance mixed with the night air, filling my lungs as if she were still here, as if she'd never left at all.

If I could turn back time...

If I could return to that morning five years ago, to the moment she stood before me, laying her heart bare, what would I do?

I would pull her into my arms, tell her I was Drake, tell her that night had shattered me too, tell her she was my fated mate, and I would never let her go.

But reality offers no second chances.

I opened my eyes. Moonlight fell across the weathered wooden door, across stone paths in the courtyard, across my solitary shadow.

The shadow stretched long and lonely.

"Phoebe..." I whispered, my voice dissolving into the night wind.

No answer came.

Only rustling leaves and distant barking dogs.

I stood outside that gate for what felt like hours, until the moon traced new angles across the sky, until dew began forming on grass blades.

I just wanted to stand here, in the place where she'd once lived, surrounded by traces she'd left behind. Even if her scent had faded to almost nothing, even if this was pure self-deception.

At least here, I could still feel that she'd once been real.

Before I destroyed everything, she had truly loved me.

CHAPTER SEVENTEEN

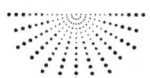

Phoebe

The night outside blurred into streaks of darkness, streetlights dissolving into watery halos through my tears.

I gripped the steering wheel tight, knuckles white from the pressure. Tears streamed down uncontrollably, blurring my vision until I had to slow down and finally pull over.

After I killed the engine, silence wrapped around me.

Why? Why was I always so damn stupid?

I slumped against the steering wheel and finally let myself sob.

I don't know how long I sat there before my phone buzzed in my bag, the ringtone sharp in the cramped space.

I took a shaky breath, wiped my eyes, and pulled out my phone.

Elena's name lit up the screen.

I hesitated, then answered.

"Hello?" My voice came out raw and broken.

"Phoebe." Elena's voice was careful, testing the waters. "Are you... okay?"

Okay?

How could I possibly be okay?

"I'm fine." I forced the words out. "If you're calling to defend Drake, don't bother."

"I'm not here to defend him." Elena's voice was soft. "I just... There are things you need to know. As a friend from the same pack, as a woman—whatever you decide to do, I think you have the right to know the truth."

Same pack...

Right. Elena and I were both from Grayclaw Pack.

Years ago, when the pack was facing bankruptcy, I'd accepted that contract, pretending to be the missing heir to seal a marriage alliance with the Ironspine Pack Alpha.

"Phoebe, I know Drake hurt you." Elena continued. "He did lie, hid his identity, treated you wrong. Those are facts. I won't make excuses for him."

"Then why are you calling?" I asked coldly.

"But..." Elena paused. "His feelings for you, his care—that's real too."

My heart lurched, tears threatening again.

"Phoebe, did you know? Drake has a folder on his computer." Elena's voice was barely a whisper. "It's called 'Grayclaw Pack Resettlement Plan.' He asked for my input and showed me the proposal."

I froze.

"What?"

"Detailed site selection, resource allocation plans, even arrangements for the elderly and weak in the pack," Elena said. "He applied to the Werewolf Council not long after you left Ironspine Pack, fighting for new territory for Grayclaw Pack. Phoebe, our pack's new beginning, that new territory—Drake made it happen."

My breath caught.

New territory?

I thought of Elias.

Five years ago, Elias told me Grayclaw Pack had found a new path, that the pack members' lives had improved. I'd been happy then, thinking at least my leaving hadn't burdened the pack too much.

But now...

"Wait." My voice shook. "You're saying... Grayclaw Pack's new territory—Drake fought for that?"

"Yes." Elena's voice was certain. "When Elias contacted Grayclaw Pack, he was told all these details. He should know everything."

I felt something explode in my chest.

Elias knew?

"When you left five years ago," Elena continued, "many elders in Ironspine Pack wanted to hold Grayclaw Pack accountable. After all, you impersonating me for the marriage alliance was deception against Ironspine Pack."

My heart started racing.

Grayclaw Pack... I'd never thought my leaving would cause the pack such trouble.

"But Drake shut down all opposition." Elena's voice carried an emotion I couldn't read. "He told the elders it was his fault, nothing to do with Grayclaw Pack. He even clashed with the most conservative elders over this. All these years, Drake's been helping Grayclaw Pack in various ways."

I covered my mouth, unable to believe it.

"Phoebe, I'm not making excuses for him," Elena said softly. "He definitely did wrong. But... his feelings for you are real."

My hands trembled, barely able to hold the phone.

"Think about it," Elena said. "If you need anything, call me anytime."

She hung up, leaving only the dial tone.

I clutched the phone, my mind reeling.

Elias knew everything Drake had done for Grayclaw Pack, yet told me it was the pack Alpha's achievement. Drake had been protecting my pack all along, but Elias never mentioned a word.

Why?

My phone buzzed again. Kay this time.

I answered mechanically.

"Miss Phoebe." Kay's voice was respectful but cautious. "Sorry to disturb you. I think... I need to tell you some things."

"About five years ago?" My voice sounded hollow.

Kay went quiet, seeming surprised I'd ask that.

"Yes." He said. "Five years ago, when you were preparing to leave Ironspine Pack, Darkfang Pack was stirring up trouble within our pack. They wanted to use your relationship with Drake to start a war between the packs, throw Ironspine Pack into chaos."

My breath stopped.

"If you'd stayed at Ironspine Pack, Darkfang Pack would've used your identity as leverage, dragged you into the conflict between the packs." Kay's voice was heavy. "So Drake made a decision—use the cruelest way to make you leave, make everyone believe you had nothing to do with Ironspine Pack anymore."

So... those brutal words were to protect me?

"What he said to you that morning," Kay's voice carried a hint of guilt, "he didn't mean any of it. He had to make you believe he didn't care, so Darkfang Pack wouldn't target you, so you'd leave decisively instead of staying to face danger with him."

My breathing stopped. He didn't mean it?

Those words that tortured me for five years, that woke me screaming in countless nights, that made me feel worthless—they were all lies?

"Are you alright, Miss Phoebe?" Kay's voice came through the phone, worried.

I realized tears were streaming down my face again.

"After you left, Drake arranged protection for you." Kay continued. "But at the city outskirts, the protection team was attacked by Darkfang Pack. In the chaos, they lost track of you."

"Lost track?" I repeated shakily.

So... he'd been protecting me all along?

That night when Elias and I escaped the castle, I'd vaguely heard Elias mention the usually tight security was unusually lax that night. It was all Drake's arrangement.

He'd even arranged guards to protect us. I never knew. While I was heartbroken over his coldness, he was protecting me in his own way.

"Yes." Kay's voice grew heavier. "After the fighting calmed down,

Drake went crazy looking for you. He used every connection and resource he had, even infiltrated Darkfang Pack territory himself."

"He never stopped searching." Kay's voice softened, like approaching a frightened deer. "Until the Ironspine Group bidding meeting, when he finally... finally saw you again. He was afraid you still hadn't forgiven him for five years ago. So he approached you through business cooperation, hoping to... win you back."

"But he lied again." My voice broke. "He hid his identity again."

"Because he felt unworthy," Kay said quietly. "He said he was the one who pushed you away, made you suffer so much. He didn't have the right to ask forgiveness then, plus you were very resistant to him at the time."

"Why..." I choked out. "Why didn't he tell me any of this?"

"I know." Kay sighed. "He was wrong. He should've told you the truth from the beginning. But Miss Phoebe, you need to know how much he's sacrificed these five years to protect you and your pack."

I covered my face, shoulders shaking.

"Miss Phoebe, Drake's methods might be clumsy, even cruel." Kay's voice held helplessness. "But he really wanted to protect you. These five years, he's been secretly watching over Grayclaw Pack, making sure no faction could harm you or your family."

"Miss Phoebe, I'm not making excuses for Drake." Kay's tone grew serious. "He definitely did wrong, hurt you. But I want you to know the truth, to know... his love for you is real. What you do with that is your choice. I just hope you'll think about it seriously."

"I understand." I forced the words from my throat. "Thank you for telling me."

After hanging up, I tossed the phone onto the passenger seat and collapsed into my chair.

The night outside remained deep, moonlight streaming through the glass, cold and piercing.

Think about it seriously... How was I supposed to think?

Drake lied. Elias lied too.

One pushed me away with coldness and cruelty, the other trapped me with gentleness and companionship.

They both claimed it was for my own good. But why didn't anyone ask what I actually wanted?

I remembered what Elias had told me these five years.

"Phoebe, you deserve better."

"Don't look back."

"Grayclaw Pack is doing well now, don't worry."

"I'll always be here for you."

Every word now had a different meaning.

I tried to calm myself. I needed to be sure, so I called Elias.

"It's me, Phoebe."

"Phoebe, where did you go? I was so worried," Elias's anxious voice came through.

"I'm fine, I... I need to confirm something." I had no idea how to approach this without crushing his dignity. "Is there anything you want to tell me? Any well-meaning omissions?"

Elias obviously hadn't expected my question, hesitating before responding. "Phoebe, let me come find you. We should talk face to face."

"It's too late today. Tomorrow." I didn't have the strength for another emotional blow today.

He didn't want me to know what Drake had done. Didn't want me to soften toward Drake. Wanted me to stay with him forever.

This wasn't protection. This was manipulation. Selfishness disguised as love.

But...

Elias had been with me for five years, helped me care for Ryan, helped me run the studio, silently protecting me. I'd always thought he was the person I trusted most, my only support in this world.

My mind was in chaos, countless thoughts colliding.

Drake...

Did he really love me?

If he loved me, why push me away so cruelly? Why hide his identity when approaching me again?

But...

If he didn't love me, why risk his life going to Darkfang Pack? Why fight for new territory for Grayclaw Pack? Why endure pressure from pack elders to protect my family? Why spend five years searching for me?

Who should I... believe?

Taking a deep breath, I restarted the engine.

The car pulled slowly into the night, heading home.

Streetlights passed one by one, casting shifting shadows inside the car.

I thought of Ryan.

That sweet little boy, that child with Drake's features.

He had the right to know who his father was.

He had the right to a complete family.

And I...

I had the right to know the truth.

Elena and Kay's words echoed in my mind.

"Think about it seriously."

Yes, I needed to think seriously.

Not for Drake, not for Elias.

For myself. For Ryan.

But in my heart, I wasn't as resolute as before.

Something was shifting, and in that wall I thought was unbreakable, a tiny crack had appeared.

CHAPTER EIGHTEEN

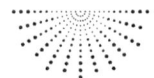

Phoebe

I hadn't slept all night.

Outside the window, the sky shifted from deep black to hazy blue-gray, then golden dawn slowly crept up the buildings across the street. I sat on the living room couch, phone clutched in my hand, the screen flickering on and off.

Drake's number was right there.

Elena and Kay's words had been spinning through my head all night. Grayclaw Pack's new territory, five years of searching, Darkfang Pack's danger... Everything told me he'd never given up.

What should I do?

Keep hating him? Or give him a chance?

I thought about the hope in Ryan's eyes every time he mentioned "Daddy," the loneliness when he watched other kids get picked up by their fathers.

He deserved to know who his father was.

And I... I wanted to know if we still had a future.

Taking a deep breath, I hit dial.

Three rings, then he picked up.

"Phoebe?" Drake's voice came through, filled with disbelief and joy, but clearly exhausted.

"Drake, where are you right now?" My voice was hoarse.

Silence on the other end, then a soft sigh.

"I'm... downstairs. Outside your building." His voice carried embarrassment. "I'm sorry, you told me not to show up anymore, but I couldn't help myself. I didn't mean to bother you, I just... wanted to be close to you."

I froze, instinctively walking to the window and pulling back a corner of the curtain.

In the morning light, that black sedan sat parked below. In the driver's seat, Drake's silhouette leaned against the window, phone still in his hand.

He was really here.

Who knows how long he'd been waiting.

My heart clenched tight, tears instantly blurring my vision. This fool—had he stayed awake all night, keeping watch down there?

I heard my voice trembling. "Tonight... come for dinner tonight."

Sharp breathing came through the phone.

"Phoebe, you... You mean it?" His voice was full of disbelief.

"Yeah. We need to talk. Really talk," I said, "But now, go get some rest. You look... exhausted."

"I'm not tired," He said immediately.

"Drake." My tone turned stern. "Did you sleep in the car again last night? You barely slept, I can tell. Go home and rest. Six o'clock tonight, come for dinner."

He was quiet for a few seconds, then finally gave in. "Okay. Then... see you tonight."

"See you tonight."

After hanging up, I leaned against the window, watching the black sedan slowly drive away.

I'd made a decision.

I didn't know if it was right, but at least... at least I had to give him a chance. Give myself a chance too.

For Ryan, and for my own heart.

After finishing my daily work, I prepared early for dinner.

Grocery shopping, cleaning the house, prepping ingredients. Ryan noticed something was different and followed me around curiously.

"Mommy, are we having company tonight?" he asked, tilting his little head.

I crouched down. "Ryan, Mr. Gray... he's coming for dinner tonight."

Ryan didn't know Alexander had changed his name to Drake yet. How was I going to explain that?

Ryan's eyes lit up instantly, like two little stars. "Really? That's great! I like Mr. Gray!"

"You really like him?"

"Yes!" Ryan nodded vigorously. "He is so gentle and patient when he plays with me. I feel comfortable with him, I just like him."

Blood calling to blood.

Children of fated mates felt naturally drawn to both parents.

My heart ached. This child had never met his father before, yet was instinctively attracted to him.

"And," Ryan continued, "Mr. Gray looks at mommy the same way the prince looks at the princess in fairy tales. He must really like mommy, right?"

My eyes instantly welled up.

"Go play." I touched his head. "Mommy needs to make dinner."

Ryan bounced away happily, and I stood up, taking a deep breath.

Tonight, I was going to clear everything up.

At six o'clock sharp, the doorbell rang.

I took a deep breath, smoothed my clothes, and went to answer it.

Drake stood outside wearing a clean navy shirt and black casual pants, hair neatly combed back. His eyes were still slightly red, but he looked much better. He held a large bouquet of champagne roses and an elegant gift box.

"For you." He handed me the flowers, nervous, acting like a guy on his first date. "I remembered you like champagne roses. And... this is for Ryan."

I took the flowers, their subtle fragrance washing over me. He actually remembered.

"Come in."

"Mr. Gray!" Ryan charged out from the living room like a little cannonball, launching himself at Drake.

Drake crouched down and caught him steadily, his face breaking into a gentle smile. "Ryan."

"Mr. Gray, you're here!" Ryan happily nuzzled against him. "I missed you so much!"

Drake's eyes instantly reddened. He held Ryan tight, his voice choking up. "I missed you too. This is your gift."

Watching them embrace, complex emotions swirled in my chest.

Father and son by nature, connected by blood. Even having never met, even not knowing their relationship, that instinctive closeness couldn't be hidden.

Drake handed him the box. "Open it and see if you like it."

Ryan eagerly opened it to find an exquisite set of dinosaur models—T-rex, triceratops, stegosaurus, each one lifelike.

"Wow! Dinosaurs!" He cheered excitedly. "So many dinosaurs! Thank you!"

"I'm glad you like them." Drake ruffled his hair, eyes full of tenderness.

"Go play in the living room," I said. "Mommy and Mr. Gray need to talk, then we'll eat."

Ryan nodded obediently and ran into the living room with his gift.

Drake and I stood in the entryway, the atmosphere slightly awkward.

"Sit down," I put the flowers on the table. "Dinner's almost ready."

"Let me help," He said immediately.

"No need, just keep Ryan company."

I turned toward the kitchen, but could feel his gaze following me.

Through the half-open kitchen door, I could hear sounds from the living room. Ryan excitedly told Drake about kindergarten while Drake patiently responded, occasionally letting out deep chuckles.

"Mr. Gray, you know what? The teacher praised me today!"

"Really? You're amazing."

"Mr. Gray, will you keep coming to see me? I missed you so much these past few days when you weren't here."

"I will, as long as mommy allows it, I will keep coming."

"That's wonderful! I like you the most!"

Listening to their conversation, tears unconsciously slid down my cheeks.

If there hadn't been those misunderstandings five years ago, if we'd stayed together, would every day have been this warm?

I wiped away the tears, took a deep breath, and continued preparing dinner.

"Dinner's ready." I walked out carrying the last dish.

Drake immediately stood up and took the plate from my hands. "Let me."

We sat at the dining table with Ryan in the middle, Drake and I on either side of him.

Warm yellow light from the pendant lamp cast a soft glow over the steaming food. Perfectly grilled steak, creamy mushroom soup, roasted vegetable medley, and Ryan's favorite spaghetti with meat sauce filled the air with delicious aromas.

Outside, night was falling, but inside it was warm as spring.

The scene looked exactly like a family of three.

"Mommy's cooking is the best!" Ryan waved his spoon happily.

"Absolutely." Drake tasted the steak, his eyes lighting up. "Phoebe, this dinner is incredible."

His voice grew lower, a flash of disbelief in his eyes.

I knew what he was thinking. Like me, he couldn't believe this was real—after everything we'd been through, all the misunderstandings, separation, pain, we could still be together like this, experiencing such warmth.

The atmosphere grew quiet, with only Ryan chattering occasionally, bringing life to the table.

I stole glances at Drake as he carefully served Ryan food, his movements gentle and careful.

He'd be a good father.

If... if we could start over.

Halfway through dinner, Ryan suddenly put down his spoon.

He tilted his little head, looking seriously at Drake, those big eyes full of curiosity and expectation.

"Mr. Gray," his voice was soft and sweet, yet carried a seriousness beyond his years, "can I ask you a question?"

"Of course." Drake put down his chopsticks and looked at him seriously. "What do you want to ask?"

Ryan bit his lower lip, then suddenly leaned close to Drake and sniffed gently.

"You smell like me. Teacher said only family smells the same."

He looked up, eyes bright as he gazed at Drake.

"When you and mommy stand together, it smells even better, and I'm happiest then."

His big eyes blinked as his gaze moved between Drake and me, filled with expectation.

"Are you... are you my Daddy?"

The air froze instantly.

I sat there with my bowl halfway to my mouth, heart pounding violently.

Drake's body jerked, and he looked at Ryan, complex emotions flooding his deep eyes—joy, guilt, longing, and disbelief.

Then he turned to look at me, eyes full of hope and uncertainty, but not daring to speak.

He was waiting for my answer, waiting for my decision.

I looked at Ryan's expectant face, then at Drake barely breathing from nervousness.

In that moment, I suddenly understood.

No matter what had happened, no matter how many misunderstandings and hurts still lay between us—

Ryan deserved to know the truth. He deserved a complete family.

And I... I was tired. Tired of running, tired of hiding, tired of carrying everything alone.

"Ryan," I put down my bowl, my voice trembling, "Drake... he is your Daddy."

"Drake?" Ryan looked confused.

Drake obviously hadn't expected me to confirm he was Ryan's father. Overjoyed, hearing Ryan's confusion, he quickly explained, "I'm sorry, Ryan. I hid my identity for certain reasons. Let me reintroduce myself—I'm Alpha Drake of Ironspine Pack."

Ryan didn't seem to understand what Drake was saying, but he understood that the man he liked was his Daddy.

His eyes lit up instantly, like two of the brightest stars.

"Really?!" He jumped up from his chair excitedly.

Drake shot to his feet, the chair scraping loudly. He walked over and crouched in front of Ryan, hands trembling slightly, eyes instantly red.

"Ryan," his voice choked with emotion, "I'm your Daddy. I'm sorry... I'm sorry I came so late..."

"Daddy!" Ryan cheered and threw himself into Drake's arms, little hands gripping his neck tight. "I knew it! I knew you were my Daddy! I could smell it!"

Drake held him tight, shoulders shaking violently. He buried his face in Ryan's shoulder, crying like a child.

"I'm sorry, I'm sorry, Ryan... Daddy came too late... I missed your birth, missed you learning to walk, missed your first 'Daddy'... I'm sorry..."

He repeated it over and over, every word heavy with guilt and heartbreak.

I sat in my chair, covering my mouth as tears streamed down.

This scene was too heartwarming, yet too heartbreaking.

Father and son meeting for the first time should have happened in a delivery room, the moment the child opened his eyes.

But now, Ryan was already four years old.

Over fourteen hundred days and nights, lost forever.

"Daddy, don't cry." Ryan wiped Drake's tears with his chubby little hands. "Daddy's not late now. We can always be together from now on, right?"

"Yes... yes..." Drake nodded through his tears. "We'll always be together now."

Ryan smiled contentedly, then turned to look at me. "Mommy, why are you crying?"

I wiped my tears and forced a smile. "Mommy is... too happy."

"That's good!" Ryan said happily. "With Daddy and mommy both here, we're a family!"

A family.

Those three words hit my heart hard.

Drake also looked up at me, eyes full of longing and hope.

"Ryan," my voice still trembled, "mommy needs to apologize to you and Daddy."

"Apologize?" Ryan looked at me, confused.

"It's mommy's fault you met Daddy so late." I took a deep breath. "Five years ago, mommy left Daddy. Mommy thought... thought Daddy didn't want us anymore. So mommy took you and left alone. I'm sorry."

"Daddy, mommy, it's okay. I feel so happy right now." Ryan's innocent words touched my heart. He suddenly stood up excitedly.

"Daddy, I painted a new picture today. Wait, I want to give it to you!" Before he finished speaking, he ran back to his room on his little legs, leaving only his cheerful voice echoing in the air.

Drake immediately stood and walked over to me.

"Phoebe, no... this isn't your fault." He crouched down, eyes full of guilt. "It's all my fault."

"But," my voice turned serious, "Drake, you deceived me too."

His body went rigid.

"Five years ago, you used those cruel words to push me away, made me think you didn't care. Five years later, when I thought I could finally start over, when I thought Alexander was fate giving me a second chance," tears started flowing again, "you told me it was all another lie."

"I know Kay and Elena told me everything—you were trying to protect me, keep me out of danger. But Drake," I looked into his eyes, "understanding doesn't mean I can easily forgive. Those words, those cold words... and your deception, your lies, do you know how deep the scars they left in my heart?"

"I know... I know it all..." Drake's voice choked. "Phoebe, I'm sorry. It's all my fault. I hurt you in the wrong way."

He reached out to touch me but didn't dare, his hand trembling in the air.

"I don't expect you to forgive me now." He continued. "I just hope... you'll give me a chance to make up for these five years. Even if it takes a lifetime..."

I looked at his red eyes, at the tear tracks on his face, complex emotions swirling inside me.

"Drake," I took a deep breath, "I need time."

Disappointment flashed in his eyes, but quickly turned to understanding.

"I understand." He nodded. "However long you need, I'll wait."

"But," I looked toward Ryan running out of his room, "he's your son. He has the right to know his father, to receive a father's love. So... you can come see him, spend time with him."

Drake's eyes instantly brightened. "Really?"

"Yes." I nodded. "But that's all. As for us... let's take it slow."

"Okay." He nodded vigorously, eyes full of gratitude. "Thank you, Phoebe. Thank you for letting me... letting me be part of your lives again."

"Daddy, look how pretty my painting is today," Ryan said excitedly.

Drake hugged Ryan, praising happily, "My baby, it's the most beautiful painting ever."

Watching their joyful interaction, warmth and bittersweet emotion filled my chest. This was a scene that had appeared countless times in my dreams.

"Can Daddy stay tonight?" Ryan suddenly asked, eyes bright. "I want Daddy to tell me a bedtime story!"

Drake and I both froze.

Drake looked at me hopefully but didn't dare ask.

I looked at Ryan's expectant face, then at Drake's careful expression, and finally sighed.

"Okay."

"Yay!" Ryan cheered.

Drake's eyes lit up, his voice choking. "Thank you, Phoebe."

"Let's finish eating," I said. "The food's getting cold."

The dinner table came alive again. Ryan chatted happily, Drake responded gently, occasionally serving me food.

Warm yellow light bathed us, night deepening outside while inside remained warm as spring.

In this moment, we really looked like a family.

Late into the night.

Putting Ryan to bed took a long time because he was too excited, constantly pestering Drake for stories and asking endless questions. Drake was incredibly patient, seriously answering every question until the little guy finally fell asleep in his father's arms.

Drake carefully placed Ryan on the bed, tucked him in, and gently kissed his forehead.

"Good night, my child." He whispered tenderly.

I stood in the doorway watching this scene, complex emotions filling my heart.

Leaving Ryan's room, only the two of us remained in the hallway.

"The guest room is over there." I pointed right. "Towels and toiletries are in the bathroom."

"Okay." Drake nodded but didn't leave immediately, just stood there looking at me.

The hallway light was dim, casting shadows on his face.

"Well... good night." I turned to leave.

"Phoebe." He suddenly called out.

I stopped and looked back.

Drake walked closer, stopping a meter away from me.

"Today... thank you." His voice was soft. "Thank you for letting me stay, for telling Ryan the truth, for... not really giving up on me."

My heart jumped hard.

"Drake..."

"I know you need time." He interrupted. "I'm not trying to pressure you. I just want you to know, no matter how long you need, I'll wait. A month, a year, ten years... as long as you're willing, I'll keep waiting."

His gaze was too sincere—I couldn't meet it directly.

"Good night, Phoebe." He said softly, then turned toward the guest room.

I stood there watching his figure disappear behind the door.

Back in my room, I lay in bed unable to sleep.

Everything from today kept replaying in my mind—Drake and Ryan's recognition scene, his apology, his tears, and that gentle kiss...

The fated mate instinct stirred restlessly inside me, as if urging me to find him, to get closer.

I rolled over, hugging my pillow. Damn this mate bond.

Just then, soft footsteps came from outside.

I held my breath.

The door handle turned gently, and the door opened a crack.

"Phoebe?" Drake's voice came through. "Are you... asleep?"

"No." I sat up.

He walked in, moonlight streaming through the curtain gaps onto him. He'd changed into pajamas, hair slightly mussed.

"What's wrong?" I asked, my heartbeat accelerating.

"I... I can't sleep." He stood in the doorway, slightly embarrassed. "The guest room feels too empty. I... I miss you."

My heart pounded violently.

"Drake..."

"Can I... can I sleep here?" He asked carefully. "I promise I won't do anything. I just... just want to be close to you."

I should refuse.

Logic told me to refuse.

But my mouth said the opposite. "...Come here."

Drake's eyes lit up instantly.

He walked over and carefully lay on the other side of the bed, keeping distance between us.

In the darkness, I could hear his breathing, feel his warmth, smell his familiar sandalwood and primal wild scent.

The fated mate bond pulled between us, the air thick with irresistible attraction.

"Phoebe." He called softly.

"Yeah?"

"Thank you."

"Alright."

We lay quietly like that, neither speaking again.

After a long time, long enough that I thought he'd fallen asleep, he suddenly turned and carefully pulled me into his arms.

Warm embrace, familiar scent, and that wildly beating heart.

"Phoebe," he whispered in my ear, "I love you. From the first moment I saw you, I've never stopped loving you. These five years, every day and night, it's never changed."

His kiss landed on the top of my head, gentle and restrained.

Then my temple, my cheek.

I looked up at his eyes in the moonlight.

Those eyes were full of love, full of longing, yet restrained and not daring to cross the line.

"Drake..." I called softly.

I didn't speak, but leaned up and kissed his lips.

His body went rigid, then responded frantically.

The kiss was passionate and deep.

When we finally broke apart, we were both breathing hard.

"Phoebe..." His voice was hoarse.

"Hold me while I sleep." I buried my head in his chest. "Tomorrow's problems can wait until tomorrow."

"Okay." He held me tight. "Whatever you say."

His hand gently stroked my hair, over and over, like soothing a frightened little animal.

Gradually, my breathing steadied.

In his warm embrace, surrounded by the fated mate's scent, I finally felt a long-lost sense of security.

"Good night, Phoebe." He whispered in my ear.

"Good night, Drake."

I closed my eyes, the corners of my mouth unconsciously curving into a small smile.

Maybe, maybe we really could start over.

Not going back to the past, but creating a new future.

A future with Ryan, with me, and with him.

Outside the window, moonlight flowed like water over our embracing figures.

That night, I slept peacefully.

For the first time in five years.

CHAPTER NINETEEN

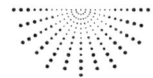

Phoebe

Sunlight streamed through the curtains, warm rays caressing my face like gentle fingers. I slowly opened my eyes to find Drake's jaw in my line of sight.

He was still holding me, his breathing steady and even, carrying that familiar scent of sandalwood and primal wildness. His arm wrapped around my waist, chin resting atop my head, body heat seeping through the thin fabric of my sleepwear—warm and reassuring.

I didn't move, simply basking in this rare moment of peace.

His steady heartbeat thrummed against my ear, each beat seeming to whisper: I'm here. I won't leave.

Five years. This was the first time I'd slept so soundly in five years. No nightmares, no startling awake—just warmth and safety.

The call in my blood sang so clearly, making my body instinctively crave his embrace, his scent. And my heart... my heart was beginning to surrender too.

"Awake?" Drake's voice rumbled above me, husky with sleep, that low timbre incredibly intimate in the quiet room.

"Yeah," I murmured softly, feeling his arm tighten slightly around me. "How long have you been up?"

"A while." His hand gently stroked my hair, fingers threading through the strands with reverence. "Couldn't bear to move. Didn't want to wake you."

My heart stuttered, heat flooding my cheeks.

"Mommy! Daddy!" Ryan's excited voice suddenly burst from the hallway, followed by the rapid patter of small feet racing toward us.

Drake and I sprang apart, startled. I could feel the reluctance in his retreating arm, matching my body's instinctive protest at the loss of contact.

The door flew open, and Ryan burst in wearing dinosaur pajamas, hair disheveled, eyes bright as stars. "Daddy's really here! I thought yesterday was just a dream!"

He launched himself onto the bed, wiggling between us, his small body radiating warmth and the sweet scent of childhood—milk and baby shampoo.

"Daddy, what are we doing today?" Ryan asked breathlessly, tiny hands clutching Drake's shirt. "Can we play together?"

Drake's expression melted as he ruffled Ryan's hair. "Of course. Where would you like to go?"

"The amusement park!" Ryan declared without hesitation, his voice so bright it made me smile. "Mommy promised, but she's always too busy. Can Daddy come with us?"

He looked between us with such hope blazing in those wide eyes.

Drake and I exchanged glances. Morning light caught his features, making his eyes appear impossibly deep.

"Would that be all right?" Drake asked carefully, hope and uncertainty warring in his expression, as if bracing for rejection.

Looking at their expectant faces—father and son mirror images of anticipation—I realized resistance was futile.

"All right. The amusement park it is."

"Yes!" Ryan cheered, bouncing on the mattress until it rippled beneath him. "Our whole family's going to the amusement park!"

Our whole family.

Those three words sent my heart skipping again.

At ten that morning, we stood before the city's largest amusement park.

Weekend crowds swarmed everywhere—families with children creating a tapestry of joy. Laughter, screams, and carnival music blended into a symphony of happiness. The air carried the rich aroma of popcorn, the cloying sweetness of cotton candy, and the savory temptation of hot dogs.

Perfect sunshine, gentle breeze lifting my hair. I'd chosen a light blue sundress—the one Ryan insisted "makes Mommy look the prettiest."

Ryan gripped Drake's hand while clutching mine with his other, face flushed with excitement, eyes sparkling like captured starlight.

His small hand felt soft and warm, fingers intertwined with mine. Through our connection, I could sense Drake's presence, creating an unbroken chain between the three of us.

This feeling of belonging was... extraordinary.

"Daddy, look! The Ferris wheel!"

"Mommy, look! The carousel!"

Ryan pointed in every direction, enthusiasm boundless. His clear voice rang above the crowd like silver bells.

Drake listened with infinite patience, responding to each exclamation, his stern features softened by genuine smiles. Sunlight transformed his entire presence, gentling the formidable Alpha into something achingly tender.

This man who commanded absolute authority in his pack was now putty in the hands of a five-year-old.

"Where shall we start?" I asked Ryan.

"Carousel!" he answered instantly.

Drake led the way with Ryan while I followed, watching their silhouettes—one towering, one tiny, large hand enveloping small, their steps finding rhythm together. My throat constricted unexpectedly.

I'd dreamed this scene countless times.

Through those endless nights and lonely moments, I'd always

imagined this day might come.

I simply never believed it would.

The carousel drew long queues, but Ryan didn't mind waiting. He chattered excitedly with Drake, questions tumbling over each other.

"Daddy, what's your favorite color horse?"

"Did you ride carousels when you were little?"

"Daddy, are you scared of roller coasters?"

Drake answered each query with thoughtful consideration, voice gentle and endlessly patient, occasionally earning delighted giggles from his son.

Standing behind them, watching Drake crouch to meet Ryan at eye level, something profound stirred in my chest.

He was truly trying.

Every response, every glance, every gesture carried such intentional care, such tender devotion.

When our turn finally came, Ryan selected a pristine white horse and scrambled up with infectious enthusiasm. Drake positioned himself protectively alongside, one large hand steadying the ornate pole.

"Isn't Mommy riding?" Ryan asked.

"Mommy's our photographer today." I raised my phone with a smile.

Music swelled, the carousel began its dreamy rotation, ethereal melodies floating through sun-dappled air. Ryan sat regally on his steed, waving with unbridled joy, his small hand painting happiness across the sky.

Drake remained vigilant beside him, one hand gripping the pole, the other hovering protectively near Ryan's waist, ready to catch him should he slip.

Golden sunlight bathed them both, father and son glowing like figures from a Renaissance painting. Drake's smile was radiant, his eyes brimming with wonder and unconditional love.

I lifted my phone, framing them through the lens.

In that viewfinder—father and son, their matching smiles telling stories of belonging.

Click.

The moment crystallized forever.

Gazing at the image on my screen, tears blurred my vision.

This photograph would become my most treasured possession.

After the carousel came the miniature train, then bumper cars. Drake accompanied Ryan on every single ride, never once showing impatience or fatigue.

By midday, Ryan was finally flagging, his cheeks rosy, tiny droplets of perspiration beading his forehead.

"Hungry, sweetheart?" I knelt down, dabbing his face with a tissue.

"Starving!" Ryan nodded emphatically, his stomach growling on cue.

"There's a restaurant just over there." Drake indicated a nearby building. "Let's refuel."

The restaurant offered blessed air conditioning and wasn't overly crowded. We secured a window table overlooking the vibrant park sprawling beneath afternoon sunshine.

"You two get comfortable. I'll handle the ordering." Drake said.

"I want a kids' meal!" Ryan announced immediately. "The kind with toys!"

Drake chuckled, affectionately mussing his hair. "One kids' meal with toy, coming up."

His gaze found mine. "Phoebe, any preferences?"

"I trust your judgment."

Drake nodded and headed for the counter.

Ryan and I settled in to wait. Through the expansive windows, the amusement park stretched before us like a child's fever dream—all primary colors and impossible architecture gleaming under crystal light.

"Mommy," Ryan said suddenly, voice soft with contentment. "Today's been perfect."

"Has it?" I smoothed his silky hair.

"Uh-huh!" His smile transformed his eyes into crescents. "Because Mommy and Daddy are both here. Now I have a complete family like all the other kids."

Emotion crashed over me, tightening my throat until speech became difficult.

This precious child had never complained, never accused. But I knew he must have envied those children with fathers present, must have wondered countless times where his daddy had gone.

"I'm sorry, Ryan." My voice wavered. "Mommy should have brought you and Daddy together sooner."

"It's okay," Ryan said with startling maturity, turning to face me fully, his small hand finding mine. "Daddy's here now. We can stay together forever, right?"

I stared into those crystalline eyes—no resentment, no blame, only pure joy and infinite hope.

"Yes. We'll... be together."

My voice cracked. I squeezed his warm little hand, drawing strength from that simple contact.

Drake returned bearing a laden tray—burgers, golden fries, cold drinks, everything steaming and aromatic.

"Lunch is served." He distributed food with practiced ease, as if he'd been doing this for years.

Ryan attacked his meal with gusto, promptly decorating his mouth with a perfect ring of ketchup.

Drake laughed and retrieved napkins, cleaning Ryan's face with surprising skill and tenderness.

"Easy there, champion. No need to inhale it." His voice carried pure affection.

Watching their natural interaction, realization dawned—Drake possessed innate paternal instincts.

Gentle, patient, attentive, with that fierce protectiveness that seemed hardwired into his very essence.

I bit into my burger, savoring familiar flavors spreading across my tongue.

Drake ate too, but his attention kept drifting to me, warm and focused with an intensity that made my pulse quicken.

Every time our eyes met, electricity arced between us.

That afternoon, Ryan's energy returned full force, ready to

conquer new territories.

The sun blazed overhead, warming our skin. Sweet carnival scents grew richer, mingling with fresh grass and the promise of adventure.

"Mommy, cotton candy!" He pointed toward a vendor's stand, eyes lighting up like Christmas morning.

"Want some?" Drake asked indulgently.

"Yes!" Ryan nodded so vigorously I worried he might injure himself.

"Let's make that happen." Drake took his hand, steering toward the stand.

I followed, watching them deliberate over flavors. Warm breeze carried sugar-spun sweetness—that innocent, childhood magic distilled into edible clouds.

"What color strikes your fancy?" Drake asked, crouching to Ryan's eye level.

"Pink!" Ryan exclaimed, practically vibrating with excitement. "Pink like fluffy clouds!"

Drake's smile could have powered the entire park. He conversed briefly with the vendor, returning with an enormous puff of rose-colored confection, gossamer-light and gleaming like spun diamonds.

"Your chariot awaits." He presented it with theatrical flourish.

Ryan accepted his prize with reverent hands, joy practically radiating from his small frame. He pinched off a wisp and let it dissolve on his tongue, expression transcending mere happiness.

"It's like eating happiness!"

"Take your time, little prince. Try not to wear it." Drake advised gently.

Predictably, Ryan managed to coat himself in pink sugar strands within minutes—nose, cheeks, even his eyebrows sporting cotton candy debris.

Drake shook his head with fond exasperation, retrieving more napkins to restore his son to human appearance.

"You're a walking sugar sculpture. How do you manage this?"

"'Cause it's too delicious to eat slowly," Ryan explained through pouty lips.

Sunlight illuminated their tableau—father tenderly cleaning son's face while said son gazed up with absolute trust and adoration.

I captured the moment instinctively.

Click.

Another memory preserved.

Drake glanced up, catching me in the act, color rising in his cheeks until even his ears flushed.

"Documenting my parenting failures?"

"Documenting perfection." I smiled, warmth blooming in my chest. "It's beautiful."

Drake rose and moved closer, his height requiring me to crane my neck to meet his gaze. He studied the photo on my screen, emotions flickering across his features—tenderness, gratitude, and something like wonder.

"Phoebe," he said quietly, voice rough with feeling. "Thank you."

"For what?"

"For this chance." His eyes held mine with devastating sincerity. "To be with you both. To feel like family."

My heart hammered against my ribs, heat flooding my face.

"Drake..."

"Mommy, Daddy, look!" Ryan's excited shout shattered our intimate bubble. "Balloon release!"

We turned to witness dozens of colorful balloons ascending skyward, rainbow orbs dancing against azure infinity like escaped dreams seeking heaven.

Ryan tugged both our hands, pulling us toward the spectacle with irrepressible enthusiasm.

Drake and I exchanged glances—understanding passing between us without words—and willingly followed our son's lead.

Perfect sunshine warmed our skin. Gentle breezes carried laughter and sweetness and the ineffable magic of family. Joy saturated every breath.

Evening descended as we departed the amusement park.

Ryan succumbed to exhaustion during the drive home. Drake

carried his sleeping form to bed with infinite care, tucking blankets around his small body like the most precious treasure.

"He overdid it today," I whispered from the doorway, watching peaceful slumber smooth away the day's excitement.

"He was radiant." Drake joined me, voice soft with reverence. "So was I."

I turned to study his face. His eyes held such contentment, such gratitude it made my chest ache.

"Thank you, Phoebe." His words came out raw with emotion. "For today... for letting us be a real family."

My heart lurched. Just as I prepared to respond, the doorbell's chime cut through the quiet.

"Who could that be at this hour?" I frowned.

Drake's expression immediately sharpened to predatory alertness. "I'll handle it."

"No." I caught his arm. "I'll go."

At the door, I peered through the peephole and froze.

Elias.

Drawing a steadying breath, I opened the door.

"Elias?"

He stood on my threshold, looking haggard, shadows beneath his eyes, something brittle in his bearing.

"Phoebe, may I... come in for a moment?" Exhaustion weighted his voice. "I need to speak with you."

I hesitated before stepping aside. "Of course."

Elias entered, his gaze sweeping the living room, lingering on scattered dinosaur toys and photographs spread across the coffee table. Today's amusement park memories, fresh from the printer.

"You went to the park?" His voice carried an odd, hollow quality.

"Yes." I nodded. "Drake took Ryan."

"Drake's here?"

"I'm here." Drake's voice carried from the hallway. He emerged, positioning himself protectively behind me, watching Elias with wolf-like intensity.

Tension crystallized instantly.

"Elias, what did you want to discuss?" I broke the charged silence.

Elias looked at me, pain flickering in his tired eyes. "Phoebe, I need to speak with you privately. Would that be possible?"

Drake's entire frame went rigid.

"Drake, could you..." I began.

"I'll be in Ryan's room." Drake's gaze lingered on me with unmistakable reluctance before he withdrew.

Alone with Elias, the air felt suddenly fragile.

"Please, sit." I gestured toward the couch.

Elias settled heavily, hands clasped so tightly his knuckles went white. His nervousness was palpable.

"Phoebe," he finally spoke, voice trembling with suppressed emotion. "I need to tell you something. Something I've carried for five years."

My pulse accelerated.

"All this time, I've stood beside you." He raised his eyes to mine, raw devotion burning there. "Caring for you, caring for Ryan, supporting your studio... I believed if I remained close enough, patient enough, you might eventually see me."

"Elias..."

"Please, let me finish." He held up a shaking hand. "Phoebe, I love you. I've loved you for longer than I can remember. Not as a friend—I mean I want to marry you, want to give you and Ryan the home you deserve."

His voice broke, tears gathering in his eyes.

"I know I was wrong to hide what Drake did for you. I was selfish, I admit it." Bitter laughter escaped him. "I was simply... terrified of losing you. Terrified that learning the truth would send you back to him."

Tears spilled down my cheeks.

"Elias... I'm so sorry." My voice fractured. "I've always treasured you as my dearest friend, like family. Everything you've done for us—I remember it all. But... my feelings for you truly are only friendship."

Elias closed his eyes, tears tracking silver paths down his face.

"I know." His voice barely registered above a whisper. "I've always known. The way you look at him—you've never looked at me that way."

"We could still be friends, couldn't we?" I asked hopefully.

Elias opened his eyes, raw and red-rimmed, shaking his head with finality.

"No." His voice emerged hoarse and broken. "Phoebe, I can't. I love you too deeply. Remaining as merely a friend would destroy me."

"Ahem."

A soft clearing of throat from the hallway.

Drake leaned against the wall, arms crossed, observing us with those penetrating eyes.

Elias turned, seeing him, and released a sound between laugh and sob.

"Eavesdropping?"

"Absolutely." Drake approached, stopping beside me. "I don't leave my fated mate alone with men who've just declared their love."

Possessiveness threaded through his words as his hand settled naturally on my shoulder.

Elias watched us, pain flickering across his features before settling into resigned acceptance.

"Drake." He stood, meeting the Alpha's gaze directly. "I have something to say to you."

"I'm listening."

"Phoebe is the finest woman I've ever known." Elias's voice steadied. "She's gentle, strong, compassionate. These five years, she's raised a child alone, endured struggles you can't imagine."

He paused, his expression hardening with protective steel.

"If you hurt her again, Alpha or not, I will make you pay. Hunt you to the ends of the earth if necessary."

"Never again." Drake's voice rang with absolute conviction. "My greatest mistake was pushing her away five years ago. That error dies with me."

"See that it does." Elias's tone carried lethal promise. "She deserves everything beautiful this world offers. Betray that trust, and I become your worst nightmare."

"I'll spend every remaining breath proving myself worthy." Drake looked at me, eyes blazing with devotion. "Her happiness is my life's purpose."

Elias studied us both for a long moment before turning to me, tears glistening but smile surprisingly gentle.

"Phoebe," his voice caught. "Chase your happiness. Stop running from it, stop second-guessing. Drake is your fated mate. You belong together."

"Elias..." My tears wouldn't stop flowing.

"Don't cry for me." He reached toward my face but caught himself, hand falling away. "I want your joy above all else. Truly."

He stepped back, drinking in my face one final time.

"Take care of yourself. Take care of Ryan," He whispered.

Then he turned and walked to the door, opening it, stepping into darkness without looking back.

The door closed with quiet finality.

I stood frozen, tears streaming unchecked.

Drake's arms encircled me from behind, pulling me against his solid warmth.

"Let it out." He murmured against my hair. "I know this hurts."

"It's not... I don't..."

"I understand." He interrupted gently. "You're grieving for a friend. A man who sacrificed five years loving you. I get it."

I turned in his arms, burying my face against his chest, finally releasing the sobs I'd been holding back.

Drake held me tightly, saying nothing, just stroking my back with infinite patience.

Outside, night claimed the world. Inside, only my weeping echoed through empty rooms.

Elias hadn't said goodbye. Hadn't mentioned when he might leave. He'd simply walked away.

But somehow I knew he wouldn't return for farewells. He'd quietly disappear back to Grayclaw Pack, vanishing like morning mist.

Just as he'd always done everything—quietly giving, quietly protecting, and now, quietly letting go.

CHAPTER TWENTY

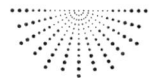

Phoebe

Three days after Elias left, I decided to take Ryan to see the Grayclaw Pack's new territory.

Part of me wanted to check on how the pack members were settling in. The other part... I wanted to see Elias. Whatever had happened between us, he'd been there for me for five years. I couldn't just let him disappear from my life like that.

At the very least, I owed him a proper thank you.

"Mommy, where are we going?" Ryan bounced in his car seat, kicking his little legs excitedly.

"To visit Mommy's pack members." I glanced at him in the rearview mirror. Sunlight hit his face just right, making him look like a little angel. "You need to be good, okay?"

"Okay!" He nodded eagerly.

The car pulled away from the city, through suburban roads, gradually entering the forest. The scenery shifted from skyscrapers to endless trees. Sunlight filtered through the canopy, casting dappled shadows on the ground like scattered gold.

The air carried that clean scent of earth and grass, mixed with something wild and primal that belonged to the forest.

I took a deep breath, letting it fill my lungs. Pure werewolf instinct—the forest was home. This scent brought peace.

The Grayclaw Pack's new territory lay deep in the woods. Drake had helped secure it for us. Supposedly it was beautiful—clear streams, open meadows. A hell of a lot better than our old, run-down place.

Following the GPS, I parked at the forest edge. When I cut the engine, everything went quiet except for wind rustling through leaves.

"We're here, Ryan." I unbuckled my seatbelt and turned to help him out of his car seat.

"Yay!" He jumped down, grabbing onto my skirt.

I took his warm little hand and headed down the forest path. His palm was slightly sweaty—excitement or nerves, I couldn't tell.

Tall trees lined both sides, their thick canopy blocking most of the sunlight. Our feet sank into soft earth and yellowed leaves that crunched with each step. The air grew cooler, carrying a hint of moisture.

"Mommy, so many trees!" Ryan looked around in wonder, his little head swiveling back and forth.

"Well, forests do have lots of trees." I smiled, though unease was creeping in. "Watch your step. Don't trip."

We kept walking, our footsteps and the rustling leaves unnaturally loud in the silent forest.

It was getting too quiet.

Way too quiet.

No birdsong. No insects. Like the entire forest was holding its breath.

A chill ran down my spine. As a werewolf, I could sense something wrong in the air—strange scents, suppressed killing intent.

"Ryan, stay close to me." I pulled him against my side, gripping his hand tighter.

"Mommy, what's wrong?" He looked up with frightened eyes.

"Nothing, it's just—"

A whooshing sound cut through the trees, followed by heavy footsteps.

My heart slammed against my ribs. Instinct kicked in as I shoved Ryan behind me, muscles coiled, ready to fight.

A dozen werewolves in dark clothing burst from the treeline. Fast and vicious, they surrounded us in seconds. Their massive forms blocked the sunlight, casting cold shadows.

Their clothing... that symbol... Darkfang Pack.

My blood turned to ice.

These wolves moved with terrifying speed, their eyes glowing an eerie green in the filtered light. Like a pack of starving predators.

"Don't touch my son!" I snarled, shifting into semi-wolf form, nails extending into razor-sharp claws.

The leader laughed coldly. A vicious scar ran from his left eye to his jaw.

"Save your strength, Phoebe. We know exactly what we're here for."

"Mommy!" Ryan screamed.

Two massive wolves rushed from the sides. One locked my arms in a crushing grip while the other ripped Ryan from my grasp. I fought like hell, my claws tearing bloody gouges in one attacker's arm, but he didn't even flinch.

"Let him go! Let go of my son!" My voice cracked with terror and rage.

Ryan thrashed in his captor's arms, his tiny hands reaching desperately for me. "Mommy! Mommy, help me!"

"Ryan!" My heart felt like it was being crushed in an invisible fist, the pain stealing my breath. I struggled against my captor, but his grip was iron. My arms twisted at painful angles, bones creaking under the pressure.

"Don't move, or things get ugly." The scarred wolf stepped closer, looking down at me with cold satisfaction.

"Relax. We won't hurt the little brat. As long as Drake cooperates, he'll be fine."

"What do you want?" I bit out through gritted teeth, tears streaming down my face.

"You'll find out soon enough." He pulled a crumpled paper from his jacket and tossed it on the ground. "Give this to Drake. He's got until tomorrow noon to make his choice."

He gestured to his pack. They melted back into the forest, Ryan slung over one man's shoulder. His cries grew fainter and fainter until they disappeared completely.

My captor released me with a hard shove. I stumbled, nearly falling. By the time I regained my balance, the Darkfang wolves had vanished.

The forest returned to its unnatural silence. Just wind through leaves and my ragged breathing.

I stumbled to where the paper had fallen, hands shaking as I picked it up. The writing was deliberately sloppy, radiating malice:

"Drake—If you want your son to live, meet us at the abandoned Moonlight Pack Castle by tomorrow noon. Come alone and prepared to renounce your position as Ironspine Pack Alpha. Otherwise, the little brat pays for your stubbornness. —Darkfang Pack"

The note slipped from my fingers, floating down to land among the dead leaves.

My mind went completely blank, like something had slammed into my skull.

Ryan, my Ryan, he was only four years old. So small, so afraid of the dark he needed a nightlight. Scared of thunder, scared of strangers, and he needed me most of all... He must be terrified right now, crying, calling for mommy...

Thinking about it broke something inside me. Tears poured down my face. No. I couldn't fall apart. I had to stay calm. I had to save Ryan.

My hands shook so violently I could barely hold my phone. Deep breath. Another one. I forced my fingers to steady.

Then I called Drake.

Two rings. "Phoebe?" His voice was warm, surprised, delighted. "What's wrong? Miss me already?"

"Drake..." My voice shattered completely. "Ryan... they took Ryan..."

Dead silence on the other end.

I could hear my heartbeat, pounding like it was trying to escape my chest.

"What?" Drake's voice went ice-cold, dangerous as a blade. "Tell me exactly what happened."

"Darkfang Pack, it was Darkfang Pack..." I choked out between sobs. "They took Ryan... they said if you want him back, you have to give up being Alpha... tomorrow noon, the abandoned Moonlight Pack Castle..."

"Phoebe, where are you right now?" His voice was urgent. I could hear him moving, things crashing in the background.

"At... at the forest entrance near Grayclaw Pack's new territory..."

"Phoebe, listen to me." Drake's voice steadied, becoming my lifeline. "Breathe. Calm down. I'm coming."

"But they said—"

"I know what they said." He cut me off. "Phoebe, trust me. I'm going to get Ryan back. I swear it."

His voice carried a strength that cut through my panic.

"Stay right there. Don't go anywhere." He continued. "I'll be there soon."

The call ended. I collapsed against a tree trunk.

My phone slipped from numb fingers, hitting the leaves with a soft thud. The screen went dark, its faint glow vanishing like my last hope.

Everything blurred—trees, sunlight, forest—all distant and unreal behind a film of tears. Only the fear and desperation stayed crystal clear, a giant hand crushing my heart until I couldn't breathe.

Ryan's screams echoed in my head.

"Mommy! Mommy, help me!" Sharp, terrified, desperate. Each cry was a knife cutting into my soul. His little hands reaching for me, those blue eyes full of tears and terror...

I buried my face in my hands, shoulders shaking violently. My palms were ice-cold and wet. My fingertips still had blood under the nails from fighting. Tears slipped through my fingers, dropping onto the dead leaves below.

Drake said he was coming.

He said he'd get Ryan back.

But what if... what if Darkfang Pack really hurt him? What if I never saw him again?

These thoughts stabbed into me like knives, each one stealing more breath.

Time crawled.

Every second felt like a year.

Then, somewhere in the distance, an engine roared to life.

The sound grew closer, cutting through the forest silence.

I jerked my head up.

A black SUV came racing through the trees, kicking up clouds of dust. It was flying, barely touching the ground.

Drake.

The car skidded to a stop in front of me, tires screaming against dirt. The door flew open and Drake leaped out.

His face was thunderous, eyes burning with barely controlled rage. But when he saw me huddled against the tree, everything changed.

"Phoebe!" His voice cracked with urgency.

He ran toward me, boots pounding the earth, sending up sprays of dirt and leaves. His shadow fell over me, blocking the sun.

I tried to stand but my legs were useless, filled with lead. I could only watch helplessly as he closed the distance.

Drake dropped to his knees in front of me, hitting the ground hard enough that the stones must have hurt. But he didn't even flinch. His hands reached out, pulling me into his arms.

"Phoebe..." His voice was rough, shaking, his breath hot against my hair. "Don't be afraid. I'm here... I'm here..."

His embrace was warm and solid, carrying that familiar scent of sandalwood and mint mixed with the salt of sweat. His heartbeat thundered against my ear—strong, fast, telling me he was here, that I wasn't alone.

In that moment, I completely fell apart.

"Drake..." I clutched his shirt like a lifeline, breaking down completely. "Ryan... they took Ryan... it's my fault... I couldn't protect him..."

"This isn't your fault." One arm crushed me against him while his other hand stroked my hair, gentle as if I were a frightened animal.

"This isn't your fault, Phoebe. Darkfang Pack planned this. One person couldn't have stopped them."

His voice was soft but carried unshakable strength, like a light in the darkness.

"But I..." I sobbed, my words breaking apart. "I'm his mother... I should have protected him..."

"Listen to me." Drake pulled back slightly, cupping my face in his hands. His palms were warm and rough, thumbs brushing away my tears with heartbreaking gentleness.

He looked straight into my eyes. His were red-rimmed, bloodshot, like he was fighting back his own tears.

"I'm going to bring Ryan home." His voice grew rougher, eyes glistening.

"I swear it, Phoebe. I'll bring him back whole and safe. No one will hurt him. That's my promise. I swear on my life."

I stared into his eyes, seeing that unwavering determination, and felt hope flicker to life.

"The note..." I fumbled in my pocket for the crumpled paper, handing it to him. "They said... you have to give up being Alpha..."

Drake took the note and stood.

He unfolded it, scanning the contents. His expression grew darker by the second, like storm clouds gathering. I watched his hands tighten until the paper creased, his knuckles white, veins standing out in sharp relief.

His jaw clenched. The vein at his temple pulsed. The fury in his eyes was ready to explode.

"Bastards..." he growled, voice loaded with killing intent.

He folded the note and pocketed it, then pulled out his phone and dialed.

Two rings. "Kay." Drake's voice could have cut steel. Every word dripped ice.

"Get every core member to the castle conference room. Now. I don't care what they're doing—twenty minutes, everyone there."

He paused, his expression growing more vicious.

"I want everything on Darkfang Pack's recent movements. Every hideout, every member, full details. Tell the security chief to prep weapons and gear."

Kay's voice came through the phone. Drake listened briefly, then replied coldly.

"I don't give a damn what they want. They touched Ryan. Now they're going to pay in blood."

He hung up.

Then he turned to me, his expression immediately softening.

"Phoebe, come on." He extended his hand. "We're going back to Ironspine Pack. Time's running short. I need to plan this rescue."

I grabbed his hand and tried to stand, but my legs were still weak. I stumbled the moment I got up.

"Can you walk?" He steadied me, worried.

"I can..." But before I could finish, Drake swept me up in his arms.

"Don't push yourself." He looked down at me, voice gentle. "You need rest."

He carried me toward the SUV, sunlight falling across his shoulders, casting a long shadow on the ground. I pressed against his chest, listening to his heartbeat—steady, strong, promising me everything would be okay.

His embrace was warm, carrying that familiar scent and that unshakable strength.

I closed my eyes. Tears still fell, but hope was growing.

At least I wasn't alone.

Drake would save Ryan.

He'd promised me.

He'd sworn on his life.

CHAPTER TWENTY-ONE

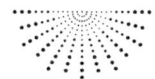

Phoebe

The moment the conference room door swung open, a wall of tension hit me.

The long conference table was packed with nearly every core member of the Ironspine Pack. Their faces were grim—some whispering in hushed tones, others staring intently at maps spread across the table. The air was thick with oppressive silence, suffocating.

The instant Drake entered, all conversation ceased. Everyone rose to their feet in perfect unison.

"Alpha." Their voices rang out, deep and commanding.

Drake led me by the hand to the conference table, his face dark as a storm cloud, eyes burning with barely restrained fury. That overwhelming Alpha presence seemed to drop the room's temperature by several degrees.

"Sit." One word, cold as winter.

Everyone dropped back into their seats like clockwork.

Kay stood at the far end of the table. The moment he saw us enter, he strode over, expression grave, brow furrowed, clutching a stack of files.

"Alpha. Phoebe." He nodded, his gaze lingering on my face for a heartbeat, sympathy flickering in his eyes.

I knew I looked terrible—eyes swollen from crying, face pale as parchment, hair disheveled, clothes stained with mud and dead leaves. But I was beyond caring.

"How's it going?" Drake's voice could have frozen hell, though his hand still gripped mine tightly.

"We've begun the investigation." Kay placed the files on the table. "I've mobilized every contact we have, including our informants in Grayclaw territory. Darkfang kept this operation under wraps, but they left traces."

He opened the files, revealing satellite maps and hand-drawn route charts.

"Based on current intelligence, Darkfang most likely has Ryan hidden in the abandoned Moonlight Pack Castle." Kay's finger stabbed a location on the map. "Remote location, surrounded by mountains and dense forest. Easily defended, difficult to assault. The castle has been deserted for years—civilians avoid it. Perfect hideout."

I stared at that mark on the map, my heart clenching like a fist.

Ryan was there. My baby was trapped in that strange, dark, terrifying place.

"You're certain?" Drake's voice grew even colder.

"Eighty percent positive." Kay's expression darkened further. "We found recent Darkfang activity around the castle perimeter, and informants spotted them moving supplies inside. Timeline suggests they're preparing for extended occupation."

"How many?" Drake asked.

"At least twenty, all Darkfang elite warriors." Kay looked increasingly troubled. "Castle defenses are tight—perimeter sentries, complex internal structure. Direct assault carries significant risk."

"Then we go smart." Drake's eyes remained fixed on the map, clearly strategizing.

Suddenly, a knock echoed at the conference room door.

"Come in." Drake didn't look up.

The door opened and a young guard in Ironspine uniform poked his head in. "Alpha, someone's here to see Miss Phoebe."

"Who?" Drake's frown deepened, displeasure evident.

"Says he's... Elias from Grayclaw Pack." The guard spoke carefully.

My head snapped up.

Elias? Why was he here? Hadn't he returned to Grayclaw territory?

Drake's face instantly grew even darker, his grip on my hand tightening. I could feel his displeasure radiating outward—that mixture of possessiveness and wariness almost tangible.

"Let him in." I spoke before Drake could respond.

Drake turned to me, his expression unreadable.

"Drake," I said softly, squeezing his hand. "Elias might be able to help. He has extensive contacts on the Grayclaw side, and... he knows Moonlight territory well. He grew up in that area."

Drake remained silent for a long moment, finally nodding, though his expression stayed stormy.

The guard departed, and soon Elias entered.

He wore simple gray clothes and black pants, hair slightly mussed, face showing the weariness of hard travel. But those gentle eyes filled with concern the instant they found me.

"Phoebe." He hurried over, taking in my swollen eyes, pain flickering across his features. "I heard about... Ryan..."

"How did you know?" My voice came out hoarse.

"Word reached Grayclaw Pack." Elias said. "News travels fast. I came immediately."

He turned to Drake, his expression growing serious. "Drake, I'm here to help. Ryan... he's like family to me. I can't stand by and do nothing."

Drake stared at him coldly, saying nothing, the wariness and hostility in his eyes completely undisguised.

The atmosphere grew tense, the air practically crackling with electricity.

"Elias," Kay broke the silence, his tone more diplomatic. "Since you're here, perhaps you can assist. Are you familiar with Moonlight Castle's layout?"

"Very." Elias nodded, approaching the conference table to study the map. "I spent considerable time in that region as a child. I know the castle's internal structure well."

He pointed to several locations on the map. "The castle has three main entrances—front gate, side entrance, and rear door. The front gate will be heavily guarded, the side entrance leads to the dungeons, the rear door connects to kitchens and storage. For infiltration, the rear approach is optimal."

Kay nodded thoughtfully. "The dungeons... Ryan might be held there."

"Unlikely." Elias shook his head. "If I were Darkfang, I wouldn't keep such a valuable hostage in the dungeons. Too damp, single exit point—poor for quick evacuation. More likely the tower. Better visibility, easier to monitor surroundings, superior defensive position."

His analysis was sound. Everyone in the room listened intently.

"Your recommendation?" Kay asked.

Elias took a deep breath, meeting Drake's gaze. "I can disguise myself as a Darkfang member and infiltrate the castle."

The conference room fell silent. All eyes fixed on him.

"What?" My eyes widened in shock.

"Phoebe, hear me out." Elias turned to me, expression earnest and determined. "Darkfang has complex recruitment—many mercenaries from various packs. I can pose as one of them, infiltrate to locate Ryan precisely, then relay intelligence. You coordinate from outside—working in tandem dramatically improves our odds."

"Too dangerous." I immediately shook my head. "If you're discovered, you're dead."

"I understand the risks." Elias looked at me, his gaze gentle. "But this gives us the best chance. Direct assault might drive Darkfang to desperation—they could harm Ryan. Only by confirming his location first can we ensure a flawless rescue."

"He makes a valid point." Kay said gravely. "Internal support would significantly improve our success rate."

"Absolutely not." Drake suddenly spoke, voice ice-cold. "I refuse.

Moonlight Castle has changed considerably over the years. You've been absent for five years—your intelligence is likely obsolete."

Everyone turned to him.

Drake rose, his commanding Alpha presence making direct eye contact difficult. He stared at Elias, gaze sharp as a blade. "My son's affairs don't require outside interference. Besides, Ryan was taken from Grayclaw territory—clearly they understand your pack well. How can you guarantee they won't see through your disguise?"

"Drake!" I caught his hand.

"Outside interference?" Color flickered across Elias's face, but he quickly composed himself. "I know you have reservations about me, but this isn't the time for personal grievances. Ryan's safety is paramount."

"I will retrieve my son." Drake said coldly, each word seemingly forced through clenched teeth. "Your false sympathy isn't needed. I've battled Darkfang long enough—I know them intimately."

"Drake!" I raised my voice, frustration and anger building. "What are you saying? Elias genuinely wants to help!"

"Does he?" Drake turned to me, hurt flashing in his eyes. "You trust him so completely?"

I froze.

I suddenly understood—Drake was jealous.

In this crisis, he was actually jealous of Elias.

"Drake," I took a steadying breath, trying to remain calm. "I know you can save Ryan. I believe in you completely. But Elias's plan is sound and could minimize risk. Right now we should unite every available resource, shouldn't we?"

Drake studied me, his face still dark.

The conference room atmosphere was suffocating. Everyone held their breath, afraid to speak.

"Alpha." Kay ventured carefully. "Phoebe's right. Elias's plan could improve our odds, and... time is critical. We can't afford delays."

Drake remained silent so long I thought he'd refuse.

Finally, he spoke slowly. "Fine. But with conditions."

He fixed Elias with a razor-sharp stare. "You scout intelligence only. Confirm Ryan's location then extract immediately. I personally lead the rescue operation. Their combat capabilities exceed your limits. Clear?"

"Clear." Elias nodded.

"Furthermore," Drake's voice grew even colder, "if anything happens to Ryan, you'll answer to me."

Elias met his gaze unflinchingly. "If something happens, you won't need to act—I won't forgive myself."

The two men locked eyes, tension crackling between them.

"Drake," I tugged gently at his sleeve. "I want to come with you."

"What?" Drake whirled to face me, eyes wide. "Absolutely not!"

"I'm Ryan's mother." I met his gaze, forcing my voice to stay steady. "I can't do nothing and wait here for news. I won't."

"Phoebe, it's too dangerous." Drake's brow furrowed, worry evident in his voice. "Darkfang won't show mercy."

"I know." I gripped his hand tighter, palm slick with sweat. "But I have to go. Drake, if positions were reversed, could you simply stand aside?"

Drake looked at me, his expression conflicted.

I could see the struggle in his eyes—wanting to protect me, keep me from danger, yet understanding my maternal instincts.

"Phoebe," Elias spoke up, voice gentle. "This truly is dangerous. Stay here and wait for us to bring Ryan back safely."

"No." I shook my head, turning to him. "Elias, you should understand. I can't remain here doing nothing—I'll lose my mind."

My voice began trembling, tears threatening again. "He's only four... he must be terrified... he needs me... I'm his mother... I have to go..."

"Phoebe..." Drake's voice suddenly softened.

He cupped my face, thumb gently brushing away my tears. Those cold eyes melted into warm pools when they looked at me.

I turned to Elias. "I can help. I'm skilled at mimicry—I can disguise myself as Darkfang too. Two infiltrators are safer than one."

Elias considered this, then nodded. "She's right. And Phoebe has exceptional senses—she could help us locate Ryan faster."

Drake's face was grim, eyes full of internal conflict. He studied me with that complex expression, finally taking a deep breath. "Very well. But you follow orders. No independent action."

"I promise."

An hour later, I stood in Ironspine's armory, staring at the stranger in the mirror.

I'd changed into rough gray clothing captured from Darkfang prisoners, coarse fabric reeking of stale sweat. Elias helped me smear mud across my face to mask my refined features. I pulled my hair into a crude ponytail, deliberately messing several strands.

"Relax your shoulders," Elias coached quietly. "Darkfang members move more casually, with underlying aggression. Try it."

I adjusted my posture, recalling the Darkfang warriors I'd observed—shoulders swaying slightly, heavy footfalls, eyes alert and predatory.

I took a deep breath and began mimicking.

Relaxed shoulders, heavier steps, sharper gaze...

"Excellent." Elias nodded. "You're a natural."

Drake stood in the doorway, watching silently. His face looked haggard, jaw clenched, eyes flickering with worry and unease.

I approached him and took his hand. "Trust me. I'll be careful."

"Phoebe..." His voice was strained. "If you encounter danger, retreat immediately. Ryan matters, but so do you. I can't lose either of you."

"I understand." I rose on tiptoes and kissed him softly. "Wait for me to come back."

When darkness fell, we departed.

The SUV raced through the night, headlights cutting through winding mountain roads. I sat in back, hands clenched, palms damp with perspiration.

My heart hammered frantically—so loud I could hear each beat like war drums.

Ryan... Mommy's coming... hold on...

The vehicle stopped two kilometers from the castle. Drake killed the engine and turned to Elias and me.

"Twenty minutes," his voice was low and serious. "Locate Ryan and signal immediately. Remember—avoid direct confrontation."

"Understood." Elias nodded.

"Phoebe." Drake gripped my hand, that warm contact steadying me slightly. "Stay with Elias. Don't leave his sight."

"I will."

He pressed a kiss to my forehead. "Be careful."

Elias and I exited the vehicle and melted into the darkness.

The forest was pitch black, moonlight obscured by clouds, only scattered starlight visible. I followed Elias, stepping on soft earth, trying to move silently.

Night wind carried forest scents—soil, pine, and the stench of decay from the distant castle.

I inhaled deeply, letting these scents fill my lungs. As a werewolf, my sense of smell far exceeded human capabilities—I could detect subtle atmospheric changes.

The castle loomed closer.

That abandoned structure appeared sinister in the darkness, crumbling stone walls shrouded in vines. Faint light flickered from windows, wavering ominously.

We circled to the castle's rear, where security was lighter.

"Wait," Elias whispered, pointing ahead. "Two sentries."

I squinted and spotted two shadowy figures positioned in the darkness.

"We'll go around."

We pressed against the walls, staying in shadows. The stone was cold and damp, with a slimy texture. The air reeked of mold and old blood.

Suddenly, a sentry turned, his gaze sweeping toward our position.

I immediately froze, flattening against the wall, holding my breath.

The sentry stared in our direction for several tense seconds before finally turning away.

I exhaled quietly, heart pounding.

"Move," Elias whispered.

We located the rear entrance—an old wooden door, slightly ajar.

Elias carefully pushed it open. The hinges creaked softly, making my pulse spike.

Beyond was a long corridor lined with dim oil lamps, flames dancing.

We entered, the door closing softly behind us.

The corridor was eerily quiet except for distant footsteps and muted conversation. I controlled my breathing, staying calm while adopting Darkfang posture—relaxed shoulders, heavy gait, alert expression.

"This way." Elias indicated stairs to the right. "According to intelligence, the tower is in that direction."

Just as we prepared to turn, I suddenly stopped. A strange sensation welled up from deep within, as if something was drawing me, calling to me. The feeling was intense, making my heart race.

Not the tower. Not there.

"Wait." I grasped Elias's arm, whispering urgently. "Not the tower."

"What?" Elias frowned. "Intelligence indicates..."

"I can sense it," I pressed my hand to my chest, where waves of recognition pulsed. "Ryan isn't in the tower. He's... below."

"You're certain?"

"I'm certain." My voice trembled. "I'm his mother. I can feel him. He's... underground."

Elias hesitated momentarily, then nodded. "I trust you."

I closed my eyes, breathing deeply. The air contained countless scents—mold, blood, sweat, rotting wood... I strained to distinguish them, seeking that most precious smell.

Ryan's scent—faint grass fragrance mixed with his unique, sweet aroma. Very subtle, nearly masked by other odors, but I caught it.

"This way." I led Elias toward the left corridor.

We navigated several passages, the scent strengthening. The pull in my heart intensified, like an invisible thread guiding me toward my son.

Finally, we reached an iron door, half-open, revealing stone steps descending into darkness—the basement.

"Here," I whispered, voice shaking with anticipation.

Elias surveyed our surroundings alertly, then nodded. "Go."

We carefully descended the stone steps.

The stairs were narrow and treacherous, slick with moisture. A few guttering oil lamps provided minimal illumination. The deeper we went, the colder and damper it became, like entering a tomb.

I could hear distant water dripping—methodical, echoing. Rats scurried in the shadows, squeaking.

Ryan's scent grew stronger. My heart raced, palms sweating.

We reached the underground corridor. It stretched endlessly, lined with tightly shut wooden doors. Wall lamps became scarcer, darkness deepening. Following my maternal instincts, I pressed forward.

"Here." My voice barely a whisper. "Ryan's inside."

Elias nodded, signaling caution. He quietly eased the door open—it creaked softly.

My breathing stopped. Inside was a damp stone chamber, a single flickering oil lamp casting sickly light. The floor was wet, shallow puddles reeking of decay. Broken sacks and rusted chains littered the corners.

In the room's center, bound to a crude wooden chair, sat Ryan.

Time froze.

My precious child was secured with coarse rope, tiny hands and feet tightly bound. His small face was deathly pale, eyes red and swollen, tears clinging to his lashes. Dirty streaks marked his cheeks, lips cracked and dry. His clothes were filthy and soaked, clinging miserably to his small frame.

His head drooped forward, looking unconscious.

"Ryan..." My voice broke.

Ryan's head jerked up.

The moment our eyes met, those blue eyes blazed to life like stars igniting in darkness.

"Mommy... Mommy..." His voice was weak and hoarse, thick with emotion, but carefully quiet. "Is it really you... I'm not dreaming..."

Tears instantly blurred my vision.

"Mommy's here, sweetheart, Mommy came to save you..." I rushed forward, nearly stumbling as I dropped beside him.

My knees struck the cold, wet stone, water soaking through my clothing. But I didn't care, my trembling hands working frantically at the ropes.

"Mommy, I was so scared..." Ryan's tears fell steadily, warm drops hitting my hands. "They-they wouldn't let me sleep... kept asking about Daddy... I didn't tell them anything... I remembered what Mommy said about strangers..."

"You were so brave, baby, the bravest boy..." I choked out, desperately attacking the knots.

But my fingers trembled violently from emotion, the cursed knots pulled impossibly tight, multiple deadlocks resisting every effort.

The coarse rope had carved deep red welts into his tender skin, some areas broken and bleeding. The sight shattered my heart.

"Does it hurt? Baby, I'm so sorry... Mommy should have come sooner..." Tears dropped onto the ropes.

"It doesn't hurt. Don't cry, Mommy..." Ryan said maturely, though tears still streamed down his face. "I-I was brave... I kept waiting for you... I knew you'd come..."

"Mommy's brave boy..." I attacked the final knot desperately, my nail splitting, blood seeping to stain the hemp.

"Phoebe, hurry," Elias warned from the doorway. "We're making too much noise."

"Almost... almost..."

Finally, I tore the last knot free.

I immediately lifted Ryan from the chair, crushing him against me.

His small body was ice-cold and frighteningly light, trembling violently. He clutched my clothes desperately, small face buried in my neck, warm tears dampening my skin.

"Mommy, Mommy... I thought I'd never see you again..." He sobbed, voice breaking with relief and lingering fear. "I missed you so much, missed Daddy... I want to go home..."

"Sweetheart, Mommy will never leave you..." I held him fiercely, one hand stroking his back. "We're going home right now..."

I kissed his forehead, cheeks, hair, tears flowing freely.

His forehead was cold and clammy. His hair was damp and dirty. His clothes reeked of mold. His hands were like ice.

But none of that mattered.

What mattered was my baby was alive, safe in my arms.

"We need to move," Elias urged.

I stood on unsteady legs, Ryan clinging to me like I might vanish. He buried his face in my neck, tiny hands gripping my shirt.

Just as we reached the door, heavy footsteps echoed outside.

Deliberate, measured steps, each one like a hammer blow.

Elias's face went white, immediately positioning himself protectively in front of us.

The door swung slowly open.

A tall figure appeared silhouetted in the doorway, features obscured but radiating menace that made the air thick.

"Such a touching reunion." A low voice dripped with mockery. "How heartwarming."

The man stepped into the lamplight, revealing a face marked by a vicious scar running from forehead to chin, eyes glowing with predatory intensity.

Coleman. Darkfang Pack Alpha.

"Did you really think I wouldn't anticipate this?" He sneered as a dozen Darkfang warriors filed in behind him. "I deliberately kept the little whelp here as bait. You walked right into my trap."

My blood turned to ice as I clutched Ryan protectively.

Coleman's cruel gaze fixed on my son. "Now none of you are leaving."

At that critical moment, Ryan stirred in my arms.

"Mommy... let me down..." His voice was soft but carried unexpected authority.

"Ryan? No sweetheart, it's dangerous..." I tightened my grip, trying to shield him.

"Mommy, trust me." Ryan looked up, those blue eyes suddenly blazing with golden fire—exactly like Drake's when he shifted.

He broke free with surprising strength, his small body landing gracefully on the ground.

"Ryan!" I reached for him desperately.

Coleman observed Ryan with contempt. "A four-year-old brat thinks he can..."

His words died abruptly.

Ryan stood perfectly straight, small chin raised defiantly as he opened his mouth toward Coleman.

The next instant, a howl erupted from his throat—

"Awoooo—!"

The sound was young but filled with impossible Alpha dominance!

The entire chamber shook, dust cascading from the walls. Darkfang warriors clutched their ears, crying out in pain, several dropping to their knees.

Even Coleman staggered, his sneer freezing, eyes going glassy.

"Impossible... Alpha howl at four years old..."

"Now! Move!" Elias roared.

I snapped into action, grabbing Ryan's hand. His small palm burned with fever, still trembling from exertion.

"Follow me!" Elias blazed ahead, striking down any warrior who blocked our path.

I clutched Ryan tight, racing after Elias.

"Don't let them escape!" Coleman bellowed behind us.

We burst from the basement, taking the stone steps two at a time. Ryan's legs were too short to keep pace, so I swept him into my arms.

"Mommy, I'm so tired..." His voice was weak, that howl having drained his small reserves.

"Hold on, baby, we're almost safe..."

Chaos erupted behind us—shouting voices and pounding feet growing closer.

We exploded from the castle into the night air.

CHAPTER TWENTY-TWO

Drake

I stood at the edge of the woods outside the castle, my gaze locked on that ominous structure.

Moonlight spilled across the crumbling stone walls, illuminating ivy-covered windows that gleamed like the eyes of predators. Night wind swept through, rustling the vines with a sound like countless serpents slithering. The air reeked of decay mixed with earth and blood—a scent that set my nerves on edge.

I could feel blood surging through my veins, my heart pounding so violently that each beat felt like war drums in my chest. My palms were slick with sweat, nails digging deep into my flesh, but the pain kept me focused.

Phoebe and Ryan were both inside.

My mate, my son—trapped in that godforsaken place.

Every second was agony. I could feel the fated mate bond pulling at my very core, like an invisible thread connecting me to Phoebe. That thread was stretched so taut now it felt ready to snap, tearing my heart in two.

"Alpha," Kay murmured beside me, his voice barely above a whisper. "The warriors are in position. The moment they signal, we move."

I nodded, my eyes never leaving the castle, afraid to blink and miss something crucial.

Fifty elite Ironspine warriors were hidden throughout the surrounding woods, scattered at strategic positions, their bodies melted into the shadows, ready to strike. Everyone held their breath, watching the castle with such intense focus that the very air seemed to thicken around us.

Moonlight filtered through the canopy, casting dappled shadows across the forest floor. Night insects chirped in the distance, their calls only making the silence feel more ominous.

I drew a deep breath, cold air flooding my lungs with the forest's damp scent, but it did nothing to calm my restless spirit.

Letting Phoebe go in with Elias had been one of the hardest decisions of my life. Every instinct screamed at me to charge in myself, to shoulder all the danger, to carry Ryan out in my own arms, to shield them both with my body.

But I couldn't.

As Alpha, I had to remain calm, rational. Elias and Phoebe's infiltration was our safest bet, and commanding from out here meant I could provide maximum support when it mattered most.

But this waiting was driving me to the brink of madness.

Every second stretched like an eternity. I could feel my jaw clenching, teeth grinding until my muscles ached. The wolf within me was restless, roaring, urging me to charge in and tear apart anyone who dared harm my family.

I glanced at my watch.

Twenty minutes. If they weren't out in twenty minutes, I was taking everyone in. To hell with the plan. To hell with the risks.

My family was in there. I wouldn't let them remain in danger a moment longer than necessary.

Suddenly, Elias's voice crackled through my earpiece, urgent and breathless. "Found him! We found Ryan! Prepare for extraction!"

My heart slammed against my ribs like a sledgehammer, every muscle in my body coiling for action.

"Location?" I asked, my voice hoarse with tension.

"Basement, moving out now... shit, we're blown! They're on us!" Panic edged Elias's voice, and I could hear the clash of weapons in the background.

"All units, prepare for battle!" I commanded, feeling the wolf within me stirring, blood heating, muscles beginning to swell beneath my skin.

The warriors around me rose from the woods in unison, weapons drawn, eyes beginning to glow that familiar predatory green. The atmosphere turned lethal in an instant, thick with killing intent.

Alarm bells suddenly shrieked from the castle, their piercing wail cutting through the night and echoing through the silent forest. Then the main gate burst open with a thunderous crash. Torchlight flooded the courtyard, orange flames dancing in the darkness like hellfire.

"Eyes on the gate," I growled, my gaze riveted to that spot.

Seconds later, three figures burst through the entrance.

In the moonlight, I saw them clearly—Elias in the lead, moving with desperate agility; Phoebe behind him carrying Ryan, running with everything she had, her body stumbling with exhaustion.

My heart clenched so violently I thought my chest might split open.

Phoebe's hair whipped wildly in the night wind, her clothes stained with dirt and worse. She looked utterly spent. Ryan was pressed against her chest, his tiny body clinging to her, small hands fisted in her clothes. Even from this distance, I could feel her trembling, see her faltering steps, sense her terror and exhaustion.

"Prepare for extraction!" I roared, about to charge forward.

Then more figures poured from the castle—at least twenty Darkfang warriors, all massive and imposing, eyes glowing with predatory hunger as they gave chase. Their footsteps pounded the ground in rhythmic thunder, like Death's own march.

I recognized the one leading them.

Coleman. Darkfang Pack Alpha.

Moonlight gleamed off the long silver blade in his grip, that cold radiance like Death's own scythe.

Silver.

The one weapon that could truly kill us.

Ice shot through my veins, a chill racing from my spine straight to my skull.

"Charge!" I roared, my voice tearing through the night.

My body began its violent shift.

Bones cracked and reformed, each break bringing white-hot agony, but I welcomed the familiar pain. Muscles swelled, power flooding through me as thick black fur erupted from my skin. My spine elongated, limbs hitting the ground as I rapidly shifted into my massive wolf form.

The strength roared through my body, sharpening every sense to a razor's edge—I could smell Phoebe's familiar scent mixed with the salt of fear-sweat; could hear Ryan's rapid, shallow breathing and his muffled whimpers; could feel their heartbeats, racing fast enough to burst.

Ironspine warriors shifted around me, wolf after wolf charging from the treeline with deep, resonant howls as they launched themselves at the Darkfang Pack. The ground shook beneath our combined weight, the night air filled with our battle cries.

I was the fastest among them.

My legs devoured the distance, each stride powerful and precise, claws carving furrows in the earth. Night wind howled past me, whipping through my fur as I closed the gap between us and them.

Phoebe was still running, clutching Ryan, giving everything she had left.

I could see her face, pale as death, lips tinged blue, forehead slick with sweat. Ryan was buried against her neck, his tiny face pressed into her shoulder, small body shaking with terror.

But she was too slow—a woman carrying a child couldn't outrun shifted werewolves. The Darkfang warriors were gaining ground with every second, the distance closing relentlessly.

Coleman ran at their head, eyes wild with bloodlust, face twisted in a savage grin as he raised his silver blade high. The weapon caught the moonlight, reflecting it back in deadly brilliance.

He was less than ten meters from Phoebe. Nine. Eight. Seven.

I could see his arm muscles coiling, preparing to strike. Could see the cruel anticipation in his expression, feel the murderous intent radiating from him.

"Aooooo!" I howled, the sound deep and primal, filled with terror and rage.

Phoebe heard me and glanced back.

Our eyes met across the distance.

Hers were wide with fear, tears streaming down her face, her complexion ghostly pale. Ryan gripped her clothes with desperate fingers, his small face buried against her neck, tiny body trembling uncontrollably.

Coleman's arm was already drawing back.

He released the blade with practiced precision, silver death spinning through the air with a whistle, aimed straight for Phoebe's back.

The angle, the speed, the distance—she had no chance to dodge. If that blade found its mark, she would die.

The thought of it piercing her heart, of her collapsing in a pool of blood, of watching the light fade from her eyes...

My mate would die before my eyes. No. Never. I would not allow it.

I exploded forward with superhuman speed, legs driving me across the ground, muscles screaming with the effort, claws gouging deep trenches in the earth.

Time seemed to slow.

I watched the silver blade spinning through the air, inching closer to Phoebe's vulnerable back, moonlight dancing along its edge.

Ryan, in her arms, opened his eyes, looking around in confusion and terror, his tiny mouth forming a silent cry for his daddy.

My heart felt ready to explode, my chest burning with desperate fire.

I could not let that blade touch her. Would not.

I launched myself upward, my massive form cutting a dark arc through the moonlit air, shadow and silver light washing over me.

In the instant before the blade would have found Phoebe's back, I intercepted it. The silver drove deep into my shoulder.

Agony exploded through my entire body. This wasn't ordinary pain—silver to a werewolf was like liquid fire, like poison, like death itself coursing through my veins.

The agony spread from the wound, burning along every nerve, searing through muscle and bone. My blood felt like it was boiling, the wound hissing and smoking as I caught the acrid stench of my own burning fur. Silver toxin raced through my bloodstream, every vessel feeling like it was being eaten by acid, every nerve shrieking in protest.

A low, agonized sound escaped my throat as my body convulsed, nearly stumbling.

"Drake!" Phoebe's scream tore through the night, raw with horror.

Fighting through the pain, I steadied myself, all four paws hitting the ground hard enough to crater the earth. The silver blade remained buried in my shoulder, its hilt trembling with each labored breath. Every movement sent fresh waves of agony through me, like someone repeatedly pressing a white-hot brand into the wound.

Blood ran down my dark fur in rivulets, dripping steadily to pool beneath me, gleaming crimson in the moonlight.

But I remained standing. My legs shook, my vision blurred, but I gritted my teeth and forced myself upright.

I opened my muzzle and unleashed a threatening howl at Coleman —"Aooooooo!"

The sound was deep and intimidating, an Alpha's challenge, a warning to enemies, and a promise of protection to my family. It echoed through the night, shaking the very trees around us.

The air itself seemed to vibrate with the force of it. Even the Darkfang warriors faltered, instinctive fear flickering in their eyes as they took involuntary steps backward.

Coleman's triumphant expression vanished, replaced by shock and grudging respect. He hadn't expected that even grievously wounded by silver, I could still stand, still project such raw dominance.

Before my howl had fully faded, I was already moving, shooting toward Coleman like black lightning. My claws tore through the air, carrying all my accumulated rage and desperate love, slashing toward his exposed throat.

Coleman snarled and leaped backward, trying to escape. Too late. My claws raked across his throat, opening a gaping wound that sent dark blood spurting across his matted fur.

Screaming in pain and fury, he lashed out with his own claws. I twisted aside, avoiding the worst of it, though his strike still caught my shoulder, tearing at the silver wound with renewed agony. But that pain only fed my primal fury.

I pressed my attack, driving my full weight into his chest with bone-crushing force.

"Uragh!"

Coleman was launched backward by the impact, his heavy form tumbling across the ground in a cloud of dust and debris. He struggled to rise, but his legs were shaking uncontrollably, his breathing labored and pained. Those wolf eyes stared at me in disbelief, as if unable to comprehend how I could still fight with such ferocity while carrying a silver wound.

I didn't give him time to recover, advancing with a low, threatening growl that promised violence. The silver poison burned through my system, but right now, that pain was fuel—behind me stood everything worth dying for.

The remaining Darkfang warriors were frozen by my display, not daring to advance.

"Drake..." Phoebe's voice came from behind me, thick with tears and breaking with emotion.

I felt her approach, felt her trembling hand touch my flank. Her touch was warm and gentle, carrying her unique, beloved scent.

"Drake... you're hurt... Goddess, there's so much blood..." She choked on the words, her voice fracturing. "This is all my fault... I did this to you..."

I turned my head and gently nuzzled her tear-stained face, her warmth dampening my fur.

It's all right, I wanted to tell her. As long as you and Ryan are safe, this wound means nothing.

"Daddy..." Ryan's voice reached me, small and scared but filled with awe. "Daddy got hurt... saving us..."

Hearing my son's voice sent a different kind of pain through my chest.

I looked at Ryan in Phoebe's arms. He lifted his small face, those blue eyes red-rimmed and swimming with tears as he stared at me. His tiny hand stretched toward me, wanting to touch but afraid of causing more pain, hovering uncertainly in the air.

"Daddy's so brave..." he whispered, tears streaming down his cheeks. "Daddy's a real superhero..."

I nuzzled his small hand with my nose, that soft, warm touch easing some of the fire in my chest.

"Drake... your wound..." Phoebe's hand hovered near the silver blade still embedded in my shoulder. I couldn't suppress a shudder at her proximity to it, agony clouding my vision with red.

"Don't touch it!" I wanted to warn her, but only low whines emerged from my throat.

"We have to get the blade out... but..." Her voice trembled with pain and self-recrimination. "It's going to hurt so much... I'm sorry... I'm so sorry..."

Her hand closed around the blade's handle. I could feel her fingers shaking violently.

"Drake, hold on," she whispered, her voice breaking with anguish.

Then she yanked the silver blade free.

"Aaarrgh!" The sound tore from my throat as my body convulsed, legs nearly buckling beneath me.

The pain defied description—like molten metal poured directly into my veins, like a thousand knives flaying me from within, like my very soul being torn apart. Silver poison spread from the wound with an audible hiss, white smoke rising as it ate at my flesh.

Blood gushed from the wound, soaking the ground beneath me. The metallic scent filled the air as my vision grayed at the edges, my legs threatening to give out entirely.

"Drake!" Phoebe hurled the blade aside—it clattered against stone—and threw herself against me, arms wrapping around my neck. "I'm sorry... I'm so sorry... I should never have let you get hurt... this is all my fault... if it wasn't for us, you wouldn't have..."

Her tears soaked into my fur, warm droplets mixing with my blood. I could feel her whole body shaking, hear her muffled sobs, sense the guilt and heartbreak radiating from her.

I pressed my muzzle against her cheek, trying to offer comfort. It's all right. This is nothing. As long as you're both safe, everything is worth it.

Kay's voice cut through the night from somewhere nearby. "Alpha's down! Form a perimeter!"

Ironspine warriors immediately surrounded us, creating a protective barrier between us and the Darkfang Pack. They growled low and menacing, eyes blazing with fierce loyalty as they took defensive positions.

Coleman stared at me, clearly stunned that I could still fight after taking a silver blade. The Darkfang warriors behind him had lost their nerve entirely, backing away with fear plain in their eyes.

Calculation flickered across Coleman's features as he assessed the situation.

He looked around—Ironspine warriors had formed a complete encirclement, at least thirty massive wolves whose eyes glowed with murderous intent in the moonlight, all focused on him and his remaining forces.

Coleman signaled a retreat to his warriors, then turned and fled toward the castle.

The other Darkfang fighters hesitated only a moment before following in chaotic retreat, their footsteps scattered and panicked, looking like whipped dogs. Their retreating forms were pathetic in the moonlight, all their earlier arrogance completely stripped away.

CHAPTER TWENTY-THREE

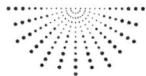

Drake

The Darkfang Pack warriors turned and fled, their silhouettes pathetic and panicked in the moonlight.

But I couldn't let them escape.

"Stop them!" I slowly shifted back to human form, my bones cracking audibly. I roared, my voice hoarse from pain but still filled with authority.

I couldn't let them retreat to the castle. Once they fell back to those fortifications, we'd pay a much steeper price to break through. And Coleman still had intel on Ryan, still knew our personnel deployment. He couldn't leave here alive.

Today, we had to end the Darkfang Pack threat once and for all.

The Ironspine Pack warriors immediately understood, dozens of massive wolves flanking from both sides, cutting off the Darkfang Pack's retreat. Under the moonlight, black, gray, and brown wolf shadows intertwined, low growls rising and falling, shaking the night sky.

"Damn it!" Coleman stopped in his tracks, turned around, his face dark as thunder. He raised another silver blade in his hand, his eyes glowing with crazed green light.

"Drake, you think with injuries this bad, you can still stop me?"

I stood between Phoebe and Ryan, my legs trembling slightly but still steady. Blood was still flowing from the shoulder wound, dripping down my leg and forming a pool on the ground. Every breath pulled at the wound, pain shooting through my entire body like electric current.

But I couldn't fall.

"You're not going anywhere." My voice was pure killing intent.

Coleman suddenly burst into maniacal laughter, the sound piercing and insane, echoing through the night sky. "Drake, you're such a foolish Alpha! For a woman and a pup, you actually got yourself this messed up!"

His gaze turned even more sinister. "You think we just guessed today was the perfect time to strike? You think we just happened to know about the pup's existence?"

My heart clenched.

"It was your good friend who told us!" Coleman grinned wickedly, his voice dripping with mockery. "Your childhood sweetheart, that omega called Sera! She personally called us, said if we grabbed Ryan, we could force you to give up your Alpha position!"

What? Sera? My body froze, my mind spinning in chaos. No... impossible...

"That's right, her!" Coleman continued, savoring my shocked expression. "She said she was the one who deserved you, said that outsider woman wasn't worthy of you! She hates you, hates that you abandoned her for some fake omega! So she contacted us, provided all the intel—the pup's existence, your whereabouts, even today's plan!"

"No... it's not like that..." A trembling voice came from behind. I turned around. From the back of the crowd, a familiar figure stumbled forward.

Sera.

She wore a dark cloak, her long hair disheveled, her face deathly pale. Tears streamed down her cheeks, her eyes red and swollen, her whole body shaking like a leaf in autumn.

"Sera?" Kay looked at her in surprise. "What are you doing here?"

"I... I..." Sera's voice trembled, barely able to speak. Her gaze fell on the wound on my shoulder, seeing that blood-soaked injury, her face grew even paler, her body swaying, nearly unable to stand.

"Sera!" Coleman saw her, his face breaking into a triumphant smile. "Perfect timing! Come see your handiwork! Come see the man you personally destroyed!"

"No... it's not..." Sera shook her head, tears flowing endlessly. "I didn't mean... I just wanted..."

"You just wanted Drake to come back to you, right?" Coleman sneered.

"Too bad, you were too naive. You thought we'd actually help you? We don't want to help you win back some Alpha—we want the entire Ironspine Pack!"

He raised the silver blade in his hand, moonlight reflecting off the steel with blinding coldness.

"Once Drake's dead, the Ironspine Pack will be leaderless, and we can take over the whole territory! By then, this land, these pack members—all ours!"

Sera's face went ashen, her whole body shaking as if struck by lightning.

"You... you used me..." Her voice trembled. "From the beginning you... you just wanted to use me to destroy the Ironspine Pack..."

"Just figured it out? Too late!" Coleman laughed maniacally. "Thank you, Sera! Thank you for helping us eliminate the biggest obstacle! Once Drake's dead, the Ironspine Pack is ours!"

He stepped toward me, the silver blade raised high. In the moonlight, his shadow stretched long like Death's scythe.

"Drake, die!"

I gritted my teeth, ready to fight. Though the wound was still bleeding, though my body was weak to the extreme, I couldn't fall. Phoebe and Ryan were behind me, Ironspine Pack warriors were watching me. As Alpha, I had to fight to the last moment.

Just then, Sera suddenly screamed, "No!"

She rushed forward, arms spread wide, blocking my path, tears streaming. "Enough! Stop hurting him! It's all my fault! If you want to kill someone, kill me!"

"Sera, move aside," I growled, my voice hoarse.

"No!" She shook her head, tears flowing endlessly.

"Drake, I'm sorry, I'm so sorry... I didn't know it would turn out like this... I was just so jealous. I saw you and Phoebe so happy, saw you had a child, and I just... I lost my mind..."

Her voice grew more choked:

"But I never wanted to hurt you... I swear! I just wanted... wanted you to notice me... wanted you to know she wasn't worthy of you... but I really never thought about taking your life... I never thought the Darkfang Pack would..."

"Enough." I cut her off, my voice low. "What's the point of saying this now?"

"I know..." Sera sobbed uncontrollably.

"I know I committed an unforgivable sin... but please... please let me make amends... even with my life..."

Coleman sneered, "Touching confession. Too bad, it's too late. You all have to die!"

He raised the silver blade, about to strike down.

I was about to lunge forward when Sera suddenly turned around, desperately grabbing Coleman's arm. "Run! Drake, take them and run!"

"You asked for it!" Coleman kicked Sera, sending her crashing to the ground with a scream.

In that instant, my mind raced.

Sera had indeed committed an unforgivable error. Her jealousy and stupidity had nearly cost me Ryan, nearly put Phoebe in danger.

But now wasn't the time for blame.

The Darkfang Pack was the real enemy. And Sera... though she'd made mistakes, as one of the few pack members skilled in the ancient mechanisms, her knowledge might be the key to breaking this deadlock.

I needed to use that.

"Sera." I suddenly spoke, my voice low and powerful.

She looked up, her face covered in tears, her eyes full of guilt and despair.

"You want to make amends?" I stared into her eyes.

"Yes... I'll do anything..." she sobbed.

"Good." My voice became cold and determined. "Listen, the Darkfang Pack couldn't have built such tight defenses from nothing. They must be using the castle's original Moonlight Pack System. Find the core that controls these systems!"

Sera froze. As an expert in ancient mechanisms, she immediately understood what I meant.

I didn't give her time to hesitate. "I don't care where it's hidden. Based on Moonlight Pack's architectural conventions, go find it, shut down all defenses—alarms, traps, mechanisms, leave nothing operational! This is your only chance."

"West side!" Sera practically blurted out, her eyes sharpening with professional instinct. "The Moonlight Pack always put the core in the western underground... I can find it!"

"Ten minutes." My command brooked no argument.

Sera looked at me, tears still flowing, but hope flickered in her eyes: "I... I'll definitely complete it!"

"Wait!" Coleman caught on, his face changing drastically. "You can't—"

"Kay!" I roared. "Cover her!"

"Yes!" Kay immediately charged with several warriors, blocking Coleman.

Sera took the chance to turn and run, her figure quickly disappearing into the night.

"Damn it! Damn it!" Coleman frantically swung the silver blade, trying to chase after her, but Kay's team held him tight. "You idiots! Let me go!"

I took a deep breath, fighting through the wound's agony, and commanded all the warriors:

"Everyone listen! We have ten minutes! When the defense system shuts down, we storm the castle with everything we've got and wipe out the Darkfang Pack completely!"

"Yes!" The warriors responded in unison, their voices shaking the sky.

"But Alpha, your injury..." Kay looked at me worriedly.

"I'm fine," I said through gritted teeth, though my body was weak to the extreme. "Kay, take Phoebe and Ryan somewhere safe."

"No, I want to fight alongside you." Phoebe's voice came from behind, firm and stubborn.

I turned around to see her holding Ryan, her eyes red and swollen but filled with determination. Ryan was also looking at me, his small hand reaching out, wanting to touch me.

"Mom's right, we stick together." Ryan's voice was small but serious. "Dad's hurt, we need to protect Dad."

My heart jumped, warmth flooding through me.

"Alright," I said quietly. "Then stay close to me, don't leave my side."

"Okay!"

Coleman saw this scene, and his face twisted into a savage grin. "What a touching family moment! Too bad, you're all going to die here!"

He barked an order, and the remaining Darkfang Pack warriors all charged forward.

The battle erupted again.

Under the moonlight, wolf shadows intertwined, blades clashed, blood sprayed. The air was thick with the smell of blood and gunpowder, mixed with beast roars and human screams.

I fought through the pain, shifting again, clamping my jaws around a Darkfang Pack warrior's throat, tearing hard as warm blood sprayed across my face. He screamed and fell, twitching a few times before going still.

Another enemy lunged from the side. I dodged and raked my claws across his belly, spilling his guts.

Each attack pulled at my shoulder wound, the pain nearly making me lose consciousness. Blood kept flowing, my vision blurred more and more, my body grew heavier and heavier.

But I couldn't fall.

Absolutely couldn't.

Phoebe shifted to half-wolf state, protecting Ryan while joining the fight, covering my flanks against sudden attacks.

"Drake, watch out!" Phoebe suddenly screamed.

I spun around to see a Darkfang Pack warrior dropping from a tree, dagger in hand, aimed straight at my neck.

No time to dodge. Just then, a black shadow shot forward, knocking the warrior aside.

It was Kay. He shifted back to human form, grappling with the warrior and quickly subduing him.

"Alpha, your injury's too severe!" Kay panted. "You need treatment now!"

"Not yet," I said through gritted teeth in human form. "We have to wait for the defense system to shut down..."

"Report!" A warrior suddenly ran over. "The alarms at the castle have stopped!"

My heart jumped. Sera succeeded?

Sure enough, seconds later, the castle gates slowly creaked open with heavy groans. The defensive lights that had been blazing went out one by one, plunging the entire castle into darkness.

"No! No!" Coleman's face changed drastically. "Damn Sera! Damn her!"

"Now!" I roared. "Everyone, storm the castle! Leave no one alive!"

"Yes!"

The warriors howled as they charged toward the castle like a black flood.

I forced my body forward, following the pack. Phoebe stayed close with Ryan, never leaving my side.

Inside the castle was chaos.

The air was thick with the heavy smell of blood, mixed with the sweat of fear and the stench of entrails, sharp and nauseating.

Screams echoed throughout the castle.

These people had kidnapped my son, threatened my mate, wanted to destroy my pack. They didn't deserve to live.

"Kill them all," I repeated the command coldly.

The warriors attacked even more savagely, showing no mercy.

I walked through the corridors to the great hall.

Coleman was there with only several followers left, their backs against the wall, terror in their eyes.

"Drake..." Coleman's voice shook. "We can talk... I can give you anything... territory, wealth, just spare me..."

I walked toward him slowly, each step heavy. Blood dripped down my leg, leaving a trail on the floor.

"Please... I was wrong..." Coleman dropped to his knees, tears streaming. "Spare me... please..."

I stopped in front of him, looking down.

This once arrogant Darkfang Pack Alpha now knelt, trembling all over, snot and tears flowing.

"You threatened my family," I said quietly, my voice cold as ice. "This is the price." I quickly bared my fangs—half-wolf state—and stepped forward, clamping down on his throat.

"No—"

His words cut off.

Warm blood flooded my mouth, tasting of salt and metal. His body convulsed violently, hands struggling uselessly before going limp.

I released him, his corpse hitting the ground hard, eyes wide open, dying with unfinished business.

The remaining Darkfang Pack warriors completely crumbled, some begging on their knees, others turning to flee.

But none escaped.

Ironspine Pack warriors appeared like ghosts in every corner, harvesting every life.

Half an hour later, the battle was over.

"Alpha." Kay approached, also covered in blood. "The Darkfang Pack has been completely eliminated. Our casualties... twelve injured, three seriously wounded, no deaths."

I nodded. Though my shoulder wound still throbbed, hearing this result brought relief.

"Well done," I said, my voice hoarse from pain. "Get the medical team to treat the wounded, increase security, watch for stragglers."

"Yes!" Kay immediately went to make arrangements.

After the battle ended, Phoebe's tense nerves finally relaxed. Ryan had exhausted his strength and fallen into deep sleep. She gently placed Ryan on a spread blanket, her fingers softly stroking his sweat-dampened hair. Taking a deep breath, she turned toward me.

"Let me look at your wound first." Phoebe's voice trembled, her eyes red and swollen, clearly having cried again. "You've lost so much blood... it must hurt terribly..."

In the moonlight, her face was pale, her hair disheveled, her clothes stained with dirt and grime. But when those eyes looked at me, they were full of heartache and worry.

"Sit down." She helped me sit on a stone, her voice carrying a commanding tone. "Let me see."

I let her examine the wound.

Phoebe gently touched my shoulder, her movements light and careful, afraid of causing pain. When she saw the deep gash, tears welled up again.

"So deep..." she choked out, her trembling fingers hovering near the wound's edge. "It must hurt so much..."

"It's alright," I said quietly, reaching out to hold her hand. "The silver poisoning's troublesome, but not fatal. A few days' rest and I'll be fine."

"It's all my fault..." Phoebe's tears fell like raindrops. "If it wasn't for saving me and Ryan, you wouldn't have gotten hurt this badly..."

"Don't talk nonsense." I lifted my hand to wipe the tears from her face, my thumb gently stroking her cheek. "Protecting you two is my responsibility and my instinct. I don't regret it."

"But..."

"No buts." I interrupted her. "You and Ryan are safe. That's enough."

Phoebe looked at me, tears still flowing, but her eyes were full of tenderness and emotion.

"Where's the medical kit?" she asked Kay.

"Right here!" Kay immediately brought over a medical kit.

Phoebe opened the box, taking out antiseptic and bandages. Her movements were careful and gentle, like handling the most precious treasure.

"This might sting a bit, bear with it," she said softly.

The cold liquid hit the wound, pain instantly shooting through my body. I gritted my teeth, suppressing a groan.

Phoebe treated the wound while constantly blowing on it, like comforting a child. "There, it won't hurt soon..."

Her voice was soft, trembling, tears still flowing endlessly.

I watched her focused profile, warmth filling my heart.

Just then, footsteps approached.

"Drake..."

A trembling voice spoke. I turned to see Sera being supported by two warriors.

She looked terrible—clothes torn and ragged, cuts and bruises covering her face and arms. Her hair was disheveled, matted with blood and dust. Her eyes were severely swollen, tear tracks marking her face.

She stopped a few meters away. The warriors released her, but her legs gave out, struggling to stay upright.

"Drake..." her voice choked, tears flowing endlessly. "I'm sorry, truly sorry..."

"I-I committed an unforgivable sin..." her voice grew more choked, her whole body trembling. "I shouldn't have betrayed you all out of jealousy... betrayed Ryan... I almost got you killed..."

She raised her head, face covered in tears, eyes full of regret, pain, and despair. "I was wrong. If I could do it over, I wouldn't do such a thing... I..."

The clearing fell silent except for her suppressed sobs echoing in the night sky.

I looked at her, complex emotions stirring within me.

Sera had grown up with me since childhood, once a good friend.

"Sera," I spoke, my voice low and calm.

She jerked her head up, hope and fear flashing in her eyes.

"You did make a serious mistake." I looked directly into her eyes.

"Your jealousy and foolishness put my son in danger, frightened my mate, and nearly destroyed the Ironspine Pack."

Sera's face went even paler, her body shaking violently.

"But..." I paused. "You did shut down the defense system at the end, allowing us to quickly defeat the Darkfang Pack. That counts as redemption through merit."

"Drake..." Sera's tears flowed even harder.

"Reflect well," I continued. "I hope you understand that jealousy and hatred only destroy everything."

"I understand now." Sera nodded vigorously, sobbing uncontrollably. "Thank you for still giving me a chance..."

She turned to look at Phoebe, her eyes full of guilt and pleading. "Phoebe, I'm sorry. I-I was too jealous that you could be with Drake and that you had Ryan, but I really shouldn't have done such things. I'm sorry..."

Phoebe stopped her work and looked up at Sera.

"Honestly, you put Ryan in danger, and I'm filled with anger toward you." Her voice was soft, but every word clear. "As a mother, I can't forgive anyone who might harm my child."

Sera's body trembled slightly, not daring to meet Phoebe's eyes.

"But," Phoebe sighed softly, "I also saw your final choice. At the crucial moment, you found your conscience again and used your actions to make amends."

Her gaze fell on the wounds covering Sera's body, her tone becoming gentler. "These injuries must have made you deeply understand the price of your mistakes. Since Ryan returned safely, and you are truly repentant, I think we all need to give each other a chance to move forward."

Sera cried so hard her whole body shook, unable to speak.

"Go," Phoebe said gently. "Heal well, reflect well. I hope you can find true happiness in the future."

Sera looked at Phoebe with shock, gratitude, and guilt in her eyes, then stumbled away with the warriors' support.

I looked at Phoebe, deeply moved.

"You're so kind," I said quietly.

"I just..." Phoebe lowered her head, continuing to treat my wound. "I just don't want the hatred to continue. Ryan is safe, the Darkfang Pack is defeated, what should be let go should be let go."

She looked up into my eyes. "Besides, if I don't forgive her, she'll live in guilt and pain for the rest of her life. I don't want that."

I reached out to caress her cheek, my thumb gently wiping away the tear tracks on her face.

"I'm so lucky to have you," I said softly.

Phoebe blushed, but her eyes grew brighter. "Because we're fated mates."

She continued treating the wound, her movements gentle and careful. Moonlight bathed her, making her seem to glow.

Not far away, Ryan turned over, mumbling "Mommy..." then continued sleeping soundly.

CHAPTER TWENTY-FOUR

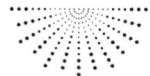

Phoebe

After the Darkfang Pack was completely defeated, I sat in the car on our way back, holding Ryan tightly.

He was sleeping deeply, his small face nestled in the curve of my neck, his breathing steady and gentle. After everything we'd been through, he could finally sleep peacefully. I gently patted his back while keeping my eyes fixed on the window.

Night was gradually fading, and a pale glow appeared on the horizon. Dawn filtered through the gaps in the forest, casting dappled shadows on the ground. The air carried that distinctive morning humidity, mixed with the scents of earth and dew.

But my heart remained clenched with worry.

Drake was in another car. Kay said he needed to lie flat to prevent his wound from worsening. I had wanted to stay with him, but Kay insisted that vehicle had more space and was better suited for an injured person.

I had no choice but to agree.

When our convoy stopped in front of the Ironspine Pack castle, daylight had fully arrived.

Sunlight bathed the castle's stone walls, illuminating the ivy-covered windows. Warriors began bustling about—some taking inventory of supplies, others tending to the wounded.

I stepped out of the car with Ryan in my arms and immediately looked toward Drake's vehicle.

Several warriors were carefully lifting a stretcher from the car. Drake lay on it.

My heart lurched, and my feet moved of their own accord.

Drake's eyes were closed, his face pallid in the morning light. His shoulder was wrapped in thick gauze, the white bandages stark in the sunlight. His brow was slightly furrowed, as if he were enduring pain.

"Drake..." I called softly, my voice trembling.

No response. His eyes remained closed.

"The Alpha needs rest," a warrior said quietly to me. "We're taking him to the master bedroom to recover."

I nodded, my throat tight, unable to speak.

The warriors carried the stretcher into the castle, and I followed. The castle was quiet except for footsteps echoing through the corridors. Sunlight streamed through the tall windows, casting long shadows across the floor.

We first stopped at a guest room on the second floor, where Kay had me settle Ryan.

The room was warm and comfortable, with a large, soft bed. I gently placed Ryan on it and tucked him in. He rolled over and continued sleeping.

I kissed his forehead and whispered, "Mama's going to check on Papa. Sleep well."

Leaving the guest room, I hurried upstairs. In the hallway, I encountered Kay and a white-coated doctor emerging from a room.

"Phoebe." Kay nodded when he saw me. "This is Dr. Brown, the best private physician in our pack. He just finished examining the Alpha."

"Doctor, how is Drake?" I rushed over, asking anxiously, my fingers unconsciously gripping my clothes. "His injury... is it serious?"

Dr. Brown adjusted his glasses, his expression grave. "The Alpha's wound is deep, and silver poisoning has spread through his system.

Fortunately, we cleaned the toxins from the wound in time, but recovery will take time."

"How... how long before he's better?" My voice grew smaller, my heart pounding as if it might burst from my chest.

"At least a week of bed rest." After providing some care instructions, Dr. Brown departed.

Kay's expression grew somber. He remained silent for a moment before speaking. "Phoebe... the Alpha's condition... isn't very good."

"What the doctor said was the basic situation," Kay continued, his expression serious, his voice lowered. "But in reality, the silver poisoning has spread more severely than expected. The Alpha has been coughing constantly, and he's very pale—he looks quite weak. He needs proper rest, at least a week... no, possibly longer."

"How could this..." Tears instantly welled up in my eyes, blurring my vision.

The doctor had just said he'd be fine with rest. How had it suddenly become worse?

"Try not to worry too much," Kay consoled me, patting my shoulder. "With proper care, the Alpha will be fine. During this time, it'll be hard on you to look after him. He really... needs you now."

"I understand." I wiped away my tears, took a deep breath, and tried to calm myself. "I'll take good care of him."

Kay nodded and left.

I stood in the hallway, my mind in turmoil.

Drake's injury was worse than I had imagined... He must be in so much pain, yet still trying to act normal in front of me...

No, I had to go see him.

I took several deep breaths, dried my tears, and quietly pushed open the door to enter the room.

Drake was lying in bed, his brow furrowed, his face indeed somewhat pale. Sunlight fell across him, making him appear even more fragile.

Just then, he began coughing.

The coughing sounded weak and raspy, as if something were lodged in his throat. It was heartbreaking to hear.

"Drake!" I hurried to the bedside. "Are you all right?"

"I'm... fine..." He opened his eyes to look at me, forcing a weak smile. "Just... a little uncomfortable..."

"Don't speak." I sat beside the bed and gently took his hand. It was burning hot—clearly he had a fever. "Just rest."

I leaned down and softly kissed his injured shoulder.

The moment my lips touched the gauze, I could feel the temperature of the wound beneath—much hotter than anywhere else. Through the bandage, I seemed to sense the wound pulsing, as if it had its own heartbeat. That heat made my chest ache so intensely I could barely breathe.

Tears dripped onto the gauze, dampening a small area and spreading dark stains across the white bandage.

"It's all my fault..." I sobbed, my voice breaking. "If you hadn't saved me and Ryan, you wouldn't be hurt this badly... wouldn't be suffering like this..."

More tears fell, one after another, like unstoppable rain.

"Phoebe..." Drake's voice suddenly changed—no longer weak, but filled with deep guilt.

I looked up, puzzled.

His expression grew awkward, his eyes shifting, unable to meet mine directly, like a child caught misbehaving.

"What's wrong?" I wiped my tears. "Are you feeling worse? Should I call the doctor..."

"No." Drake suddenly sat up, moving with agility that completely contradicted someone who should be bedridden with serious injuries.

I froze, tears still on my face.

"How are you..."

"I..." Drake ran his hand through his hair, looking extremely embarrassed, his ears even reddening. "I'm actually... not that badly hurt."

"What?" I didn't comprehend, my mind blank.

"I mean," Drake cleared his throat, his voice returning to normal strength, "my injury does hurt, but it's not as serious as Kay described.

The silver poisoning is spreading, but not enough to make me as weak as I appeared."

I stared at him wide-eyed, my mind in chaos, taking a long time to understand what he was saying.

"So... you were... pretending to be sicker than you are?" My voice began trembling.

"Not exactly pretending." Drake tried to defend himself awkwardly, his voice growing smaller. "Just exaggerated a little bit. I asked Kay to say those things. And that coughing just now was deliberate..."

"A little bit?!" My voice rose, a mixture of anger and hurt. "Kay said your condition wasn't good! Said you'd been coughing constantly! Said you needed at least a week of rest, possibly longer!"

"Well, I do need a few days of rest..." Drake attempted to justify himself, but his voice grew quieter.

I was too angry to speak, tears still streaking my face.

"You deceived me?" My voice shook. "Do you know how worried I was? Do you know how terrified I was just now? I thought you really..."

"I'm sorry, I'm sorry." Drake immediately reached out to embrace me, his expression full of remorse. "I truly didn't mean to. I just wanted—"

"What?" I pushed his hands away, glaring at him furiously, tears still flowing.

"I wanted..." Drake scratched his head, his voice becoming tiny as a whisper. "I wanted you to care about me more, wanted you to pay more attention to me. As an injured person, shouldn't I receive some special treatment?"

I looked at him, torn between anger and amusement, tears still on my face.

This formidable Alpha of the Ironspine Pack, who had just yesterday triumphantly defeated the Darkfang Pack, was now acting like a child wheedling for candy?

"Are you being childish?" I poked his forehead.

"I am not." Drake caught my hand, speaking earnestly. "I just...

wanted you to spend more time with me... wanted you to know that I need you..."

Looking at his serious yet aggrieved expression, I took a deep breath and suddenly laughed.

"You know," I wiped my tears, my voice carrying a hint of mischief as I pinched the soft flesh at his waist hard, "I was just thinking that if you really became unconscious, I'd go find a new Alpha."

Drake's face instantly transformed, his eyes widening in shock. "What?!"

"That's right," I said deliberately, pinching him again. "Since you're practically at death's door anyway, and I'd be lonely with just Ryan, I might as well find someone new. There are so many excellent betas in the Ironspine Pack. Kay is quite nice—reliable, good with Ryan, and handsome too..."

"Phoebe!" Drake bolted upright, his previous weakness vanishing completely.

He pulled me into his arms in one swift motion, his voice filled with obvious tension, jealousy, and anger. "You wouldn't dare! I'm perfectly alive! And Kay is my subordinate—don't even think about it!"

"Oh, but aren't you practically dying?" I struggled in his embrace, unable to suppress my laughter. "Kay said you need at least a week of rest, possibly longer. Who knows..."

"I feel like I could live for decades more! No, centuries!" Drake said through gritted teeth, his eyes blazing with fire. "Don't even think about finding someone else. You're mine! Forever!"

"But your injury..." I reminded him teasingly.

"What injury? I'm perfectly fine!" Drake declared, then leaned down to capture my lips.

His kiss was punishing—dominant and scorching, as if he wanted to melt me entirely. His tongue forced past my lips, claiming every inch of sweetness within my mouth. I struggled briefly before surrendering to his kiss, my arms winding around his neck.

"Do you still dare talk about finding someone else?" He released my lips, his voice husky, his breath hot against my face.

"I wouldn't dare..." I gasped, my cheeks burning, my entire body soft in his arms.

"I don't believe you." Drake leaned down, trailing kisses along my neck, each one sending electric currents through me. "I need to make sure you remember exactly who you belong to."

His hands became bold, unbuttoning my clothes. The instant his fingers touched my skin, I couldn't help but tremble.

"Drake..." My voice quavered.

"Yeah?" He looked up at me, his eyes burning with desire.

His scorching palm pressed against my bare spine with undeniable force, pulling me deeper against him...

His lips crashed back onto mine like he was starving, all desperate hunger and raw need that hit me like a freight train. I could taste it on him—the sharp tang of salt from his skin, like he'd been holding back for hours and now the dam had busted wide open. His tongue swept in, demanding, teasing, and I met him stroke for stroke, my own hunger clawing its way up from deep in my gut. Goddess, it felt like every nerve in my body was lit up, buzzing.

His hands—those big, calloused hands that I'd fantasized about more times than I could count—roamed over me with this slight tremble, like he was barely holding it together. Fingers traced the curve of my waist, dipped into the hollow of my hip, then slid up to cup my breast, thumb brushing over my nipple in a way that made me gasp into his mouth. Fire shot straight through me, hot and electric, pooling low in my belly. I arched up against him without thinking, my body begging for more, a soft moan slipping out that I couldn't stifle even if I'd wanted to. It was embarrassing how needy I sounded, but screw it—this was Drake, and after five damn years, I wasn't holding back shit.

He pulled back just enough to trail his mouth down my jaw, nipping at the skin there before burying his face in the crook of my neck. His breath came hot and ragged against my throat, sending shivers racing down my spine. "You're mine," he growled, voice all gravel and smoke, roughened by that thick desire he couldn't hide. It wasn't a question; it was a brand, sinking into me like ink under skin. "Say it, Phoebe. I need to hear you say it."

The words hung there, heavy and electric, and something twisted inside me—equal parts thrill and terror at how much I wanted this, wanted him owning every inch of me. I tilted my head back, giving him better access, my fingers diving into that thick hair of his, tugging just hard enough to make him hiss. "I'm yours," I breathed out, the confession tumbling free like it'd been bottled up forever. "All yours, Drake. Have been since the second you walked back into my life."

That did it. His response hit like a summer storm—immediate, overwhelming, no warning. Those strong hands of his hooked under my thighs, lifting me off the bed like I weighed nothing, all easy power and zero hesitation. I wrapped my legs around his waist on instinct, feeling the heat of him pressing right where I ached most, and damn if that didn't make my head spin. He shifted us in one fluid move, settling me back against the pillows with my back propped up just so, knees bent and spread wide like an invitation he was dying to accept. The cool sheets contrasted with the furnace of his body, and when he lowered himself over me, skin sliding against skin—smooth and slick with a light sheen of sweat—it was intoxicating. Warm, solid, every inch of him screaming male in the best way: the broad span of his shoulders blocking out the dim lamplight, the flex of his abs against my belly, the rough scrape of stubble on my inner thigh as he nudged it wider.

I could feel his heart hammering against my chest, this wild, frantic drum that synced up perfectly with mine—like we'd been tuned to the same beat all along, just waiting for this moment to let loose. My own pulse thundered in my ears, a roar that drowned out everything but us, and I pressed my palm flat over his pec, feeling the heat radiate through him. "Drake," I whispered, half plea, half prayer, my nails digging in just a little because I needed to ground myself in something real.

His eyes locked on mine then, dark and stormy, pupils blown wide with want. He didn't say a word at first, just let one hand drift lower, bolder now, fingers tracing the slick heat between my legs with a possessiveness that made my breath hitch. He circled slow, teasing, watching my face like he was memorizing every twitch, every flutter of my lashes. "Tell me you need me," he demanded, voice dropping an octave, all command wrapped in velvet. It wasn't gentle; it was a challenge, his touch growing firmer, more insistent, like he was staking his claim right there.

The words ripped out of me before I could think to play coy. "I need you," I gasped, the admission tearing free from that raw, hidden place inside where I'd buried all my loneliness these past years. My hips bucked up into his hand, chasing the friction, and I didn't care how desperate it sounded. "Only you, Drake. Goddess, only you —please."

That broke him. Whatever thin thread of restraint he'd been clinging to snapped like a guitar string under too much tension. His mouth slammed down on mine again, fierce and devouring, swallowing my gasp whole as he angled his hips and thrust home in one smooth, deep stroke. I cried out his name—sharp and broken—my back bowing off the mattress as he filled me completely, stretching me in that perfect, aching way that blurred the line between pleasure and pain. He froze for a beat, buried to the hilt, our breaths mingling in harsh pants, his forehead pressed to mine like he was afraid I'd vanish if he blinked.

"Easy, baby," he murmured, voice wrecked, one hand stroking down my side in long, soothing sweeps while the other braced beside my head. But there was no easing into it after that—time lost all meaning, dissolving into this hazy blur where the world narrowed to just Drake. Just the exquisite torment of his hands gripping my hips hard enough to bruise, guiding me into his rhythm; just the wet slide of his lips over my collarbone, sucking marks into the skin like he wanted to tattoo his name there. The heat between us built slow at first, a smoldering fire that licked higher with every roll of his hips, every grind that hit that spot inside me just right. It threatened to swallow us both, this inferno of need that had simmered for years, now roaring out of control.

I lost myself in it—the way his muscles bunched under my palms as I clawed at his back, leaving red trails I'd apologize for later; the low, guttural groans he let loose against my ear, each one vibrating through me like a bass line I could feel in my bones. Sweat slicked our skin, making us glide together slick and seamless, and I wrapped my legs tighter around him, heels digging into the small of his back to pull him deeper. "More," I begged, voice hoarse, head thrashing on the pillow. "Don't stop—fuck, Drake, don't you dare stop."

He didn't. If anything, he ramped it up, thrusts turning harder, faster, the bed creaking under us like it might give out any second. When the wave finally crested, it hit me like a goddamn tsunami—pleasure exploding outward in white-hot bursts, my walls clenching around him as I shattered, crying out his name in a sob that echoed off the walls. Stars burst behind my eyelids, my whole body seizing up in the best kind of overload, toes curling into the sheets.

Drake held me through every shudder, every aftershock, his arms like steel bands around me, one hand fisting the sheets beside my head while the other tangled in my hair, tilting my face up so he could watch. "That's it, Phoebe," he whispered, lips brushing my temple, my cheek, the shell of my ear—words of possession and devotion spilling out like he'd been saving them up. "Mine. All mine. Love how you feel, how you take me... fuck, you're everything." It marked me deeper than any hickey or scratch, sinking into my soul, rewriting the lonely chapters I'd written alone.

I collapsed onto his chest, boneless and spent, his arms wrapping around me tight as release pulsed between us, hot and endless. "Yours, forever," I promised, the word muffled against his neck, tasting salt and skin and home. I meant it with every damn fiber of my being—through the ache in my muscles, the throb in my heart, the quiet certainty settling in my bones. This was us, finally whole. No more running, no more waiting. Just Drake and me, tangled up and unbreakable.

Much later, I lay completely spent in Drake's arms, feeling as though every bone in my body had dissolved, lacking the strength to lift even a finger.

My cheek rested against his sweat-dampened chest, still rising and falling gently, and I listened to his gradually steadying heartbeat like the most soothing lullaby.

The air still carried the lingering scent of our passion, a reminder of how wild and consuming everything had been.

His strong arms encircled my waist, keeping me securely within his domain, his chin resting gently atop my head.

"Will you do that again?" His voice carried post-passion languor and huskiness, along with a trace of lingering dominance.

I didn't even have the energy to shake my head, managing only a soft hum through my nose to indicate I wouldn't dare.

My heart swelled with a mixture of sweetness and helpless affection. This powerful werewolf, who could sometimes be as childish as a little boy, had used his most direct method to dispel all my insecurities while declaring his undeniable ownership over me.

CHAPTER TWENTY-FIVE

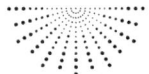

Drake

The full moon hung like a silver disk overhead, its pale light spilling across the ancient open-air assembly square of the Ironspine Pack. A massive bonfire blazed at the center of the grounds, its dancing flames weaving with the bright moonlight to cast a sacred glow over this special night.

My injuries had healed quickly this past week. The silver poison had been mostly purged from my system, and the wound on my shoulder had begun to close. Though I still couldn't handle intense physical activity, daily movements posed no problem.

Phoebe had been watching over me these past few days, terrified something else might happen. Every time she changed my bandages, she'd clean the wound with the careful touch of someone handling their most precious treasure.

Ryan came to see me every day, too. The little guy would climb onto the bed and carefully lean against my uninjured side, telling me about his day—what he'd done, what he'd seen.

This feeling of being surrounded by family brought me happiness I'd never known before.

But I knew there was one important thing left to do—tonight, under this full moon's radiance, at this solemn Pack Meeting.

Pack members sat in circles around the bonfire, their faces mixing confusion and anticipation. Moonlight and firelight illuminated every face with startling clarity. The air carried the clean scent of burning pine, mingled with the faint pheromones of the werewolves and that unique energy pulsing through our blood on full moon nights.

The elders sat in the front row, expressions grave. I stood on the stone platform built before the bonfire, my gaze sweeping over everyone present.

Phoebe sat in the first row, Ryan cradled in her arms. Moonlight draped her gently, making her seem to glow. She looked at me with eyes full of encouragement and support.

Kay stood beside me, holding a stack of documents.

I took a deep breath and began, my voice carrying clear and strong in the moonlight.

"Elders, pack members. Tonight, under the moon's witness, at this Pack Meeting, there are things I need to publicly explain to everyone."

The square fell quiet. Everyone looked at me—only the fire's crackling and distant forest winds broke the silence.

"Five years ago, for the Ironspine Pack's benefit, I agreed to a marriage alliance with another pack." I continued. "At the time, the Grayclaw Pack was facing bankruptcy from territorial invasion and proposed an arranged marriage. As Alpha, I accepted this arrangement."

The elders nodded. They knew all this.

"But in reality," I paused, looking toward Phoebe as moonlight caught her beautiful face, "she isn't the real Grayclaw Pack heir. Her name is Phoebe, also from the Grayclaw Pack. To save her pack, she accepted the contract and assumed Elena's identity."

Murmurs rippled through the crowd, whispers spreading in the moonlight.

"Quiet." I raised my voice, and the square fell silent again.

"At the time, I was deeply suspicious of this sudden arranged marriage," I continued. "I suspected she was a spy from a rival pack, so

I arranged for my beta Kay to take my place in the arranged marriage while I posed as a business advisor to observe from the sidelines."

I looked at Kay, who nodded.

"That was my first mistake." My voice carried self-reproach. "I treated her with suspicion and testing, subjecting her to coldness and grievances she never deserved."

Phoebe's eyes reddened, and in the moonlight I could clearly see the tears she was fighting back.

"Later, on a full moon night, we discovered we were fated mates." I continued. "That attraction from deep in our bloodline was impossible to resist. But afterward, I used cruel words to reject her and told her to leave."

My voice grew hoarse. "That was my second mistake, and my greatest one."

The square was dead silent. Everyone held their breath as the full moon quietly poured down its light.

"Phoebe left carrying my child and hid in the human city for five years," I said.

"For five years, she bore everything alone—the pain of childbirth, the hardship of raising a child, uncertainty about the future. And I, through my own stupidity and arrogance, missed my child's birth and his first five years."

I paused, glancing up at the perfect moon overhead, taking a deep breath.

"Five years later, I was lucky enough to encounter Phoebe again, giving me a chance to atone for my past wrongs. Though we faced obstacles, she ultimately chose to forgive me, and we fell in love again." My voice continued echoing in the air.

"A few days ago, the Darkfang Pack tried to force me to abandon my Alpha position by kidnapping my son, Ryan. During the rescue, Phoebe showed incredible courage and wisdom. We fought side by side, successfully rescued Ryan, and defeated the Darkfang Pack."

My gaze fell on Phoebe again. Her eyes were rimmed with red, but she gave me a brilliant smile through her tears. No words were needed—I understood everything.

"Through this, I finally understood what it means to have a partner, what family truly is," I said. "Phoebe isn't a tool for a marriage alliance or some fake heir. She's my fated mate, Ryan's mother, the most important person in my life."

I stepped down from the platform and approached Phoebe. Moonlight spilled like mercury across the stone slabs between us.

I dropped to one knee and took her trembling hands.

"Phoebe." I looked into her eyes, where I could see myself reflected alongside the full moon behind me. "I owe you so much. I owe you a sincere apology, a formal commitment, a complete ceremony."

Her tears finally spilled over, dropping onto my hands like falling pearls in the moonlight.

"I'm sorry." My voice was full of sincerity. "Sorry for the suspicion and coldness, sorry for making you bear so much alone, sorry for missing Ryan's birth and childhood. All of this was my fault, my sin."

"Drake..." she choked out.

"But now, I want to make up for everything." I continued. "I want to formally propose to you in front of everyone, under the moon's witness. Not because of a marriage alliance, not because of pack interests, but because I love you. I love your courage, your kindness, your wisdom, everything about you."

I pulled a small box from my pocket and opened it, revealing a ring. It was silver, set with a blue gemstone that sparkled brilliantly in the interplay of moonlight and firelight.

I looked into Phoebe's eyes and asked in a gentle but firm tone:

"Phoebe, will you be my Luna? Not as an object of a marriage alliance, but as the other half of my life? Will you help me raise Ryan and face whatever storms the future brings?"

The square fell completely silent. Everyone held their breath, waiting for Phoebe's answer. Even the full moon seemed suspended, waiting for this crucial moment.

"I will." She said through tears, her voice trembling but firm. "I will, Drake."

The square exploded in thunderous applause and cheers.

I stood and slipped the ring onto her finger. Then I kissed her.

This kiss was gentle and brief. When I lifted my head and saw the happy tears on her lashes, it took every ounce of restraint to step back.

I released Phoebe and turned to face the crowd.

"There's one more thing," I said, signaling Kay to bring the documents over.

"This is a cooperation agreement between the Grayclaw Pack and the Ironspine Pack." I held up the papers. "I declare that the Ironspine Pack will ally with the Grayclaw Pack, supporting each other and developing together."

The Grayclaw Pack elders sat in the viewing section, their eyes shining with tears and gratitude.

I looked toward the Ironspine Pack's elders. "The Grayclaw Pack is my mate's family. They deserve our support and assistance."

Elder Eld stood up, moonlight illuminating his aged but dignified face.

"The Alpha's honesty shows us his responsibility. Phoebe is indeed his fated mate—this is destiny, and we have no reason to oppose it. And the Grayclaw Pack, as the Luna's family, deserves our support."

The other elders nodded in agreement. Pack members applauded, showing their support.

Just then, Elder Eld raised his voice in solemn proclamation.

"Since the truth is clear and the alliance is sealed, let the full moon continue witnessing the final union of this couple!"

Pack members erupted in understanding cheers, and the bonfire blazed higher.

Ryan was being held by Elias, the little guy excitedly watching us and waving his small hands.

Under the moonlight, Phoebe and I shared a smile. We walked to the bonfire.

I wore the Ironspine Pack's traditional ceremonial clothing—deep blue robes with the clan emblem embroidered on the chest, silver buttons gleaming in the firelight. The wound on my shoulder had completely healed, leaving only a faint scar like a badge of honor.

She wore a white dress with silver moon and star patterns embroidered on the hem. Her long hair flowed freely, shimmering softly in the moonlight. Around her neck was a simple necklace with a blue gemstone—matching the stone on the ring I'd given her.

I could clearly hear my own excited heartbeat. My palms were sweating, and I took a deep breath, trying to calm myself.

Her face carried a faint blush, her eyes nervous, but the moment they met mine, they filled with tenderness and love.

My breath caught.

She was beautiful.

So beautiful she made my heart race, so beautiful I almost forgot to breathe.

"Phoebe," I said quietly, my voice hoarse, "you're gorgeous tonight."

"So are you," she whispered back, blushing deeper. "I'm... a little nervous."

"Me too." I reached for her hand, and the warm, soft touch calmed me somewhat. "But don't be afraid. We're together."

She nodded, her fingers gently gripping mine back.

Elder Eld stood up, walking to the bonfire with his cane.

"Pack members," his voice was deep and powerful, echoing in the night sky, "we now formally begin the marking ritual for Alpha Drake and Luna Phoebe."

Pack members fell quiet, all eyes focused on us.

"The mate mark is sacred." Elder Eld continued. "It's not just a physical mark, but a union of souls. Once marking is complete, two lives become forever intertwined, through poverty or wealth, sickness or health, good times or bad—never to be separated."

He looked at us. "Drake, Phoebe, are you ready?"

"We're ready." We said in unison.

"Good." Elder Eld nodded. "Then let the ceremony begin."

He produced a small bowl from his robes, containing the moonlight oil Kay had given me before.

"This is moonlight oil," he said, "made from full moon dew and sacred tree resin. It purifies the body and strengthens the mark's power."

He dipped his finger in the oil and drew a symbol on my forehead, then drew the same symbol on Phoebe's.

The moment the oil touched skin, it brought a cool sensation, like moonlight itself flowing. A gentle power moved through my body, sharpening my senses.

"Now," Elder Eld said, "face each other and complete the marking."

I turned to face Phoebe, and she looked at me.

Moonlight bathed us both while firelight danced in her eyes, making them especially bright.

Her rapid breathing, the flush on her cheeks, her subtle fragrance—that unique scent belonging to her, mixing jasmine and morning dew. Everything about her was more alluring, impossible to look away from.

"Phoebe," I said quietly, a voice only we could hear. "I love you. From the first moment we met, the fated mate bond has been calling me. Though I stupidly resisted for so long, now I can finally have you without reservation."

"Drake..." tears welled up in her eyes again. I seemed to be making her cry enough tears tonight for a lifetime.

"Don't cry." I reached up to wipe the tears from her eyes, my heart aching as I comforted her. "This is our happiest moment."

"I know." She laughed through her tears. "I'm just... so happy."

I leaned down and pressed a gentle kiss to her lips.

Then I gently lifted her long hair, exposing the pale skin of her neck.

Moonlight spilled across that skin, making it appear even more fragile and tempting. I could see tiny blood vessels pulsing beneath the surface, could feel her pulse quickening.

"It'll hurt a little," I whispered, my lips against her ear. "But only for an instant."

"It's okay." Her voice was soft and trembling. "I'm not afraid."

My canines began to lengthen—a werewolf's instinctive response during marking. I could feel power surging through my body, the fated mate bond urging me to complete the mark.

I gently bit down on the skin of her neck.

The moment my teeth pierced her skin, Phoebe trembled slightly and let out a small whimper.

Warm blood flowed into my mouth, carrying her unique taste—sweetness mixed with a hint of bitter freshness, like ripe wild berries blended with herbal clarity.

The mark was forming. This wasn't just a physical wound, but a deeper connection. Our souls intertwined in this moment, the fated mate bond becoming unbreakably strong.

I felt her emotions—nervousness, pain, but more than anything, happiness and love.

I felt her heartbeat gradually syncing with mine, becoming the same rhythm.

I released my teeth and gently licked the wound, helping it stop bleeding. My saliva contained healing properties that would help the wound scab quickly.

"Done," I whispered, placing a kiss near her ear. "Now it's your turn."

Phoebe turned to look at me. Her eyes shone with golden light—the sign of awakened werewolf instincts.

She rose on her tiptoes as I cooperatively lowered my head.

Her hands rested lightly on my shoulders, fingertips trembling slightly. Then her lips approached my neck, warm breath spilling across my skin. I felt the touch of her lips—soft as feathers.

"Drake," She whispered. "Thank you for giving me a complete family."

Then she bit down.

The pain was instant, but more than that was an indescribable sense of satisfaction.

Her canines pierced my skin, and my blood flowed. But simultaneously, the mark formed on me like a warm brand, deeply carved into my soul.

Our bond was complete.

From now on, no matter how far apart we were, I would feel her presence. Feel her emotions, feel whether she was safe, feel her love for me.

This was the power of the permanent mate mark.

Phoebe released her teeth and gently licked the wound. Her movements were tender, filled with careful love.

We looked at each other, both our eyes shining with golden light.

"It's done," I whispered.

"Yes." She smiled, tears sliding down her cheeks—but they were tears of happiness.

I pulled her into my arms and held her tight.

Thunderous applause and cheers erupted around us.

Pack members stood up, howling—one voice after another echoing through the night sky.

Ryan was also waving his small hands in Elias's arms. "Daddy! Mommy!"

I loosened my hold on Phoebe slightly and waved at Ryan.

Elias set him down, and the little guy immediately ran over and threw himself into our embrace.

"Daddy and Mommy are a real family now!" he said happily.

"Yes, we're a real family now," I said, one arm around Phoebe, the other holding Ryan.

Moonlight bathed us as the bonfire's glow remained warm and bright.

Pack members began dancing around the bonfire, their songs and laughter echoing through the forest.

CHAPTER TWENTY-SIX

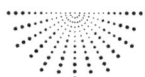

Phoebe

On this autumn evening, I stood on the Ironspine Pack castle's terrace, watching the bonfire gradually come to life in the center of the square below.

The flames danced against the twilight, casting warm, golden light across our entire pack territory. I drew in a deep breath of the crisp air, catching the scent of burning pine mixed with the aroma of roasted meat drifting from the distant kitchens.

One year.

I raised my hand to touch the back of my neck, where Drake's permanent mark rested beneath my skin. Every time I touched that spot, I could vividly recall our marking ritual on that full moon night —how tenderly, how reverently he'd kissed my neck, whispering.

"From this moment forward, you are my Luna, and I am your Alpha. Until forever."

"Mom! Come down! Everyone's waiting for you!"

Ryan's excited voice carried up from below. I leaned forward and spotted the five-year-old in his deep blue ceremonial clothing, waving enthusiastically at me from the square's edge. Drake stood beside him, his tall silhouette striking against the firelight.

Drake looked up, his deep eyes finding mine across the distance. He raised his hand, gesturing for me to join them.

I smiled and hurried down the stairs.

My moon-white gown flowed behind me, cinched at the waist with the traditional Ironspine Pack silver belt adorned with crescent-moon gems that marked my status as Luna. Drake had specially chosen it for tonight's celebration.

As I entered the square, pack members turned toward me, their faces glowing with respect and warmth.

"Luna!"

"Luna's here!"

They naturally parted to create a path, the bonfire's glow reflecting off every smiling face. All of this was real—no longer the terror of living under false pretenses, no longer the anxiety of being questioned, but genuine, heartfelt acceptance and recognition.

"Phoebe." Drake approached me, his large hand finding mine with practiced ease. "Ready?"

"Yes." I nodded, our fingers intertwining naturally.

Drake led me toward the main platform with Ryan close behind, his small hands gripping my dress.

"Everyone." Drake stood at the platform's center, his voice resonating with quiet authority. "Tonight marks the full moon and our Ironspine Pack celebration. We thank the Moon Goddess for her blessings, for granting us this year of peace and prosperity."

The pack erupted in unified cheers. Someone sounded an ancient horn, its haunting melody echoing through the night sky.

"Additionally," Drake gestured toward the large screen positioned at the square's edge, "tonight features a special presentation. We've invited distant friends to share their blessings with us."

The screen suddenly illuminated, revealing a familiar forest landscape.

My heart seized, and tears immediately welled in my eyes.

Grayclaw Pack's new territory.

Elias appeared on screen wearing traditional gray ceremonial robes, standing in the center of their pack square. Behind him, dozens of pack members had gathered, joy radiating from every face. Their new territory looked remarkably improved—lush forests, crystal-clear rivers, fertile soil.

"Phoebe, Drake, Ryan." Elias's gentle voice flowed through the speakers. "All members of Grayclaw Pack extend our most heartfelt blessings to Ironspine Pack's Luna and Alpha."

Tears spilled down my cheeks.

"Thank you for everything you've done for Grayclaw Pack," Elias continued, his voice thick with gratitude. "Phoebe, witnessing your happiness brings us immense joy. You will always remain Grayclaw Pack's most cherished daughter."

He paused, directing his gaze toward Drake.

"Drake, please treasure her. She deserves every beautiful thing this world has to offer."

Then he crouched down, waving at the camera.

"Ryan, grow strong and remember to visit Uncle Elias."

On screen, Grayclaw Pack members cheered in unison. Some raised torches high while others sounded their horns.

I couldn't stop myself from wiping my eyes, though the tears continued flowing.

Drake gently drew me closer, his arm around my shoulders as he whispered.

"Don't cry. This is a day for joy."

"I know," I managed through my tears. "I'm just so deeply moved."

Drake tenderly brushed away my tears before pressing a soft kiss to my forehead.

The screen gradually dimmed, but just as I assumed the blessing ceremony had concluded, commotion arose near the square's entrance.

I turned to see the crowd naturally parting once more.

A woman in pale purple approached slowly, carrying an enormous bouquet of vibrant wildflowers.

Sera.

The firelight played across her features, lending her an unusually gentle appearance. Her long hair cascaded over her shoulders, and her eyes held none of their former pride or hostility—only sincere warmth.

My body tensed slightly. Sensing my apprehension, Drake squeezed my hand reassuringly while whispering.

"Don't worry. She's here to offer her blessings."

Sera moved through the crowd and paused before our platform. She looked up, drawing a steadying breath.

"Phoebe, Drake." Her voice carried softly yet clearly across the entire square. "I know I've committed terrible wrongs in the past. I was consumed by jealousy, even attempted to harm you both."

She hesitated, her eyes beginning to redden.

"Yet you refused to abandon me. Drake advocated for me before the elders, and Phoebe, you chose forgiveness. Throughout this past year, I've engaged in constant self-reflection. I finally understand that genuine love isn't about possession—it's about blessing others."

Sera raised the bouquet high.

"These wildflowers were gathered by my own hands. Deep red camellias symbolize resilience, golden sunflowers represent hope, and pale pink wild roses signify new beginnings. I wish to present these to you both, blessing your future to bloom eternally like these flowers."

Her voice began trembling.

"And thank you for helping me become a better person."

Silence fell across the square.

I drew a deep breath, released Drake's hand, and descended from the platform.

Sera's body trembled slightly, uncertainty flickering across her features.

I approached her and gently accepted the bouquet.

"Thank you, Sera." My voice was quiet but deeply sincere. "And thank you for choosing to change."

Sera froze as tears immediately cascaded down her cheeks.

I embraced her gently, whispering near her ear. "What's past is finished. You're doing wonderfully now."

Sera stiffened momentarily before trembling as she returned my embrace, her voice breaking. "I'm so sorry, Phoebe. Truly sorry."

"I know," I said, patting her back softly. "But you found your way back and helped us in the end. I forgave you long ago."

When we separated, Sera's face was streaked with tears.

She turned toward Drake. "Drake, thank you for refusing to give up on me. Without your intervention, I might never have escaped that narrow, bitter version of myself."

Drake nodded, his eyes reflecting only relief. "You deserved that chance for redemption, Sera. Everyone makes mistakes. What matters is our willingness to make amends."

The square suddenly erupted in enthusiastic applause and cheers.

Ryan bounded over excitedly, tugging at Sera's dress. "Aunt Sera, will you stay for the feast?"

"Absolutely." Sera knelt down, gently stroking Ryan's hair. "I have brought you a special gift."

She retrieved an elegant wooden box from her bag. Inside lay a gleaming silver fang pendant.

"This represents our pack's most precious protective charm. Legend claims that whoever wears it receives the Moon Goddess's divine protection. Ryan, may you grow healthy and strong, becoming as formidable an Alpha as your father."

Ryan's eyes sparkled as he carefully accepted the pendant. "Thank you, Aunt Sera!"

Witnessing this scene filled my heart with profound emotion.

The bonfire blazed brighter, its light illuminating every smiling face—Drake's tender expression, Ryan's delighted laughter, Sera's tears of relief, and our pack members' heartfelt blessings.

Drake returned to my side and drew me into his embrace.

"How are you feeling?" he asked quietly.

"Wonderful." I leaned against his chest, listening to his steady heartbeat. "Better than I've ever felt."

"Good." Drake kissed my forehead. "Because this is merely the beginning, Phoebe. We still have a long journey ahead of us."

I looked up into his deep eyes and smiled, nodding.

The bonfire's glow bathed every smiling face in warmth and healing light.

In this moment, nothing from our past held any significance. What mattered was our togetherness, and whatever challenges the future might present, we would face them united, never to be separated.

The celebration continued amid joyous laughter.

I remained beside Drake, watching pack members dance and sing around the bonfire while indescribable contentment filled my heart. Ryan had long since joined the crowd, playing and chasing with the other children, their bell-like laughter ringing constantly through the air.

"By the way," Elena approached carrying two glasses of wine, offering me one. "I heard you've developed another new perfume formula?"

I accepted the cup with a nod. "Yes, an enhanced version of 'Moonlight' called 'Starlight.' I incorporated additional nerve-calming botanical elements into the original formula. It's even more effective for young wolves experiencing their first shift."

"Phoebe's 'Moonlight' perfume has been a lifesaver for so many," Kay added as he joined us, wearing an unusually cheerful expression. "During last month's group shifting ceremony, every young werewolf used 'Moonlight,' and not a single one lost control."

Drake wrapped his arm around my waist, his voice brimming with pride. "I always said my Luna was extraordinary."

"Stop that," I blushed, giving him a gentle push. "It was a team effort. Besides, without our pack members' willingness to participate in testing, I never could have developed these formulas."

Truthfully, the most fulfilling aspect of this past year had been expanding the Scent Workshop.

After relocating to Ironspine Pack territory, I gained access to more time and resources for research. I discovered that werewolves experience agony and aggression during shifting because of sudden hormonal fluctuations that overexcite the nervous system. Certain plant aromatics could effectively calm this aggression, helping werewolves adapt to shifting more smoothly.

"Moonlight" perfume emerged from this principle. Its primary components included lavender, chamomile, and mint, enhanced with herbs unique to Ironspine Pack's forests. The fragrance maintained a fresh, elegant quality while producing miraculous results during shifting.

"Phoebe," a young mother approached, cradling her cub, her eyes bright with gratitude. "Thank you for the 'Moonlight' perfume. My son experienced his first shift last week. Initially terrified, but after using your perfume, the entire process proceeded smoothly. Now he begs to practice shifting daily."

I gently touched the cub's head. "That's wonderful news. Please visit the workshop anytime if you encounter any concerns."

Each expression of appreciation from pack members reinforced my certainty that I'd discovered my true purpose.

Drake had undergone significant changes this past year as well.

He'd mastered balancing pack responsibilities with family life. Every morning, regardless of his schedule's demands, he dedicated time to help Ryan practice shifting techniques. I often watched from our window as father and son trained near the forest's edge—Drake patiently demonstrating proper form while Ryan earnestly mimicked his movements. When Ryan occasionally stumbled, Drake would approach and nuzzle him encouragingly with his wolf snout.

Evenings found us collaborating on pack administrative work. Drake would review official documents at his desk while I organized materials beside him, occasionally offering insights. During late-night sessions, I'd prepare hot tea for both of us, then lean against his shoulder while we gazed at the moon through our window.

Weekends without urgent obligations meant family forest picnics. We'd locate scenic meadows, spread blankets, and savor sunshine and gentle breezes. Ryan delighted in rolling through grass and pursuing butterflies while Drake sat beside me, monitoring his son's play and engaging in conversation.

"You know what?" Drake once said unexpectedly. "I never imagined I could have this kind of life."

"What kind of life?" I inquired.

"Having someone to love, a child, a complete family." He turned toward me, his eyes radiating tenderness. "Previously, I believed an

Alpha should devote all energy to pack welfare, that personal happiness remained secondary. After meeting you, I realized family and pack hold equal importance. Actually, family provides the strength that sustains my leadership."

That moment brought tears to my eyes.

"Come," Drake said softly, taking my hand. "Time for the next portion of our celebration."

I looked up to find the moon fully risen, suspended brilliantly in the night sky, perfectly round and luminous.

Full moon nights represented the most sacred time for werewolf packs—when the Moon Goddess granted werewolves enhanced power and when pack members traditionally gathered for collective shifting and hunting.

Drake stood prominently on the platform, his voice resonating with deep authority. "The full moon has risen. Let shifting begin!"

Pack members responded unanimously, moving toward the open ground at the square's perimeter.

I drew a deep breath and began removing my garments. Moonlight caressed my skin as I felt my wolf stirring to life, that familiar power coursing through my bloodstream.

Drake initiated his shift as well. I observed his body's gradual metamorphosis—bones elongating, muscles restructuring, dark fur emerging across his skin. Within mere seconds, he completed his shift, becoming a magnificent black wolf with amber eyes gleaming in the moonlight.

He approached and gently nuzzled my hand with his wolf snout.

I closed my eyes, relaxed completely, and allowed shifting to occur naturally. Over this past year, I'd achieved complete mastery of the shifting process. Bone reconstruction's pain had become tolerable, and my wolf nature's emergence no longer frightened me.

When I reopened my eyes, the world had been transformed.

My olfactory senses became incredibly acute—I could distinguish every scent in the air. Bonfire smoke, pack members' pheromones, and distant forest wildlife. My hearing amplified dramatically; I detected wind rustling through treetops, babbling streams, even tiny insects moving through undergrowth.

I examined myself—light brown fur, elongated limbs, and a tail swaying behind me.

"Awoo!"

Ryan's excited wolf howl echoed nearby. I turned to see a light gray young wolf bounding toward us. Though much smaller than adult wolves, his eyes held the identical brightness from his human form.

Drake lowered his head and tenderly licked his son's ear with obvious affection. Ryan circled us excitedly, occasionally nuzzling us with his small head.

"Awoo—!"

Drake raised his head and released a long howl toward the forest.

The hunting signal.

Pack members responded in unison, wolf forms charging into the forest and vanishing among moonlit tree shadows.

The forest night pulsed with life. Leaves whispered in the breeze, nocturnal creatures rustled through underbrush, and owl calls resonated in the distance.

Drake began running first, with me following closely and Ryan playfully weaving between us.

Ryan suddenly accelerated, shooting ahead of us. He glanced back and released a youthful wolf howl, apparently showing off his speed.

Drake emitted a sound resembling laughter and increased his pace to catch up. I accelerated as well—three wolves racing through the forest, leaping streams and diving through undergrowth.

Three wolves—one black, one brown, one gray—flying beneath the moonlight.

Printed in Dunstable, United Kingdom